THE THREE WOMEN

VALERIE KEOGH

BLOODHOUND
— BOOKS —

Print ISBN 978-1-913419-32-5

ALSO BY VALERIE KEOGH

THE DUBLIN MURDER MYSTERIES

No Simple Death

No Obvious Cause

For all the amazing, wonderful women in my life:
sisters and friends

Friendship between women is different than friendship between men. It's my women friends that keep starch in my spine, and without them, I don't know where I would be. **Jane Fonda**

A seasoned woman is spicy. She has been marinated in life experiences. Like a complex wine, she can be alternately sweet, tart, sparkling, mellow. She is both maternal and playful. Assured, alluring, and resourceful. She is less likely to have an agenda than a young woman—no biological clock tick-tocking beside her lover's bed, no campaign to lead him to the altar, no rescue fantasies. The seasoned woman knows who she is. She could be any one of us, as long as she is committed to living fully and passionately in the second half of her life, despite failures and false starts. **Gail Sheehy**

1

2020

Beth Anderson looked at the two women she'd known most of her life and sighed. If only they'd never met. If only she hadn't decided to go to the university bookshop that particular day, if she'd said no to joining Joanne for coffee, or if Megan hadn't chosen that day to have her lunch in the same café. But it had all happened, and in meeting, their fate was sealed.

They were standing hand in hand, only a few inches from the edge of the cliff, Beth in the middle, Joanne to her left, Megan on her right. There was nothing to hear but the wind that whistled in their ears and the thundering crash of waves breaking against rocks at the base of the cliffs far below. A sudden gust blew Joanne's long blonde hair across Beth's eyes, the wet tendrils blinding her for a moment until another stronger gust swept the hair away. Rain washed her cheeks, taking with it the tears that gathered and fell in quick succession. Her hands were wet and slippery; she felt the hold on her friends' hands loosening and tightened her grip.

The next step? There was only one thing to do, wasn't there? After all the secrets and lies, there was nothing left for any of them here. Beth looked at each of her friends, at their rain-soaked almost-calm faces, and smiled. 'Still time to change our minds,' she said, immediately feeling their hands clasp hers tightly. Nobody was letting go. Nobody was having second thoughts.

'Okay!' she shouted, her voice carrying on the wind.

And as one, the three friends took a final step forward.

2

1997

Beth Anderson had never been to London apart from a flying visit with her mother a few years before to see the sights. Applying to the City University of London had been her choice; her mother had wanted her to go to the nearer University of Bristol, but their relationship was such that whatever her mother had suggested, Beth would have done something else.

Universities with their grand lecture halls, solemn professors and mind-boggling expectations could be intimidating places, especially for those with wide-eyed optimism and little experience. Some students make quick friendships for survival, an anchor in the busy chaotic world, holding on tightly until, little by little, they find their feet. Then they migrate to more like-minded or sometimes more fun friends. Others, more self-sufficient, keep to themselves, making friends by accident rather than design. Beth was of the more self-sufficient type.

A freckled mousey-haired woman, she wasn't at all intimidated by her new surroundings and looked around with keen eyes that missed nothing. She had student accommodation in Shoreditch. A tiny studio with a small bathroom, and a kitchenette. It was on the second floor, the window looking out on the

busy street below and the ugly office buildings opposite. Beth, who'd shared a bedroom in the family home in Somerset with a much younger sister, wasn't put off by its small dimensions or the unexciting view. It was all hers, and she loved it.

Without any clear idea of a future career, she'd chosen to study criminology and, two weeks into the degree course, she was finding the subject fascinating and the lectures, so far, interesting. But the reading list was long. She borrowed some books from the library but others, ones she'd like to keep for future reference, she needed to buy. After lectures on Friday of the second week, she headed to the campus bookshop armed with her list. It was a massive place with rows of shelves stretching from floor to ceiling. She found five of the books she'd wanted almost immediately and eventually located the final one. At five feet six, she was tall enough to reach most of the shelves but not the top one where the book she wanted was sitting tantalisingly out of reach. There were steps available. She'd seen one somewhere and was looking around trying to remember where it was when a student who'd been checking books on a lower shelf, stood up and grinned at her.

'There are some advantages in being so tall,' she said, and stretching an arm up, tapped a book. 'Is it this one?'

'Yes, thanks.' Taking the book from her, Beth smiled in return. 'I thought *I* was tall.'

'Ha, you're just a little bit of a thing. I'm five eleven. Now that's tall.' Her accent was cut-glass London, the kind of accent Beth associated with old movies where everyone spoke received pronunciation English, and dialects were frowned upon. It was the kind of accent that immediately put Beth on the defensive. She smiled her thanks and went to move away, stopping when the woman reached out a beautifully manicured nail and tapped the pile of books Beth was carrying.

'What are you reading?' she asked. 'That's a lot of books.'

Beth responded to the friendly smile and the warmth in her eyes. She hadn't realised until that moment how much she missed the friends she'd left behind. 'Criminology,' she said, aware as never before of her Somerset brogue and suddenly conscious of her tracksuit trousers and baggy sweatshirt. It had seemed okay that morning, but looking at the tall elegant woman in front of her, with her dungarees, dangling earrings and long blonde hair tumbling around her shoulders, Beth felt as if she'd wandered in off her parents' farm. She shuffled the books in her arms, once again ready to leave.

'Oh, that must be interesting. I'm reading Media Studies and Sociology. Not nearly as interesting as I'd hoped, so far anyway. I'm Joanne Marsden. You're a first year?'

Slightly taken aback by Joanne's almost overpowering friendliness, Beth nodded. 'Yes, I am. Beth Anderson. Nice to meet you.'

'Me too! You free for a coffee?'

Overwhelmed and extremely flattered that Joanne wanted to have coffee with her, how could she say no? 'Yes, I suppose,' she said, trying for casual and checking her watch. She'd nothing else planned, nothing to do. Since she'd started lectures, almost two weeks earlier, she'd gone straight back to Shoreditch every day. Maybe it was time to see what university life had to offer.

Beth followed Joanne to the desk where they both paid for their books, she for the six she'd chosen, gulping when told the cost, and Joanne for the two slim volumes she held. They strolled together to the nearest café, and it didn't take long for the two women to discover they shared a similar sense of humour and the same ability to spot the ridiculous or extraordinary. In a London university, there was lots of opportunity for both, from weirdly phrased posters promoting various associations to colourfully dressed students who walked around with a confidence Beth envied.

One of three campus cafés, the one they walked into was a vast bustling space, floor-to-ceiling windows overlooking a pedestrianised area where tall maples gave shade in summer. It was noisy with chatter and too-loud background music, and jammed with people, sitting, moving about, standing. Most of the tables were full, many with students hammering away on the keyboards of neat laptops. There was little space between tables and Joanne and Beth negotiated the minefield of extended legs and carelessly placed bags and rucksacks as they hurried to one of the few remaining vacant tables. Dropping their heavy bags on the floor, they sat down.

'I'll get them,' Joanne said, jumping up almost immediately. 'What'll you have?'

Beth wanted to say a cup of tea, it's what she'd usually have had, but even in her head, it sounded so boring. 'A cappuccino,' she said, 'with lots of chocolate on top.' Joanne nodded and headed to join the long slow-moving queue. Careful not to be caught staring, Beth watched her shuffle forward, moving rhythmically to the blaring music as if she were on her own, blonde hair swinging, head bouncing. Admiring Joanne's careless self-confidence, Beth ran a hand through her long mousey brown hair and wondered how much it would cost to get highlights. Probably more than she could afford.

That night, she'd have a look at the few clothes she had and see if she could look a bit more like her new friend. She was amused at how quickly Joanne's appearance had influenced her, but she wasn't dismissing it. *Learn what you can from whomever you can*, was one of her father's favourite maxims. As she continued her surreptitious assessment, Beth remembered the charity shop she'd seen on the walk home. It might be worth calling in. She didn't have much in spare funds, but maybe a few quid would buy her some clothes that would help add that certain something. Perhaps she could bring Joanne along to give her some advice. She might like the idea of being Professor Higgins to her Eliza Doolittle. Beth's smile broadened. It was turning out to be an unexpectedly good day.

It was a few minutes before Joanne arrived back with the coffees, a cup in each hand, holding them with exaggerated caution over the heads of students she passed on her way. 'Here you go,' she said, placing one in front of Beth before taking her seat.

They both sipped silently for a moment, letting the cheerful sounds of the café roll over them. Beth wanted to know everything about her new friend but, waited, preferring to allow her to begin the conversation.

'Where are you living?' Joanne asked eventually, leaning closer to be heard over the surrounding din. She used her spoon to scoop out the foam that remained from her cappuccino and put it into her mouth with an unselfconscious action.

'Shoreditch student accommodation,' Beth said, eyeing the contents of her cup and wondering if she could get away with doing the same. Afraid of looking foolish, she decided against. 'Just a small studio.'

Joanne dropped her spoon onto the saucer. 'Me too! What floor?'

'Second.' She supposed it wasn't necessarily a coincidence. Shoreditch had the most student accommodation available, but still, it was pretty amazing. 'You?'

'Third. I would have loved a bigger studio, one of those on the top floor but the parents said they were coughing up enough.'

Curious, Beth asked, 'But you're from London, aren't you?'

'Yes, my beloved parents had a lovely home in Kensington,' Joanne tossed her hair back, 'but they sold it and retired to a villa in Portugal where Pops plays golf all day and Mums continues her attempt to preserve her youth by pickling herself in gin.'

Taken aback by this acerbic description of Joanne's parents, Beth wisely changed the subject. 'You'll have lots of friends in London, I suppose.'

'Some. Most went to Oxbridge, of course.'

Beth was about to ask why she hadn't gone there when an almighty clatter and shouts of outrage caused them both to turn in alarm.

'Oh dear.' Joanne craned to watch the drama unfold.

A student, carrying a tray laden with food, had somehow got her foot caught in a bag on the floor, stumbled and sent everything flying. A plate sailed, sending food in every direction, liquid of some sort landed in another student's lap causing her to jump up squealing, and what looked like a cream cake bounced off someone else's shoulder before landing with a squelch on the floor. For a moment, there was pandemonium. A short dumpy woman, cheeks scarlet with embarrassment, was trying to extricate her foot from the strap while at the same time pick up her tray and apologise.

'Oh, the poor thing,' Joanne said with quick sympathy, jumping up and hurrying to help.

Beth, who had been ready to giggle at the chaos, stood to follow her, stopping first to put both of their bags on the chairs. She pushed them under the table for safety and glared at those sitting nearby as if to warn against touching them. Only then did she cross the café to join Joanne where several victims were still wiping hummus from their clothes and picking salad from their hair. Their assailant holding the empty tray, muttered *sorry, sorry* as she made ineffective attempts to clean up the mess while some of the students made loud and pointed remarks about her clumsiness.

Joanne glared at them, took the tray from her and handed it

to Beth. 'Go get her some more lunch, will you?' She didn't wait for an answer. Turning, she put a hand on the woman's elbow and led her towards their table. 'Come on, sit with us,' she said gently.

Beth looked at the tray in her hand, not knowing whether to be annoyed at the cavalier treatment or impressed by the way Joanne had sorted out the situation so quickly. Turning back to the students who were still muttering, Beth swept bits of food that had landed on their table onto the tray, picked up the plate, retrieved the glass that someone else was holding out to her and then took the tray and dumped it on a tall rack.

She headed to the food counter and minutes later, was on her way back with a laden tray held high in both hands, stopping on her way to have a brief word with the students who were still scowling and shooting dirty glances towards where Joanne and the visibly trembling woman sat.

Reaching them, Beth smiled down at her. 'I got you hummus and salad, but I wasn't sure what you were drinking, so I got some water and tea for all of us,' she said, unloading and taking the third seat. 'I'm Beth, by the way.'

Taken aback by their kindness and generosity, the woman stuttered. 'T... T... Thanks b... b... but you didn't need to do this!'

'You need your lunch,' Joanne said simply, throwing a grateful smile towards Beth. 'What's your name?'

'M... Megan,' the woman said, pulling the plate towards her. She took a deep steadying breath before saying, in an accent Beth couldn't place, 'Really, you've been so nice. I'm a clumsy fool and don't blame them for being annoyed.' She waved a hand towards where the victims of her disaster sat, relieved to see they'd stopped glaring at her and were, in fact, packing up their belongings and preparing to leave.

'What did you say to them?' Joanne asked, noticing that the students were avoiding looking their way as they hurriedly left.

Beth grinned. 'I told them that if they hadn't spread out all over the floor like a particularly nasty fungus, Megan here wouldn't have tripped and that really they should be paying for her lunch. I guess they weren't willing to cough up.'

'Brilliant,' Megan said with a smile, and picked up her fork.

Beth and Joanne drank their tea while Megan ate, making small talk about lectures and the university in general. 'So, what are you studying?' Beth asked when Megan had finished eating. She was strangely fascinated by the rather dumpy little woman with the prominent crooked teeth and heavy-framed glasses.

Megan put down her knife and fork and pushed her plate away. 'Law. Afterwards, I've arranged to complete my Legal Practice course, and then I'll need to do two years of practice-based training.' Picking up her tea, she looked from one to the other. 'I eventually want to work for the Crown Prosecution Service, so I have it all carefully planned.'

'And nothing's going to stand in your way,' Beth said, surprised at the strength and determination in her voice, and envious of the focus on her career. As yet, she'd no clear idea of what she was going to do when she'd finished, her course having been chosen more out of interest and curiosity than any future career plans. Listening to someone so focused gave her food for thought.

'It's what I've always wanted to do,' Megan admitted.

They swapped stories about their various courses and their lecturers for over an hour. Joanne, adding scathing remarks about some of her lecturers, had Beth chuckling and Megan looking at her with wide-eyed admiration. 'I'd never be brave enough to criticise them,' she said.

'Stick with me,' Joanne said with a smile. 'You'll learn.'

3

Joanne, Beth and Megan chatted a little longer until Megan looked at her watch and frowned. 'I really should be going. Thank you both for being so kind. Now, I must pay you for the lunch.' She reached for her bag, but Joanne shook her head.

'Don't worry about it. It's our treat to make up for the bad experience you had.'

Beth blinked. All very well for her to say, it hadn't been her who'd paid but, short of making an issue out of it and perhaps embarrassing herself in the process, there wasn't really anything she could say.

Unaware of Beth's resentment, Joanne smiled and checked the time on her phone. 'There's a shindig in the Debating Society in about ten minutes. Do either of you fancy going?'

'I'm not a member,' Megan said, shaking her head. 'I haven't had a chance yet to join any of the societies but, anyway, I have a lot of work to get through.'

Beth added, 'I'm not a member either.'

'Nor me,' Joanne said with a chuckle. 'We'll just say we're thinking of joining, they won't care, and it's bound to be fun.' She looked at their serious faces. 'Honestly, what was the point in coming all the way to London from the wilds of...' She waved a hand at Beth.

'Somerset,' she answered the unspoken question.

'And...?' Joanne waved at Megan.

'Cowbridge,' she said and seeing their blank looks, added, 'Wales.'

'There you are then,' Joanne said as if that was the final argument.

Beth laughed and looked at Megan. 'I will if you will.'

'I have to study. I've essays due, research to do, and I really can't spare the time.' Then, suddenly, as if swept along by their enthusiasm, Megan smiled. 'Yes, why not, thank you.'

Unfortunately, as it turned out, Joanne was wrong. A rather belligerent beefy man at the door to the Debating Society's meeting room looked them up and down rudely and demanded their membership cards. He turned his nose up when Joanne trotted out her spiel about thinking of joining.

'Come back when you do,' he said curtly, ignoring her flirtatious smile.

Knowing when she was beaten, Joanne gave him a casual wave and turned back to her new friends. 'Let's go to the student bar instead.' But the others shook their heads.

'I really do need to do some work for tomorrow,' Megan said.

Beth didn't feel she needed to give an excuse. She certainly didn't want to have to admit that having spent so much in the bookshop, and having paid for Megan's lunch on top of it, she'd gone through enough money that day. Anyway, she'd already been into the student bar to have a look around. It was a low-ceilinged unattractive place with sticky floors, worn seating, and a bad smell. It wasn't the type of place she'd have thought would appeal to her new friend. But then, she knew nothing about her, did she?

'Fine,' Joanne said, the word heavy with disappointment. But she didn't stay despondent for long, linking an arm through Beth's as if they were old friends. 'I suppose I may as well head home too then.'

To their surprise, Megan lived in the same student accommodation in Shoreditch. 'How is it that I've never seen either of you coming or going?' Beth asked, curious as to why she hadn't seen the rather distinctive women in the two weeks she'd made the twice-daily journey.

Megan shrugged. 'I'm in university before lectures start and usually go to the library straight afterwards and rarely leave till late. Maybe that's why?'

'I rarely go to any lectures that start before ten,' Joanne admitted, looking not a whit embarrassed by the admission. 'And I've only been to the library once, out of curiosity, you know, in case anyone ever asks me where it is.'

That drew a gasp of disbelief from Megan and a chuckle from Beth. 'I have the walk to the lecture halls timed so I arrive with a minute to spare,' Joanne told them. 'Until today, I've gone home straight afterwards. So, that explains why we haven't met.'

They chatted amiably as they walked but, as they passed King Square Garden, Beth realised Megan was struggling to keep up with their long-legged stride. Joanne's arm was still linked through hers. With a gentle tug, Beth slowed her down, matching their pace to the smaller woman's. Joanne smiled but said nothing.

It was usually a brisk eighteen-minute walk between the university and the student accommodation, but it was nearer twenty-five before they got to the high-rise block of apartments. It was a modern, clean and well-equipped complex with communal rooms on the ground floor including a gym that only Beth had used and a cinema that, as yet, none had visited. Both Joanne and Beth had what was referred to as the standard studio, but when they went into the lift ready to press the button for their respective floors, they discovered Megan's was on the tenth where the studio apartments were the largest available.

Beth felt a twinge of envy that she didn't bother trying to hide. 'Wow, you're a lucky beggar.'

Joanne whistled. 'The tenth! Can we come and see it?'

Beth noticed conflicting emotions crossing Megan's face and wondered if she was going to say no.

But she didn't. 'You've been so kind, the least I can do is to give you a tour,' she said with her quick smile.

On the tenth floor, she unlocked the door and waved the two inside with a polite, '*Mi casa es su casa.*'

The apartment, although still a studio, was far roomier than Joanne's or Beth's, with each part, the kitchenette, bathroom, bedroom and living area all appreciably bigger. Best of all, and what drew gasps from the two visitors, was the large double window looking out over the London skyline.

'Wow,' Joanne said, making a beeline for the window and kneeling on a big padded seat to look out.

Beth, climbing up beside her, pressed her nose to the window. 'That's amazing. Wow, you're so lucky, Megan.'

There was ample room on the seat for all three to sit. Megan made coffee, and they sat and chatted, all thoughts of studies, essays, and research having been forgotten as they enjoyed getting to know one another.

They'd been there about an hour when Joanne asked Megan, 'What height are you? Five feet?'

Beth laughed, but if Megan was taken aback by the question, she didn't say. 'Four eleven. Short and dumpy.'

'It's harder to lose weight when you're smaller, without a doubt,' Joanne said, and without a word, reached over and whipped off Megan's glasses.

'Hey,' Megan yelped. 'I can't see a thing without them.'

'You're quite pretty, you know.' Joanne held the glasses out of reach. 'I'd kill for your olive skin. You should get laser treatment to your eyes, then you wouldn't need these.' She handed them back. 'And maybe you should get your teeth fixed.'

Megan scowled and put her glasses on. 'Anything else?'

Feeling suddenly sorry for her, Beth diverted Joanne's attention to her. 'What about me? What should I change?' Since she'd frequently been told she was very attractive, she wasn't expecting to hear anything too controversial so was stunned when Joanne looked at her, and said bluntly, 'I'd get rid of the accent.'

Beth could have taken offence since Joanne was virtually a stranger; could have stormed out and said she never wanted to see her again, but instead, she giggled. Soon, Megan joined in, and within minutes, the three of them were holding on to one another and belly laughing.

'Are you always so blunt and honest?' Beth said when the laughter had died down to the occasional snort.

Joanne smiled. 'I find it's the best policy. People don't get confused then.'

Beth looked at her a moment but could see no guile in her eyes. Maybe she was as honest as she said, but landing her with paying for Megan's lunch still rankled a little. She decided to hold fire on her judgement but, as it happened, she didn't have to wait long.

～

Just as they were leaving, Joanne turned to her. 'How much do I owe you for the lunch?'

Taken aback, Beth muttered what it had cost and, with a nod, Joanne reached into her pocket, took out a handful of coins, slipped a couple back into her pocket and handed Beth the rest. 'There you go.'

Three women: one honest and blunt, one uncertain and suspicious, and the third focused and determined. They'd probably never have been friends but for that chance meeting in a bookshop and the clumsy accident in a restaurant.

Whatever the reason, their friendship grew and endured for the next twenty-three years.

4

2000

They all graduated. Beth and Joanne with a respectable 2.2 and Megan with the first she'd worked so hard for. Relieved, they celebrated for a week in London before facing up to the commitments that would take them in different directions, Beth heading home to Somerset to work for the remainder of the summer on the family farm, Megan to Cowbridge to help in the family art gallery, and Joanne to join her parents in Portugal.

It had been Joanne's idea to go away for a night, a final flourish before they split up. 'Somewhere away from London,' she'd said. Beth had agreed enthusiastically and even Megan, who'd never been away with them before, decided it was a great idea. They'd all had enough of late-night party celebrations, of the noise and clamour of London. Beth and Joanne had had enough too of certain ex-boyfriends who didn't seem to get the message that whatever they'd had was over.

'Toby's being an absolute pain,' Beth complained. 'Everywhere I go, he shows up with his puppy-dog eyes, begging me to take him back.'

'I never knew what you saw in him anyway,' Megan said, rolling her eyes. 'He isn't the brightest.'

'I don't think it was his brains she was after. He is pretty fit!' Joanne said with a laugh. 'But never mind him, or Simon,' she added with an exaggerated grimace as she referred to the latest in a long string of short-lived relationships, 'we'll get away for a night, just us three. Leave it to me. I'll organise something.'

Happy to do so, Beth and Megan were taken aback a couple of days later when Joanne told them they were going to stay in a bungalow, in a village they'd never heard of, almost two hours' drive from London. They were sitting in Megan's studio. Over the years, it had become a habit to meet up there and only when exams and deadlines loomed did Megan ever beg for a bit of privacy and push them out the door.

Beth, who had been on her knees on the window seat admiring the view she never tired of, turned and looked at her with a raised eyebrow. 'A bungalow!' she said as if she couldn't believe her ears. 'Seriously?'

'Capel-le-Ferne, where's that? It sounds French,' Megan said, surprise making her distinctive Welsh lilt more noticeable. 'We're not going to France, are we?'

'Yes, it's a bungalow but no, we're not going to France, it's in Kent and you haven't heard the best yet... it's free! It's on the coast, not far from Dover. And,' she'd hurried to reassure them, 'it's only a ten-minute walk to an old country pub.'

'I think I'd prefer to pay and stay in a hotel,' Megan said unconvinced.

Beth shook her head. 'I've spent a fortune recently. Free sounds good to me.' She saw Megan's shrug with a dart of irritation. Of course, *she'd* prefer to go to a hotel. It had come as something of a shock to discover, early in their friendship, that Megan could afford to do whatever she wanted because her parents gave her what she considered a suitable allowance and Beth, when she heard how much, thought was an astronomical amount of money. That she was incredibly generous with her money and frequently paid for the three of them to go to various concerts and dinners, didn't make it any easier for her friends to accept. Sometimes, but only to Joanne, Beth would mutter about it being charity but never, in all the years, had she refused to accept it.

'How are we getting it for nothing?' Megan asked, ignoring Beth's comment.

'It belongs to friends of my parents. It was for sale but they've taken it off the market for the moment. As long as we promise to leave it as we got it, they say we can borrow it. We could stay longer, if you like.' When there was no answer, she said, 'Will I say yes then? It'll be fun. We can go for a walk along the white cliffs and have a drink or two. Relax.'

It was impossible to resist Joanne's enthusiasm. 'Fine, why not, it'll be a break from London,' Megan said.

'A bungalow,' Beth said, raising her eyes to the ceiling. 'Okay, I'm in but don't tell anyone; we have a reputation to maintain!'

The day they were leaving was their final day in the student accommodation in Shoreditch, and both Megan and Beth had brought cars from home to transport their belongings. It didn't take long; the size of their accommodation didn't lend itself to hoarding. A couple of hours later, their cars packed with their clothes and clutter, they took a last look at the building that had housed them for three years.

Beth smiled as Joanne leaned on the roof of the car she had borrowed from a friend. 'End of an era,' she said, and then tossed her hair. 'Thank God for that!' She did a twirl and tapped a drumbeat on the roof of the car with the flat of her hand. 'The world's our oyster, ladies. But first, onward to Capel-le-Ferne.'

They started their cars and drove down in a convoy with Joanne in the lead, waiting for each other when they got separated. When they were a little more than halfway there, Beth saw Joanne indicate to leave the motorway for a service station. Beth followed, with Megan close behind. Joanne was standing beside her car when Beth pulled up beside her and lowered her window. 'We stopping for a break?'

'There's no food in the bungalow,' Joanne said. 'And I'm not sure if the pub does food, so we'd better stock up now.'

The café was busy with the cross-section of people always found at such places: lorry drivers, tired shift-workers, busy sales-reps, and families with noisy children. Recognising that most people were in a hurry, the service was quick and efficient and, minutes after entering, the three friends were sitting with plates of surprisingly good fish and chips in front of them. Megan, as she always did, covered hers with tomato ketchup before starting.

When they finished, their clear plates testifying to how good the food was, Megan was the only one who insisted on having dessert. The one she chose, two meringues each almost as big as her fist joined together with a huge amount of cream, made her more health-conscious friends shiver. She looked at them with amusement through her overlarge and heavy glasses before jamming her fork into it, bits of chalky meringue flying every which way.

It was another hour's drive to their destination. Joanne indicated to turn right and pulled into the driveway of a nondescript bungalow that was third in a row of identical unexciting homes. There was plenty of parking for all three cars to fit easily and, one by one, they pulled in and switched off their engines. In the following silence, they climbed out to look around.

'What a lovely place,' Beth said with heavy sarcasm, grabbing her overnight bag from the boot and slamming it shut. Already, she was missing her studio in Shoreditch.

Megan and Joanne headed for the front door where a large ornate flowerpot overflowing with a mix of colourful flowers sat to one side. Joanne tilted it, felt underneath and pulled out a key. 'Ta-dah!' she said before slipping the key into the lock and pushing open the door.

It opened immediately into a big room that stretched to the back of the house, windows on both sides letting in plenty of light even on this grey summer's day. The owners had taken inspiration from their proximity to the sea; decorated in shades of cream and blue, there was an overabundance of sea-related ornaments, lighthouses, seagulls and sailing boats, on almost every surface. But there were also large squashy sofas. And, as they discovered when exploring the three bedrooms, big comfortable beds.

'It's perfect,' Megan said, plopping down on the sofa and kicking off her shoes.

Beth took the seat beside her. 'It's not bad inside,' she conceded.

'Just a tad over the top,' Joanne said, nodding towards the row of ceramic ducks on the windowsill. 'Okay, I'm popping back to my car, I didn't bring food, but I did bring wine.'

Perfect.

Beth watched her return, weighed down with a large canvas bag full of clinking bottles. Dumping it unceremoniously beside the sofa, Joanne pulled out a bottle and handed it to Beth. 'Open it, I'll go find some glasses.'

Beth twisted open the cap and put the bottle on the long low coffee table that sat between the two sofas.

'Best I could find,' Joanne said, returning with three glass tumblers. She put them on the table and sat between her friends, clapping each on the knee as she did so. 'Wasn't this a great idea?'

'Yes,' Beth said nudging Joanne's shoulder with her own. When Joanne made no moves towards pouring the wine, Beth leaned forward, picked up the bottle and filled each glass. She picked up one, waited until the others had theirs and raised her glass in a toast. 'Here's to us.'

'To us!' Megan and Beth said together and the three glasses met in a cheerful clink.

'It's nice to spend a last night together before we all head off,' Beth said, beginning to relax. Her voice had lost its Somerset accent. She had taken Joanne's comment to heart and when a heavy cold had left her with a husky voice that seemed to disguise her brogue, by dint of practising every day in the quiet of her tiny studio, she managed to keep it. Apart from a knowing glance from Joanne, no comment had ever been made. At first, she'd reverted back to her own accent when she went home for a visit but as time went by, as she'd grown more comfortable with the new version of herself, she'd stopped.

'One last night of freedom,' Megan said, gulping another mouthful of wine.

'When do you start your Legal Practice course?' Joanne asked her.

'September, I'm going to help out in the gallery for a while but I've a few other things planned before I start.'

'I've always admired your focus,' Joanne raised her glass to her, 'and think it's rubbed off on me. I've applied for a public relations position with Milcross and Batten. They're one of the biggest London companies. If I get it, I'll be so pleased.'

Beth propped her feet up on the coffee table. 'You'll have to find somewhere to rent; that's going to cost.'

'I'm heading to Portugal to spend a couple of weeks with my lovely parents,' Joanne said. 'I'm hoping they might help me out. They've plenty of money, but they like to spend it on themselves so I'm not holding out much hope.' Reaching for the bottle, she topped up all their glasses and when she'd drained the last drop, she took another from the bag. 'Luckily, I came well supplied.' Opening it, she left it on the table and sat back, her eyes on Beth. 'Have you made a decision?'

'Not a final one. I'm going to take a couple of months off and make a decision then.'

'But you *are* still thinking of the police, yes?'

'Yes, but I'm not completely sure yet,' Beth said. 'Right now, I'm just thinking we should go and investigate the pub.'

By consensus, they didn't bother to change clothes. Beth had long since adopted whatever fashion trend Joanne followed by finding charity shop alternatives, and both were wearing wide-legged trousers and tightly fitting low-cut T-shirts. But Megan, who found it difficult getting clothes to fit, stubbornly continued to wear the same type she'd worn since the first day.

Beth looked at Megan's billowing dark-orange cotton dress. Beth knew Megan thought it disguised her size but, instead, as she had slim shapely legs, it made her look remarkably like a toffee apple. Beth made no comment, neither did Joanne. They'd learned over the years; Megan didn't want to listen.

'We look fine as we are,' Joanne said. 'It'll probably be full of old people anyway, but it did look nice on their website.'

They headed off along the road, moving onto the grassy verge when the occasional car passed by. It was a warm balmy evening and the scenery on the ten-minute walk was pretty, with wildflowers in the hedgerows on both sides and a hazy view of the sea in the distance. Joanne pointed to a sign marking the coastal path. 'Perhaps we can walk along it for a bit in the morning?'

There were murmurs of agreement, Megan making both promise they'd walk slowly prompting the others to laugh and joke about her short legs.

Slightly inebriated after the two bottles of wine, they arrived at the old pub. Not only did it look nice but it was clearly popular as evidenced by the almost-full car park to one side and the sound of raucous laughter coming from the open windows.

'A quiet sleepy pub?' Beth grinned, thumping Joanne on the arm. 'Looks like the place is heaving.'

As they crossed to the front door, a large group of young men hanging around outside, cigarettes dangling from their fingers or lips, looked their way. Beth sent Joanne a satisfied glance.

'I don't want to be too late leaving,' Megan said, eyeing the group with a sense of foreboding. 'There are no lights on that road. It'll be a dark walk home.'

'We'll leave when they shout last orders, okay?' Joanne said to her and then glanced over to Beth. 'That okay with you?'

Beth, exchanging flirtatious smiles with one of the men, nodded. 'Yes, that's fine.' She knew by *not too late*, that Megan had meant ten at the latest. Staying till last orders meant eleven. She was right, of course, it would be dark but it was a straight road and they'd be together. Megan worried too much; they were supposed to be having fun.

They pushed the door open and walked in, Joanne and Beth leading the way. Megan trailed behind.

Inside, the pub was noisy and crowded. And mostly with young men. Joanne, who'd ordered drinks at the bar, came back with the explanation. 'They're students from a nearby boarding school celebrating the end of their own final exams.' She was holding pints of bitter for herself and Beth and a small white wine for Megan.

Beth took a gulp of beer and watched the students over the rim of her glass. They were far too young for them, many not looking old enough to buy alcohol, but their obvious admiration made age irrelevant.

Within minutes of their arrival, Beth had fallen into conversation with a small group, while Joanne was chatting to others. In the crush of the busy pub, as people moved aside to let others through to the bar, the women drifted apart.

Lost in the admiration of a couple of extremely handsome students, and pleasantly relaxed from all the alcohol she'd consumed, Beth assumed her friends were having as good a time as she was.

For the next couple of hours, she didn't give Megan or Joanne another thought.

5

Beth was having a ball but when the shout for last orders came she said goodbye without difficulty to her young Lotharios, and looked around for Megan and Joanne. Even in a room filled with testosterone-charged men, Joanne's five feet eleven stood out. Moving through the still-crowded pub to her side, Beth grinned. 'That was fun.'

'The unexpected often is,' Joanne said, grabbing her arm. 'I think I've drunk a little too much!'

Beth looked around. 'Where's Megan?'

Joanne swayed and clutched Beth's arm tighter. 'Megan? I thought she was with you. I haven't seen her since we came in.'

Beth looked at Joanne, appalled. 'I haven't seen her for ages, I thought she was with you.' Beth stood on her toes, trying to see over the crowd, feeling the first stirring of anxiety. 'I don't see her anywhere. Maybe she's in the Ladies. Jo, have a look and I'll ask the bar staff if they've seen her.'

Joanne immediately headed through the crowd towards the Ladies. Beth kept one eye on her while she struggled to get to the bar, pushing through customers who were desperately trying to get one more drink.

At the bar, it took a while to get any attention and finally, in desperation, Beth resorted to reaching across to grab the arm of one of the passing bar staff. 'I'm looking for my friend,' she said quickly. 'A short woman about this high.' She tapped the side of her arm with the edge of her hand. 'She has thick-framed glasses and dark hair, have you seen her?'

He looked at her a moment. 'Hard to miss, she's an ugly bird, isn't she?'

An ugly bird? Only anxiety over her friend made Beth keep her temper. 'Did you see where she went?' she asked him, flicking a look across to where Joanne was standing outside the Ladies.

'She left about an hour ago with the man she'd been chatting to for a while before that.'

'Are you sure?' Beth was relieved but still worried. Megan had left without saying goodbye, without letting them know. It wasn't like her to be so thoughtless; she must have known they'd be concerned. How could she be so inconsiderate? Worry gave way to righteous indignation.

'Positive,' he said. 'They looked to be getting very friendly. He bought her a couple of drinks. A local man, Matt Peters. He's in here most evenings.' The barman gave Beth a knowing look. 'He likes to escape the wife and kids.'

Beth was stunned. 'Thanks,' she said, turning away.

Joanne was still hovering near the door to the Ladies. She waved and made her way across.

'She left with a guy,' Beth said. 'About an hour ago. A local man, Matt Peters.'

'Well, well, the dark horse,' Joanne said with a drunken smirk. 'Now one of us, I could have understood, but Megan!' She swayed and reached for Beth's arm, linking her own arm through it. 'We'd better walk home slowly in case she's brought him in for a coffee.'

They weren't falling-down drunk when they left the pub but they were certainly very merry. Annoyance, however, was sobering Beth up. 'I can't believe Megan left without telling us.'

'She's a big girl. She's twenty-one after all, not eighteen. And don't forget, she has the keys in that silly little bag of hers.'

They started the short walk to the bungalow, darkness engulfing them once they left the lights of the pub behind.

'We should have brought a torch.' Beth pulled out her mobile and switched it on. It wasn't ideal, but it made them more visible to passing cars.

'Megan's never shown much interest in men up to this,' Joanne said, stumbling a little.

'Careful,' Beth said, holding her arm tighter. 'Actually, I didn't think she was into men.'

Joanne stopped, swinging around to look at her. 'Really?'

'Come on.' Beth tugged on her arm. 'I don't know, it's nothing she's ever said, just a feeling I have, it's probably wrong.'

They walked in silence for a few minutes.

'You don't think she's brought him in, do you?' Joanne asked.

'God, I hope not!' Beth groaned at the thought. 'I doubt if the walls in that damn bungalow are very thick. If she did, we'll be able to hear every grunt and groan.'

When they reached the bungalow, there was no light visible in any window. Joanne sniggered. 'They're doing it in the dark.'

Beth was still chuckling as they negotiated their way between the parked cars. 'Well, she's going to have to stop whatever she's doing to let us in, isn't she?'

They halted when they saw the front door standing ajar. Joanne was about to step forward when Beth pulled on her arm, yanking her back.

'What?' Joanne said, looking at her.

Beth pointed to the door. 'That's not right.'

'Oooh!' Joanne tittered, swaying slightly. 'They were in a biiiig hurry.'

'I suppose she might have left it open for us,' Beth said, dropping Joanne's arm. She put a hand on the door and pushed it open. Inside, there wasn't a glimmer of light from anywhere and the silence was eerily heavy. She stepped over the threshold and stood in the darkness barely able to breathe, Joanne standing so close behind that her warm breath brushed Beth's cheek.

Reaching out a hand, Beth felt along the wall for the light switch unable to remember where it was, catching her foot on a small stool as she moved forward and stumbling against the wall. Swearing loudly, she searched again and grunted in relief when she found it. Instantly, the room was flooded with light, both of them blinking to adjust before they looked around. Everything was as it had been, every over-the-top sea-related ornament, every cushion still squashed out of place from where they were sitting earlier. Nothing appeared disturbed.

They moved into the kitchen. It too, was as they'd left it, the dirty glasses lined up in a row on the draining board. 'Maybe you were right,' Beth said, brushing aside the feeling of disquiet and forcing a smile, 'maybe they were just in a hurry.'

Joanne, stumbled unsteadily, holding a hand to her head. 'I don't feel too well. Forget about her, she's probably curled up in post-coital satisfaction.'

Feeling stupid for her moment's panic, Beth picked up one of the glasses, rinsed it out and filled it with water. 'Drink,' she said, handing the glass to Joanne. 'It'll help.'

Screwing up her nose, Joanne took the glass and sipped.

And then, in the quiet, they heard it... a low gut-wrenching whimper. The glass slipped from Joanne's hand, smashing as it hit the floor, water and glass flying. 'Shit!' she said, reaching out a hand to grab Beth's arm.

Eyes wide, they hurried back to the lounge, clutching at one another, eyes frantically scanning the corners of the room before they stopped in front of the door that led down to the bedrooms. They stood hesitantly, ready to leave if the door opened and something leaped out at them, every Stephen King novel they had ever read running through their heads.

It wasn't until they heard a low-pitched moan that Beth moved closer. With Joanne panting heavily behind her, Beth reached for the handle, took a deep breath and pushed the door open, inch by inch. The corridor beyond was in darkness. Even with the door fully open, the light that filtered through from the lounge faded before it reached the end. Then, as the moan came again, a dark mass at the end took form and slowly moved towards them. Both women yelped in fright and stumbled backwards, Joanne screaming and running to the far side of the lounge; Beth, with a cry of terror, threw a final look at it before turning to follow, her head snapping back as the mass crawled forward into the dim light and horrified recognition dawned.

'Bloody hell, it's Megan!' Rushing to her, Beth dropped to her knees and reached for her. 'Oh God, Megan, what happened?' She yelled over her shoulder, 'Turn on the light, Joanne!'

Joanne, huddled by the far wall, tears spilling down her cheeks, gasped and hurried back. She found the light switch and flicked it on, flooding the short corridor with light.

'Shit!' Beth said, hugging the wild-eyed woman. She didn't bother asking what had happened; the ripped dress, scratches, bruised mouth, and especially the look of desolation, they all screamed one story. 'He raped you?' There was no reaction for a moment and then, with a moan, Megan buried her face in Beth's shoulder, and sobbed.

'The bastard,' Joanne said, moving forward to hover over the entwined women, reaching down to lay a comforting hand on Megan's head. 'The utter bastard. But don't worry, he won't get away with it, we know who he is. Matt Peters.' She spat out the name and searched her pockets for her mobile. 'I'll ring the police.'

'No!' Megan, lifting her head, put her hand out to stop her. 'No, don't! Please.'

'What?' Beth and Joanne said simultaneously, looking at Megan in confusion.

'You were raped, of course you have to report it. You can't let him get away with it,' Joanne said.

Beth, her arms wrapped tightly around the shaking woman, said quietly, 'You don't need to be ashamed. He raped you, it's not your fault. We'll be with you all the way, okay?'

'No! I don't want to report it.' Megan pushed Beth away and struggled to her feet. She dragged her ripped dress around herself and pushed past them into the lounge, her breath catching as she sobbed.

Following, the others hovered around her, their faces creased in concern. 'I don't understand,' Joanne said. 'How can you let him get away with it?'

Megan dropped onto the sofa. Tears running down her cheeks, she pulled her legs up, wrapped her arms around her knees tightly, and lifted her chin. 'Please,' she said, her trembling voice pleading, 'you have to understand, I can't go through all the questions, examinations, prodding and prying. It would get out, of course it would, and I'd be *the woman who was raped*.' She took a ragged breath and hugged herself tighter. 'I don't want that, the sympathy or the pity. I just want to forget it ever happened. Please, promise me you'll keep it a secret.'

Joanne stared at her and then looked at Beth standing behind the sofa. 'Tell her! Tell her we can't let him get away with this!'

Without a word, Beth left the room and returned almost immediately with a blanket in her hands. She draped it over Megan and tucked it down at the side before reaching out to brush a lock of hair from her eyes. Only then did she answer. 'We can't make her report it, Joanne, and I suppose I can understand what she means. He might confess but, then again,' she threw an apologetic look at Megan, 'she did leave with him voluntarily and the barman said they were very friendly. Playing devil's advocate, he might say she was up for it and was crying rape after the fact so it might very well drag through the courts and be in the papers.'

'Exactly!' Megan said, swallowing a sob.

'But your identity will be kept secret,' Joanne argued. 'You won't be *the woman who was raped*. For God's sake, Megan, you've scratches down your arms, your cheek's already turning purple and I can see bruises through your torn dress. He hurt you and he should pay.'

Megan pulled up the blanket, covering herself, and shook her head again. 'Please, Joanne, let it go. I don't want to report it.' She ran a trembling hand through her tangled hair. 'It's my choice, isn't it. And in case you're tempted to report it on your own, I'll deny anything happened.'

Joanne opened her mouth to argue but at a sharp glance from Beth, she closed it again and turned away. 'I think you're wrong but if it's what you want.'

'It is,' Megan said firmly. 'I want you both to promise you'll keep it a secret.' When neither spoke, she repeated her request, her voice an unsteady quaver but her words sharp. 'Promise me?'

Beth sat down beside her and took her hand. 'If it's really what you want, I promise.'

'This is crazy!' Joanne cried. 'What if you get pregnant? Or catch something?'

'Please!' Megan begged. 'I'll go to a clinic when I get home, I'll make sure I'm okay. Believe me, I *can* put this behind me. My future is set out. I won't let this take it from me!'

'I still think you're wrong.' Joanne dropped onto the sofa beside her. 'But, if that's what you want, Megan, then yes, I promise.' She leaned forward, and laid her hand on top of Beth and Megan's entwined fingers.

Beth, her hand sandwiched between those of her friends, felt the warm air from Megan's sigh of relief brush her cheek as Megan's head drooped to rest on her shoulder.

They stayed silent for a long time, at a loss for any words that made sense or offered comfort. Slowly, the hand under Beth's turned. She could feel Megan's fingers stretching and reaching, desperate to clasp both of their hands in hers, her fingers tightening, vice-like, as she started to cry as if determined, despite her tears, to hold them to their promise.

6

2020

It was Megan's favourite time of the day. She stood at the floor-to-ceiling window of the penthouse apartment as she watched dusk blur the edges of the city and then waited for that brief moment of dullness before it pinged to life again. Street-lights, neon signs, undefined pinpoints of light, apartment windows shining. London, day or night, she loved it. Her eyes drifted to the reflection of the woman who stood unmoving behind her. Megan closed her eyes briefly and turned.

'I wish you'd say something,' she said quietly, taking another sip of the chilled Chardonnay. It was New Year's Day. They'd partied until four a.m. and returned home for a few hours' sleep before having breakfast with some friends in the apartment below. After that, it was a late lunch in the city with a group of work colleagues and friends. Someone, and she'd no idea who, had chosen a trendy and loud Russian restaurant with food that, in her estimation, was well below average. Annoyingly too, lunch went on for far longer than she'd expected and she was beyond bored with shop talk by the time they managed to wish everyone well and get away.

All she had wanted to do afterwards was to kick off her heels, unzip and peel herself out of the uncomfortably tight dress she should never have bought, and slip on the cashmere robe Trudy had bought her for Christmas. But she'd been waiting for the right moment to speak to her partner, ever since her unexpected proposal on Christmas Eve. Stunned into silence, she had listened as Trudy had gone on and on about their honest relationship, the complete and utter trust there was between them, and how their lives were intrinsically linked through their mutual respect and love. With every word, Megan loved her more but, with every mention of honesty and trust, her secret twisted inside her.

She'd said *yes*, of course she had, she loved Trudy, had from the first day they'd met eight incredibly quick years before. But as soon as the word was out of her mouth, Megan knew she had to tell her the truth. She wasn't going to marry the woman she loved with a secret hovering in the background. It would have been better to have told her straight away, with the next breath after that ecstatic *yes*. It would have been *far* better, and she would have done it, if Trudy hadn't insisted they ring everyone, there and then, to tell them their happy news. And it was happy glorious news and, caught up in the excitement, in the absolute and utter *wonder* of it all, Megan had put it off, waiting for the right moment.

It hadn't come in the excitement of Christmas Day with Trudy's family joining in the double celebration with bottle after bottle of champagne, each popping cork accompanied by toasts made to their happy future together. Perhaps, Megan should have made time on Boxing Day, before Trudy insisted that they go to a jewellery shop to pick out engagement rings, a square diamond cluster for her, a solitaire for Trudy, the diamonds glinting in the light of the wine bar they'd gone to afterwards to celebrate with more champagne toasts and starry-eyed looks. No, the right moment just hadn't come.

Nor had it come in the days that followed, lost as they were in parties and entertaining. Every time she saw the ring on her left hand, with every twinkle as it caught the light, her heart dropped and she swore she'd find the right moment... soon. She wasn't sure why she was so reluctant; surely Trudy would understand and appreciate her honesty. Telling her would be a weight off Megan's chest and once it was gone, once she was free of a lie that had simmered inside for over twenty years, she could enjoy planning their wedding.

So, when the right moment eventually came, only one hour before, when they'd stood hand in hand looking out over the city for the first peaceful moment in days, she knew it was time to speak. They had to start the new year and their new life together in the honesty that Trudy believed was already there.

'There's something I need to tell you,' Megan had said, her eyes fixed on the city below, her fingers tightening on the hand she held. But the words she'd practised in her head in the intervening days, the calm orderly clear words of explanation, were forgotten. Instead, she blurted out the chaotic garbled truth about the secret she'd lived with for all those years. Lost as she was in the past, she wasn't aware that, somewhere in the middle of her story, Trudy had pulled her hand away, and at the end, in the silence, Megan stood isolated. She looked at Trudy now, this beautiful woman that she adored, and silently pleaded for understanding.

'I don't know what to say.' Trudy's barely audible words seemed to hang in the air. 'Such a lie... it's staggering... beyond belief.' She took another step backwards and shut her eyes as if unable to bear looking at Megan any longer. 'How could you?' Her voice cracked, and, without another word, she turned and left the room.

Watching her go, knowing there was no point in going after her, Megan took another sip of her wine and moved to the sofa.

She sat, crossed her legs and tried to believe it would all be okay. The secret had been rattling around her head for a long time; she couldn't expect Trudy to take it in, in just a few minutes, she'd need time to process it all.

Twenty years. Megan put the glass down on the side table and rubbed her eyes. It was hard to believe so many years had passed. She tried never to think about that night. Sometimes, it was as if it had happened to someone else. But, every now and then, usually in the wee hours when all that worried her was written in white chalk on the darkness of the night, the secret gnawed painfully.

Twenty years. She'd been a different person then. Gauche, confused. Even her appearance was different. She cringed now when she looked at old photos of her university days; what a mess she had been. It had taken Joanne's bluntly said words to make her see reality. When her parents had insisted on buying her a gift for obtaining the first at university, she'd known exactly what she'd wanted. To look the best she could. Thanks to a year of sometimes painful and uncomfortable orthodontic work, her teeth were now neither crooked nor prominent. Laser treatment to her eyes had taken away the need for glasses, and a better diet, along with a horrendously expensive personal trainer, had shifted the wheel of fat from around her middle. She'd never be a beauty like Trudy but, on a good day, she looked in the mirror and was content.

The only thing that hadn't changed in all the years was the focus on her career. She hadn't wanted anything to stand in her way. And nothing had, she'd made sure of that, and now she was where she'd always wanted to be, working for the Crown Prosecution Service – her dream come true.

Picking up her glass again, a frown creased her brow. She'd been right to finally tell Trudy the whole truth, but she wouldn't have had to if Beth hadn't got drunk at that party three years before. She was a sloppy drunk, becoming loose-lipped as soon as she'd had one too many and, that night, she'd had more than one. Megan, trapped in a corner by Trudy's pleasant but garrulous father, Alex, had looked across the crowded room and watched in dismay as Trudy filled Beth's glass again.

Shrugging, hoping her friend wouldn't say or do anything inappropriate, Megan had brought her attention back to Alex, answering a complicated question he'd asked her about a point of law. It wasn't the place to give free legal advice but she liked the man and really didn't mind.

It was a couple of minutes before her eyes drifted across the room with an unconscious need to catch her lover's eye, her smile fading as she saw that Beth had cornered her and was standing with her mouth close to Trudy's ear. There was no ignoring the wide eyes, the down-turned mouth and sudden pallor. With a sinking feeling, Megan knew Trudy was being told a secret that wasn't Beth's to tell.

Quickly introducing Alex to a couple chatting nearby, she'd squeezed through the crowd to their side with a forced smile. If there was any doubt as to what Beth had told her, it was dispelled immediately by Trudy's terse, 'Is it true?'

'Don't believe what Beth says when she's had too much to drink,' Megan had said with a laugh, giving her friend a none-too-kindly thump on the shoulder before leading Trudy away. 'She's drunk,' Megan had insisted, trying to brush away what Beth had said. But, for all her fragile looks, Trudy was like a bull terrier when she got hold of something so, reluctantly, she'd confirmed what Beth had told her and explained her desire to keep the rape a secret. 'I've put it behind me,' she had insisted. 'That's why I didn't tell you. It's in the past. It's where it should have stayed.'

With a gulp, she remembered that Trudy had cried for the horrific ordeal Megan had been through. She'd wanted to talk about it and had encouraged her to go for counselling, said she was certain that Megan must have buried the pain of the rape deep in her subconscious where it would fester. It had taken several weeks to persuade Trudy that she had put it all behind her. After that, it was never spoken of again. Until now.

Restless and uncomfortable in her tight dress, she finished her wine, put the glass down, and stood. There was no sound from the bedrooms. Whatever Trudy was doing, at least she wasn't sobbing. The door to the bedroom they shared was open but a glance around the spacious room told Megan she wasn't there. Crossing to the spare bedroom, she put an ear to the door. There was no sound from within. Perhaps she was sleeping or resting on the bed, staring at the ceiling trying to make sense of what she'd told her. She should go in and beg for her forgiveness. Her hand hovered over the door handle before she withdrew it, convinced it would be best to leave Trudy alone for a while to think.

Inside their bedroom, she swapped her dress for the red cashmere robe Trudy had bought her. It was the first time she'd had a chance to wear it, she wanted to show her just how lovely it was but after lingering again by the spare bedroom door, hearing nothing but silence from the other side, she turned away.

With her wine glass refilled, she switched on the TV, flicked through the channels and found a movie she hadn't seen before. She tried to concentrate on it but all she could think about was the consequences of what she'd told Trudy. Perhaps, after all, it would have been better to have said nothing, to have continued to live with the secret she'd kept for over twenty years.

When the movie ended, almost two hours later, Megan switched off the TV and sat in silence. She couldn't remember the apartment ever being so quiet; usually, Trudy would be chirruping about something or other, or humming as she cooked a meal or tidied up. Even in the middle of the night, she wasn't completely quiet. Megan smiled, remembering Trudy's horrified look when she told her, rushing to reassure her that she didn't *snore* as such, it was more a gentle snuffle.

Her smile faded; she hoped a night's sleep would put everything into perspective. She refused to give headspace to the terrifying question, *What if it didn't?* Leaving the glass where it was, she headed to their room. They had spent many nights apart; Trudy, an award-winning architect, was often required to travel to various parts of the UK, and legal conferences frequently took Megan away. There were days, weeks sometimes, when they wouldn't see one another, evenings when they spent an hour on the phone talking, as one or the other was away in some forgettable hotel in another city. Days, when the only contact was a brief text to tell their beloved that they were alive and couldn't wait to be together again. But as she slid between the sheets on the king-sized bed, her hand sliding over the wide cold emptiness at her side, Megan had never felt quite so lonely.

She didn't think she'd sleep, assumed she'd toss and turn going over everything in her head but, for a change, she slept through till morning, blinking awake when a shaft of light slipped through the not-quite-shut curtains. Moving out of its way, she lay staring at the ceiling for a long time before throwing the duvet back and swinging her feet to the floor.

After a quick shower, she pulled on jeans and a fine-knit navy jumper, ran a brush through her dark bob and took stock of herself in the mirror. Not bad for forty-two, she decided, smoothing moisturiser over her olive skin. A flick of mascara over her eyelashes, her favourite Tom Ford red lipstick on her lips, and that was as much as she was doing that morning. The door to the spare bedroom was still shut, but when she held her ear close, she could hear the faint hum of the electric shower from the en suite bathroom. It was only a hint of normality but she grabbed hold of it.

It was a lovely morning; blue skies and winter sunshine. She took a moment to admire the view before organising breakfast. Toast and coffee. It didn't require a lot of skill. The living space of the apartment was spacious; as well as a full-size dining table that would easily sit eight, there was a small bistro table and two chairs next to the window which they preferred to use when there was just the two of them. She set out plates, mugs, and cutlery, her eyes constantly flicking to the hallway for any sign of Trudy.

Toast was standing in a rack and a cafetière was filling the room with the aroma of good coffee before she heard the familiar squeaking sound of the guest bedroom door opening. She turned in her chair and waited, her heart sinking when she saw Trudy's pale woebegone face with its swollen eyes and down-turned mouth. There was a slump to her shoulders too, as if the weight of what she had told her was too much of a burden to carry. Megan wanted to leap to her feet and run to her side, take her in her arms and beg her forgiveness, but something in the rigid sadness of Trudy's expression kept Megan from moving.

Trudy took the seat opposite without a word; her eyes lowered. The face of an angel, Megan thought, as she had so many times before. She reached over and poured coffee, adding the dash of milk she knew Trudy liked. Now was the time to wait patiently. Under the table, resting in her lap, one of her hands gripped and kneaded the other.

Picking up the coffee, Trudy took a sip and put it down again, staring into it. Quietly, the words barely above a whisper, she said, 'You've never told Beth or Joanne the truth?'

Megan shook her head. 'I told you, no, they don't know. They believe the story I told them.'

Trudy's head whipped up then, eyes glinting with sudden anger. 'The *lie* you told them. The *lie* you told me–'

'I wouldn't have had to tell you anything,' Megan interrupted her quickly, 'if it hadn't been for Beth and her drunken antics. I never wanted anyone to know.'

Trudy looked at her with her top lip curling in disgust. 'Oh please, there's no point in blaming Beth for any of this. You confirmed what she told me when you should have told me the truth. You stayed silent even as I wept to think of what you'd gone through. Wept!' she cried, pushing back from the table, her head shaking in disbelief at the memory. 'All these years!' She stood and paced the floor, running a hand through her shoulder-length curly hair. 'God, I even begged you to go for counselling. And all this time...'

Megan hung her head. There was nothing she could say that justified what she had told her but she had to try. 'The story... okay, *lie*,' she said quickly, seeing the glint in Trudy's eyes, 'was so set in my head I had almost begun to believe it really happened. It seemed easier to stick to the same story. To be consistent.'

'Listen to yourself, Megan! *To be consistent.*' Trudy sat, looked at her and wiped away a tear. 'I don't know if I can forgive you for this,' she said quietly. 'It's against everything I believed about you, about us.'

Megan stretched a hand across the table, knocking against the toast rack, sending slices falling to the floor. Ignoring the mess, she pleaded, 'I'm the same person you fell in love with, Trudy. I made a mistake twenty years ago. Twenty years. A lifetime ago. I'm not the naïve stupid young woman I was then.' She kept her hand outstretched, long after she'd given up hoping it would be taken.

Trudy narrowed her eyes and crossed her arms. 'O... kay,' she said, dragging the word out. 'You told me the truth because you didn't want us to marry with this lie in your past, but telling me is only a small part of putting it behind you.'

Megan blinked, pulled her hand away, and wished she could turn the clock back to the minute before she'd told her. That precious moment when they'd been holding hands, talking about their future. A shiver slid down her backbone. Had she, with her stupid decision to confess, destroyed everything?

'If you really want to put it all behind you and to go forward in honesty, you need to tell Beth and Joanne the truth too. You need to tell them that twenty years ago, despite what you'd let them believe that night, you were not raped by that man.'

7

D etective Inspector Beth Anderson was already late when she ran down the steps of the police station, her mind on the evening ahead. She'd promised Graham, her long-suffering partner of almost six years, that for once she'd be home on time but, yet again, she was late. The Rape and Serious Sexual Offences Unit where she worked was always understaffed and overworked, and she could count on one hand the number of times she'd left the station at a reasonable hour. She hoped he'd understand. Amazingly, he usually did. Not for the first time, she thought *how lucky she was*.

Hurrying across the brightly lit car park, lost in thoughts of Graham, it took a few seconds to realise that someone was calling her, a quiet voice barely heard. She could see him but didn't turn, hurrying towards her car, wanting to ignore him, to get into her car and drive away as quickly as possible.

But she couldn't, of course, because she knew the man. Some faces never left her, no matter how many weeks, months and years passed. It had only been a week since she'd seen Bruno Forest, grey with shock when he'd arrived in the station after they'd found his twelve-year-old daughter dumped, naked, in a

44

field several miles from their home. They were lucky, she was alive but so traumatised, so bruised and broken, she was unable to speak.

Bruno was distraught and wracked with guilt because, glued to football on the television, he'd allowed her to walk the five minutes to the local shops alone... five minutes on a straight road with no major roads to cross. It was dark, but there were streetlights and he'd thought she could come to no harm.

Now, his cheeks were sunken, and his eyes looked haunted as if he had seen and heard things no parent should ever have to see or hear. Beth knew better than to ask how Lydia was doing, the long road to a recovery that wasn't guaranteed was something she knew all too much about. Instead, she asked how he was coping.

'Is it true?' he'd asked her, without answering her question, his voice cracking with the effort of keeping himself together.

'What?' she'd asked genuinely puzzled, her eyes sliding down to her watch, appalled to see how late it was.

'That you had someone in for questioning about what happened to my Lydia?'

Beth squeezed her lips shut on the groan that wanted to escape. The station was a damn leaky sieve. How information escaped despite their best efforts to secure it was beyond belief. If she ever found out who the loose-lipped idiot was, she'd... She swallowed, thinking of the lines she frequently crossed doing her job... she'd do nothing. 'We've had quite a few people in for questioning, Mr Forest,' she said, her voice carefully neutral, 'but as I told you when you rang yesterday, we've no evidence to hold anyone as yet.' She pasted on a reassuring smile. 'It's best we go slowly to ensure a conviction; we don't want to mess up our chances.'

'But you know who it is?' His eyes narrowed as he took a step closer. 'You do, don't you?'

She tried to keep knowledge from colouring her expression as she thought about the fifth man they'd interviewed the day before. Arthur Lewis, the slight, balding, myopic man with protruding ears. He was the least likely looking sexual predator she'd ever seen; it was what made him so dreadfully dangerous. He'd served fifteen years for the rape of an eleven-year-old girl when he was twenty. Since his release, he'd been on the register of sex offenders and had been careful to keep his slate clean. Not squeaky clean though. She'd seen the reports about him hanging around schools; each time he'd been caught and warned but had come up with a vaguely acceptable excuse for being in the area. She'd noted there had been nothing in the last year; she didn't think he'd stopped, she thought he'd just got cleverer.

The day before, he'd been the last person they had brought in for questioning. She'd entered the interview room with her colleague DS Sunita Kadam and had known almost immediately he was their man. There was the smug arrogance on his face and the cold lack of empathy in his eyes when they'd told him about Lydia's injuries. But although he was the most unprepossessing man she'd ever seen, he wasn't by any means stupid. There had been no DNA evidence found on Lydia, so there was nothing to match with the DNA they had on record. They questioned him for two hours, trying to shake him, to find some crack in his tale. He didn't falter, sticking to his simple story of being nowhere near where the girl had gone missing or where she was found. He'd no alibi, having been home alone. But lack of alibi, Beth knew, did not a guilty man make.

By the end of the interview, after two hours of listening to his egotistical, arrogant, self-justifying crap, she had no doubt he'd been responsible. But without a confession, evidence, or proof, there wasn't a damn thing she could do; they didn't even have sufficient cause to apply for a warrant to search his house.

He had smiled when they told him he could go, had looked at them with cocky contempt that made her wish, not for the first time, that they lived in an era when she could have taken him into a cell and beat the shit out of him until he begged to confess.

'You think he's guilty?' she'd asked DS Kadam, who was tidying away the paperwork. Beth didn't really expect an answer so was surprised when Kadam in her softly spoken, very slightly accented English, said, 'Oh yes. I watched his eyes carefully when you spoke about Lydia. He quickly disguised it, but I didn't miss the lick of pleasure that appeared for a millisecond.'

Beth smiled briefly. Her quiet colleague was far more intuitive than she. If Sunita saw it, it had been there. But it wasn't enough for a warrant to search his house. Without one, they wouldn't find the proof they needed to put the slimy toad away. They'd keep an eye on him; someday he'd put a foot wrong and they'd catch him.

But that wasn't going to help poor Lydia and Bruno Forest.

Standing in the car park, Beth saw his distress, the sad eyes and drooping mouth; it was a testament to their failure to get justice for his child and with that weight pushing down her shoulders, she turned to walk away. She'd taken one step when she felt his hand on her arm, bringing her to a halt. It would have been easy to shake it off; there was no strength in the long slim hand or in the bony fingers topped with chewed grubby nails. She would have done without compunction had he not spoken, his words sending a chill down her spine.

'Lydia won't get out of her bed; she won't eat or speak to us.' His voice cracked, and his fingers tightened their grip on Beth's arm. 'She refuses to even look at us, just lies in her darkened room day and night, crying pitiful tears. My wife sits in the kitchen hunched over the table, sobbing helplessly, while I hover between the two with guilt whipping me because I allowed this to happen. We've called in counsellors and doctors. The counsellor tried to speak to her, but Lydia screamed and only stopped when she left. The doctor says we need to give her time. Time!' he said, his voice filled with anguish and despair. 'She's fading away in front of our eyes. My darling beautiful Lydia.'

Beth had seen the photograph of the child the parents had given them when she went missing. Pale skin, shining blonde hair, fine delicate features. A pretty girl, she had the right to grow into a beautiful woman. Arthur Lewis might have destroyed that for good.

Bruno's grief was almost tangible. She contrasted it with Arthur Lewis' arrogant cruelty and made a decision. With a quick look around, she pulled out a pen and scribbled an address on the back of an old receipt. She put it into Bruno's hand without a word, and hurried away.

She sat in her car and watched as he walked away with the scrap of paper held tightly in one hand as if he was afraid he might lose it. What would he do with the information she'd given him? Turn vigilante? Get the justice for his child she had failed to get? Remembering the injuries that had been inflicted on Lydia, Beth turned the key in the ignition and hoped that Arthur Lewis got exactly what he deserved.

It wasn't until she pulled into the last remaining parking space on Fawcett Road that she thought about Graham. He was going to be annoyed; they might even have yet another row, but their rows were usually short, and the make-up sex was unbelievably good. Climbing wearily from the car, she didn't feel in the mood for either. She did feel a twinge of guilt when she considered all the times she had let him down over the years. He didn't usually complain, but lately his patience seemed to be fraying ever so slightly at the edges. She'd find a way to make it up to him tonight, she decided, slipping her key into the lock and pushing the front door open.

It was the quiet that struck her. The first thing Graham usually did when he arrived home was to turn on the radio or shove a CD into the player. She was rarely home before him, and usually opened the door to the strains of whatever music had taken his fancy. He had a thing for Johnny Cash, knew every word of *Folsom Prison Blues*, and would put on a smoky husky voice and do the worst impersonation of the man she'd ever seen. It never failed to make her smile. 'Hello,' she called, shutting the door behind her and dropping the folders she carried onto the bottom stair. She frowned, wondering when she'd get a chance to read them.

Deciding to worry about them later, she felt a chill run through her when she saw no crack of light shining from underneath the doors of either the small front sitting room or the kitchen-diner. 'Hello,' she said again, pushing open the first door. The room was not only dark but cold. Grasping the handle of the kitchen door, she hesitated a second before taking a deep breath and turning it. This room too was in darkness but enough light shone through the window from outside to cast a soft glow over the small dining area.

Her breath caught and she shut her eyes in dismay as a pang of regret hit her. The table was set for dinner, wine glasses, flowers and the burnt-out remnant of a candle showing how much trouble he'd gone to. *Promise me, you'll be home on time*, he'd said. And she'd forgotten all about him, and her promise.

She checked her watch. Nine. Three hours late. With a groan, she switched on the kitchen light. On a small side table, a bottle of champagne listed drunkenly in a basin filled with melting ice. A slightly overdone roast chicken sat on the counter.

She lifted the lids from the pots and groaned out loud when she saw he'd done all her favourites. He'd even gone to the trouble of making a white sauce. Dropping the lids, she returned to the hall.

The silence was unnerving. 'Graham?' she called, and stood to listen for a reply that didn't come. She supposed she deserved the silent treatment, but it wasn't like him, he believed in saying what he felt, getting things out in the open. It was one of the many things she loved about him. Gathering her folders from the bottom stair, she reconsidered her earlier idea to read them in bed and dropped them onto the sitting-room sofa before heading slowly up the stairs.

When they'd moved into the small terraced house a few years before, it had a tiny galley kitchen, a downstairs bathroom and three small bedrooms upstairs. As money became available, they'd altered it by installing a bathroom in the smallest of the three bedrooms, extending the kitchen into the old bathroom, and finally, knocking down walls between the other two bedrooms and changing the layout to give them one large bedroom and a tiny spare bedroom used mostly as an office and for extra storage space.

Beth opened the door into their bedroom, words of apology on her tongue. She expected to find Graham splayed across the bed with an irritated hard-done-by expression on his handsome face. But the bed was undisturbed. Puzzled, she turned, crossed the small landing and opened the door into the spare room. But it too was empty.

A sense of dread overcame her and she rushed back into their bedroom, flicking on the light, spinning around as if, for a brief moment, she hoped he was hiding out of sight, ready to pounce on her and complain about her lateness. And then, with widening eyes, she noticed the wardrobe door hanging ajar and the bottom two drawers of a chest unit sitting open.

His side of the wardrobe, and *his* drawers. They were all empty.

There was no note; there didn't have to be, his actions had made his intentions clear enough. He'd left her.

Feeling suddenly weak, she collapsed onto the bed. When they'd met, both had been working all hours; her in the police, him trying to build up his personal training business. They'd made the most of the time they had together, dreaming of the day when it would be easier, when it wouldn't always be pressure to succeed and constant unrelenting stress.

Success had come at the same time for both of them five years earlier, but whereas Graham's success allowed him to work fewer hours, her promotion to detective inspector resulted in increased responsibility, pressure from both up and down the ranks, longer, pitiless hours and brain-curdling stress.

Graham had struggled with what he considered the unreasonable demands of her new position when, time after time, she had to let him down. There were cancelled dinner plans and cinema visits; they were late for parties and, once, when they'd arrived after the curtain call of a play he'd been desperate to see, they weren't allowed in until the end of the first act.

She explained, every time, how it had been impossible to walk away from a devastated stricken woman who'd been sexually abused, and he'd listen to her, sympathise and seem to understand. And afterward, when they'd made up, as they always did, he'd look at her with his big brown eyes and say she had to make room in her life for him and he was giving her one more chance. So many *one more chances*. It had become almost a joke between them. At least it had to her, maybe it had never been funny to him.

Now, looking at the empty wardrobe and drawers, and hearing the silence, it didn't seem remotely amusing to her either.

8

———————

Beth pulled her mobile from her pocket and checked for messages. There were some, but none from Graham. Shoving it back into her pocket, she headed downstairs. The smell of food in the kitchen made her stomach lurch. She made a mug of tea and, with it cupped between her hands, she went into the small front room and gazed out the window. Streetlights cast an eerie glow over the dark narrow road.

On the other side, the terraced houses were a mirror image of the row she lived in; she could see the house directly opposite, lights showing in some of the windows, the flicker of a TV screen, the occasional figure moving across a brightly lit room, neighbours going about their normal everyday lives. Not a mirror image of her house where everything had changed. A wave of terror washed over her. Was this emptiness going to be her new normal? She was so good at sorting out the broken lives of others, why couldn't she do it for herself?

Restless, she took her tea and went back to the dining room. She pulled out the chair and sat at the table he'd set with such care. A bunch of yellow freesias was set into a small glass vase.

She picked it up, held it close, taking in their sweet scent. She couldn't remember the last time he'd bought her flowers; it made these all the more special, all the more heart breaking. If she'd been the crying type, she'd have sobbed. Instead, she held a hand over her trembling mouth and wondered if this were the end.

After so many years together, she couldn't imagine her life without him. She'd thought, despite their problems, that he felt the same. Was there someone else? He was such a handsome man: shaggy blond hair, gorgeous eyes and a fit athletic body he insisted was the best advert for his personal training business. She took out her mobile again. Still nothing from him. Should she send him a message? Her fingers hovered over the keys. What could she say that she hadn't said a hundred times before, even when she didn't mean it but said it to end an argument? *Sorry.* She guessed it no longer had any meaning, but she couldn't think of another suitable word. Tapping it out, she added several xs, sent it, and then stared at the phone for several minutes willing him to reply. When he didn't, when it stayed stubbornly quiet, she threw it onto the table.

She was damned if she was going to sit there pining, not when she had work crying out to be done. Back in the sitting room, she sat on the sofa, and picked up the first of the folders she'd brought home.

Minutes later, she was lost in her job, all worries about Graham temporarily forgotten. The notes she'd written made for the inevitable sad read. The woman... girl... had been groomed and raped by a man she met on the internet. How many times would Beth have to read the same story? She rubbed tired eyes and turned to the next page. This victim was unusually observant; it had made Beth's job easier, made the case against the defendant almost solid. But she was too good an officer to make the mistake of being cocky. She'd make sure the case was watertight before handing it over to the Crown Prosecution Service in the morning – too often she'd seen them throw out cases for lack of evidence.

She moved on to the next file, the case she'd been involved with that afternoon. She'd spent the last few hours in the nearest specialist centre for victims of rape and sexual assault. Usually, she'd have been able to hand the fourteen-year-old victim into the care of a Sexual Offence Investigative Technique officer but there had been a problem in one of the other centres and two of the SOIT officers had been temporarily reassigned over there, leaving her office short.

It didn't make any difference to the case. Beth, as the Officer in the Case, had equivalent training. It just required her to stretch herself even further than she usually did. It also meant, of course, that she couldn't get away until the victim's statement was taken and the examination done. Then she'd sat with the victim and her shocked parents, explaining what would happen next, and advising them of the help that was available. The whole process wasn't something you could rush.

Somewhere in the crazy afternoon, she should have rung Graham to let him know, but there just hadn't been a minute free. She refused to acknowledge the tiny voice that said she hadn't given him a second's thought the whole day.

She checked over the notes she'd written. Tomorrow, she'd update the computer at the station. Dropping the bundle of files onto the floor, she swung her legs up and rested her head on the arm of the sofa. Truth was, every day in her job was crazy busy. Every morning, she checked the briefing slide provided by the Jigsaw team who managed registered sex and violent offenders; every day there were new people to watch out for so that no matter where she was, or what she was doing, her eyes were constantly checking out the faces of the men and women around her.

Graham had found it amusing at first. Less so in the last couple of years. And the previous week, when they were out for dinner, he'd been unusually irritable. 'Can't you, please, stop checking out people,' he'd growled.

'Sorry. Hadn't even realised I was doing it,' she said, thinking her confession would make it easier between them.

It hadn't. It had made things much worse. 'That's the problem,' he'd said, screwing up his mouth, 'you do it automatically. I see your eyes examine every face, male or female. I can almost see you tick them off that list in your head, one at a time. And then you relax, just for a moment, until new people walk in and you do it again.'

His words had stung, partly because he was right, it had become second nature to check everyone, but mostly because she thought he understood how important her role was. Keeping women and children safe from sexual predators and ensuring that the ones who got caught and arrested were prosecuted and put in jail, that was her job, more, it was her life. She thought he understood, that he was proud of the work she did and his criticism had cut her deeply.

Was that the start of the end? There had been an uneasy distance between them ever since, their conversation polite and careful, as if they'd been strangers forced to spend time together.

Her eyes followed a thin crack that crossed their sitting room ceiling. This house had been the second one they'd viewed when they'd decided to pool their savings and buy rather than continue to waste money renting. It was small but the location was ideal. Graham had been concerned about the crack but she'd dismissed it, as had the expensive surveyor he'd insisted they hire. Were there cracks in their relationship, even before last week, that she had dismissed just as easily? She'd thought they were solid, it looked like she was wrong.

She wondered where he'd gone. They... no, *he* had plenty of friends who would happily offer him a bed. Perhaps, when he got to wherever he was going, he'd send her a text. With a sliver of hope, she got to her feet and went to get her phone, the hope slipping away when there was nothing. She hesitated only a moment before she sent him another message, *Let me know you're ok.*

There was nothing more to be done. Ignoring the chicken, the pots of cold vegetables and the sad table setting, she switched out the lights and headed upstairs. The hanging wardrobe door and open empty drawers seemed to be taunting her. She slammed them shut.

The night seemed endless. Beth couldn't remember the last time she'd slept alone. Her hand stretched out to Graham's side of the bed, the cotton sheet where his warm body should be lying felt cold and empty. She tossed and turned for hours before falling into a restless sleep to dream of cracks opening in walls and on the streets and everyone falling into them despite her screams of warning.

Waking in the early morning, convinced she'd heard the front door open, she jumped out of bed and tore naked down the stairs, words of love ready and waiting to be blurted out as soon as she saw him. But all she saw was the front door, shut tight. Standing on the bottom stair, all she could hear was the cold silence of the house and the sad thump of her heart.

She trudged back to her room. It was impossible to get back to sleep but she lay for another hour before giving up. Dragging herself from the bed, she took a long shower that she hoped would make her feel better. It didn't. Nor did it make her look any better. Always pale, her complexion looked deathly, the smattering of freckles over her nose and across her cheeks standing out in sharp relief. The minimal make-up she wore at work didn't help but she resisted the temptation to lay it on thickly. It would attract questions she didn't want to answer. With a shrug, she dressed quickly in her standard workday dark jeans, pale blue shirt and navy jacket, pulled a brush through her hair and tied it back in a knot at the base of her neck.

It was early, she had plenty of time to sort out the mess in the kitchen, but she couldn't bring herself to open the door and see that sad table set for a romantic dinner they'd never have. Instead, she picked up the files from the sitting-room floor and headed out. Getting to the office early would give her a head start on a day that was going to be exhausting.

It only took her an hour and several mugs of vile coffee to get everything ready to present to the Crown Prosecution Service. An hour later, Beth was walking into their offices in Westminster with a clear case to present. There were some members of the CPS's Rape and Serious Sexual Offences Unit who were difficult to deal with, pernickety and awkward at the best of times, rude and uncooperative at the worst. That morning she was in luck; her case had been assigned to Megan Reece, one of the best on the team and her close friend.

'Thank God it's you,' Beth said, collapsing into a chair in front of the desk in the small cluttered office. 'I really didn't need a hard time today.'

Megan smiled briefly. 'Let me see what you've got. I never make promises.'

Beth watched her slowly and methodically read the contents

of the file. As she usually did, Megan read straight through once and then reviewed the more pertinent parts more closely. Beth didn't realise she was holding her breath until she heard her say what she'd been waiting for.

'Seems pretty cut and dried,' Megan said. 'We'll proceed with prosecution.'

'Another bastard put away,' Beth said, releasing her breath. Then, with the relief of that decision out of the way, she glanced at her friend more closely. Megan was, as usual, dressed neatly in a dark grey silk blouse with a neck tie tied in a bow, slightly off-centre. It looked effortlessly classy, but Beth knew she worked hard at it. She favoured ridiculously expensive red lipstick and usually it looked well on her olive skin. But today that skin was pale, almost colourless, and her red lips stood out in a bizarrely creepy contrast. 'You look like hell,' she said with the bluntness of friendship. 'Is everything okay?'

Megan arched one perfectly plucked eyebrow. 'You don't look so bloody amazing yourself. Any paler, I'd have to check for a pulse.'

'I've been busy, and not sleeping too well.' It was a half-truth; Beth didn't want to tell her the whole, didn't want to say words that would make everything seem even more final than she guessed it was. It was better to put her troubles to the back of her mind and focus on Megan's. They'd been friends for a long time and Beth could tell something wasn't right. 'Have you set a date for the wedding yet?' It was a roundabout way of asking if Trudy was okay; she would know from her response if there was trouble in that quarter.

But Megan surprised her by ignoring her question, and asking, 'How would you like to go away for a night? Just the three of us, you, me and Joanne? A girlie night. We can put the world to rights.'

Beth frowned. She didn't need to be a detective to know

there was something wrong, but it looked as though her friend wasn't going to talk about whatever was worrying her. That made two of them. Sometimes emotional pain was too difficult to vocalise. She hoped the reason for her friend's pallor wasn't the same as hers. Beth gave herself a mental kick. It couldn't be; Megan and Trudy were solid, made for each other. It wasn't a good idea to transfer her relationship woes onto everyone else. Megan was probably working too hard which was why she was suggesting a break.

A girlie night away? It might be just what she needed. 'Yes. I think that's a brilliant idea.' *A girlie night away.*

The idea had lost its lustre by the time Beth arrived home that night. She pushed open the door, weary and heartsick. The blast of heat took her by surprise and she shut her eyes in dismay. She'd left the heating on full. With the front door shut, she screwed up her nose as the stench hit her. She dropped her bag and pushed open the kitchen door, almost gagging as she stepped into the small overheated room. Trying not to breathe, she pulled out a black refuse sack and quickly emptied all the food inside, tied a knot in the top and put it outside the back door. Opening the door wide, she pushed it back and forth to create a draught and then left it propped open to clear the smell.

Her house stank, her life stank. She wanted Graham's arms around her; wanted to hear him say he was sorry for leaving and this time, he'd be the one begging for one more chance. And they'd laugh, talk, make love, and everything would be back on track. And this time, *this time*, no matter what it took, they'd get past their problems; they'd make time for each other, she'd make more space in her life for him. Sitting, she dropped her face into her hands as she felt her heart crack. She knew she was fooling herself; much as she loved Graham, her job was always going to come first. Perhaps, he'd finally realised that himself.

The room was cold by the time she moved. Shutting the door, she trudged up to bed, kicked off her shoes and climbed, fully dressed, under the duvet. Eventually, warming up, she pulled her clothes off and threw them onto the floor. She curled up, hugged her knees to her chest, and tried to ignore the chilling sense of loss she felt deep inside.

9

Joanne Marsden stretched like a lazy cat on the 800-thread count Egyptian cotton bed sheets. It had been a nice evening. The dinner had been delicious and the wine extraordinarily good. Felix was a generous host and an attentive companion. She liked spending time with him. Through half-opened eyes, she watched as he dressed. He was a very handsome man and, apart from a slight paunch, his body wasn't bad either.

'I'll be back in a few weeks,' he said, tying his tie. He tightened the knot, then bent to look in the mirror and straighten it. 'Will I see you then?'

She shuffled into a sitting position and let the sheet slip down to show her breasts. Reaching up with both hands, she caught her expensively highlighted blonde hair and lifted it off her neck. It was a position that showed off her figure to its best advantage. She knew it, the man who watched appreciatively knew it. Dropping her hair, she smiled. 'I think that could be arranged. Let me know when.'

After he left, she lay back, enjoying the peace and comfort

for another hour before she climbed from the bed. Unusually, she was free until that evening and it was lovely to be able to enjoy the luxury The Ritz had to offer without having to rush away. She had a leisurely shower, wrapped herself in a soft cotton bathrobe and ordered room service from the very extensive menu. It was better to avoid the restaurant in the morning; there was always the chance she'd see someone she knew. Far better to have a relaxing breakfast in the comfort of the extremely plush room.

Half an hour later, room service knocked on the door, delivering excellent bacon and eggs, toast and coffee. She switched on the TV and sat watching the news as she ate. It had been an enjoyable evening, a good night, and now, a relaxing morning. Really, Felix was a dream customer, she wished they were all like that.

The room was hers until eleven. Enjoying the luxurious surroundings, she waited until the last minute before gathering her few belongings and leaving the room. She'd have asked the concierge to order a taxi but the foyer was busy, the concierge surrounded by a group of anxious-looking tourists. She threw him a smile that he acknowledged with a pleasant wave and headed out onto the street.

Her thin coat and skimpy dress were no match for the bitterly cold wind that swirled around the front of the hotel. Shivering, she wrapped her arms around herself as she waited for a taxi, relieved when one pulled up just a minute later to drop people off. She climbed into its welcome warmth, gave the driver her address and sat back with her eyes shut as the taxi made its way through the busy streets to her apartment.

King Edward's Road, in Hackney, was a relatively quiet tree-lined street. Her apartment was on the fifth floor of a six-storey apartment block, an ugly building which stood out for all the wrong reasons among its more attractive neighbours. Joanne didn't care; it was functional and she spent little time there. Surprisingly, there wasn't a lift, just one main central stairwell that served all the floors, and emergency exit stairs at the end of each block. The stairwell invariably stank of human waste, homeless people finding it a good place to spend the night despite the security men's endeavours.

She didn't think they tried very hard but she never complained even when she returned late one night and had to step over a young man curled up in a distinctly malodorous sleeping bag. One flight of stairs up, she'd grunted with annoyance. It wasn't in her nature to do nothing. Returning to his unmoving body, she took a closer look. 'Well, you're breathing,' she muttered, opening her purse. She took out two tens and tucked them under his cheek. He didn't stir.

There was nobody to step over today; she climbed the stairs to her apartment and pushed open the door. Her landlord rented it as an apartment, but it was, in fact, a tiny bedsit. A sofa bed that she rarely used sat against one wall. In one corner, a tiny fridge, a two-ring hob and a microwave formed a compact kitchenette; in the other corner, a door opened into a small room that was euphemistically called the bathroom. It was a wet room, slightly bigger than the average shower tray. There was a toilet, the tiniest wash-hand basin Joanne had ever seen, and a shower that trickled barely-warm water any time she had the misfortune to need to use it. Luckily, that wasn't very often.

She had a few hours to spare. Taking off the dress and underwear she'd put on the day before, she dropped them into the suitcase that lay open on the tiny table in front of the apartment's only window. She shrugged into a robe, picked up the book she'd brought from home, and sat on the sofa with her legs curled under her. Her life was so neatly compartmentalised that she had no problem switching off and relaxing for a few hours.

～

Mid-afternoon, she put down the book and made a mug of coffee. She'd never bothered plugging the fridge in so, while she was there, she drank it black. The mug, a jar of coffee and a teaspoon were the only items in the apartment's single kitchen cupboard. Nothing else. She never ate there, rarely ate while she was working; that Ritz breakfast earlier being an unusual luxury. She worked three days in a row, sometimes with barely a break, and afterwards, she'd head home exhausted to her house in Royal Tunbridge Wells where she would relax and eat well for a week before doing another three-day stretch.

Compartmentalised, it worked well for her.

At seven, she took underwear from a drawer, and a tight-fitting low-cut black dress from the single wardrobe. Her next customer didn't appreciate subtlety so she applied make-up with a heavy hand, thick eyeliner, lashings of mascara, loud red lipstick. She was smiling at her reflection in the small mirror on the wall when her personal mobile rang.

She stared at it, first in surprise and then with suspicion. It rarely rang. She preferred to be the one doing the calling. It was better for her, easier, and the few friends she had knew that. Picking up her phone, she looked at the screen. *Megan*. With a quick look at her watch, Joanne decided she had time to spare. 'Hi, this is a surprise.'

'Joanne, hi! Yes, listen, I'm sorry, I know you don't like us calling you but this is important.'

She was fond of Megan, they'd been friends for a long time, but there was something in her voice, a barely discernible undercurrent of distress and, suddenly, Joanne was sorry she'd answered. 'What is it?' Her voice was cool rather than encouraging.

'I was speaking to Beth earlier, and we're going to go away for a night. Just us. The three of us, like old times.' There was silence for a few seconds. 'Next week, Joanne. Just one night. It's really important to me. Do say you'll come.'

Her fingers clenched the phone. *Like old times?* The three of them had only been away together once. One night, over twenty years ago, and it had been a disaster. She'd say no. It was a silly idea.

'Please,' Megan said.

Joanne's job had made her sensitive to nuances, to the way people spoke rather than the words they used. There'd been a hint of distress in her voice and now a clear note of desperation in the *please*. She frowned. There was definitely something wrong. Megan was one of the few people she counted a friend, her and Beth. They met once a month or so, usually for dinner, sometimes for a drink, but they'd never been away together since that one night. Joanne wasn't sure if that had been a conscious decision, or if their lives had just been too busy. Now, despite her feeling that there was something bothering Megan, the idea of getting away for a night with her two old friends appealed to her. It would be fun. 'Okay,' she said before she changed her mind. 'And next week is good for me. So,' she said, checking her watch, 'where are we heading?'

'Capel-le-Ferne.'

Joanne swallowed. She must have misheard. Megan couldn't possibly have said what she thought she'd heard. 'I'm sorry, there's interference on the line, where did you say?'

'Capel-le-Ferne,' Megan repeated. 'Don't worry, I'm not suggesting the same bungalow. There's a spa hotel there now. I thought we could stay there.'

'Are you sure that's a good idea?' *Because it wasn't, it was a stupid crazy idea.*

A soft sigh came down the line. 'This is important, Jo. I'll explain when we get there.'

Why had she answered the damn phone? What possessed her to have agreed to go? She was about to say she'd changed her mind, when she heard that soft pleading voice again.

'Please, Jo.'

They had been friends for long enough to warrant doing something she didn't want to do, hadn't they? 'Okay. I'll go along with it. Text me the details.'

'You won't let me down?'

'I won't. But I don't know why you want to go back there. I think it's an absolutely crazy idea, but it's obviously important to you so, as I said, I'll go along with it even though I don't like it.'

Megan's soft laugh came down the line. 'Friday then. I'll text you the hotel's postcode. We can check in after two. Come as early as you can.' The line went dead.

Throwing her mobile on the table, Joanne stood for a moment thinking, wondering if she should call Beth and find out what the hell was going on. Joanne glanced at her watch with a groan. It would have to wait until the next day.

She slipped on her coat, checked in the mirror to make sure everything was just so and stared at her reflection, wondering again what had possessed her to say yes. The three of them had kept in touch all these years, she considered them her best friends, went to their various parties, listened to their stories, but they weren't that close anymore, were they?

Still staring at her reflection, she rubbed her lips together. That shade of red did nothing for her. What would they say, these old friends of hers if they knew the truth? They thought she worked in public relations; in truth she did, but to be accurate it was private relations, *very* private. She wasn't ashamed of what she did for a living, but she wasn't sure her two friends would view being an escort as a good career move. Even a high-class very expensive escort.

Call girl. Hooker. Prostitute. Sex worker. She lifted a trembling finger to wipe away a smudge of eyeliner. It had been her choice. And now Megan was dragging her back to the place where she'd made that decision.

10

Megan sent text messages to both Beth and Joanne with the postcode of the new boutique hotel that sat less than a mile from the white cliffs of Dover and then waited for Trudy to come back from wherever she'd gone. She thought about Joanne's reaction. Maybe it was a crazy idea to go back to Capel-le-Ferne but it seemed right to, as it were, return to the scene of the crime. Or non-crime as it really was.

The last time they'd been there, twenty years ago, they'd been students, finished with university, deliriously excited to have graduated, even more thrilled about the futures they'd mapped out for themselves. Or maybe it had been her who'd been so ecstatic, so certain about the future. Law, it was all she'd ever wanted to do. Now they were sophisticated women who'd made their way in the world. She loved her work with the Crown Prosecution Service; Beth seemed happy, if a bit stressed, in her role as detective inspector, and the ever-glamorous Joanne seemed satisfied with her corporate hospitality business. They'd all made it.

Megan rang the hotel whose reservations clerk was effusive and only too happy to accommodate her request for three of their best rooms. 'I'll be picking up the tab for all three,' she told them, thinking it was the least she could do for having lied to them. Beth and Joanne would be understandably angry at her deception; Megan hoped she'd be able to make them understand... and to forgive.

The sound of a door opening made her stand restlessly and watch as Trudy came in, shaking her umbrella and sending droplets of water everywhere. It was an action designed to annoy; the water would stain the glossy walnut floor if it weren't wiped up immediately. Instead of complaining, Megan went into the kitchen, grabbed a roll of paper towel and returned, tearing reams from it as she walked. Without a comment, she bent and mopped up the drops.

'I'm sorry,' Trudy said, putting the umbrella into the stand beside the door. 'I'm being a bitch. I can't help it; I'm just so pissed off at you.'

Megan reached out a hand and brushed the hair back from Trudy's cheek. 'I'm telling Beth and Joanne on Friday,' she said quietly. 'I decided it would be better if we went away for a night and to make it a bit like a pilgrimage of penance, I've chosen Capel-le-Ferne.'

Trudy stepped closer and, wrapping an arm around Megan's shoulders, pulled her close. 'It'll be better when it's done. I don't know how you can have lived with it all these years.'

Easily, Megan wanted to say but didn't, putting her arms around Trudy and hugging her tightly in return. She'd do anything for this woman she adored. If Beth and Joanne couldn't bring themselves to accept her apology, and she lost their friendship in the process, then that's the way it would have to be. After all, she didn't have a choice, the truth had to be told to secure her future with Trudy.

~

Megan thought Trudy would thaw once she'd taken the step to tell her friends, but over the next couple of days she remained a little cool and distant, worse, she continued to sleep in the spare bedroom, saying simply that she needed space. The fear that she had damaged their relationship permanently haunted Megan. Had she made a colossal mistake by bringing up a secret from her past that she should have let lie? Honesty, she thought with a frustrated groan, was vastly overrated. And now, she had no choice but to go ahead and tell her friends the truth. It wasn't going to be easy. She felt a tight knot in her stomach just thinking about their reaction.

When Friday morning came, half-afraid that either Beth or Joanne would cancel, Megan was pleased and relieved to see texts from both to say they'd see her there. She rang Beth and suggested that they drive down together. 'We could stop for lunch on the way, what do you think?'

'Probably not a good idea, Megan. I've asked for the afternoon off but you know what it's like with my job. Safer if I meet you there, in case I get stuck at work with some emergency.'

Disappointed, Megan had to acknowledge that her friend had a point. 'But you'll definitely make it, won't you?'

'Stop worrying, I said I'll be there. Why don't you go via Royal Tunbridge Wells and pick Joanne up?'

Stressed as she was, Megan managed a laugh. 'You just want to see if she'll invite me into the house, don't you.' It was a constant source of fascination to both women that, although Joanne had lived in Royal Tunbridge Wells for several years, neither had ever been invited down to see the house. Hints that they would call in for a visit were always politely brushed aside.

Beth sniggered. 'I live in hope.'

'It would make sense, but I can guess the answer.' The temptation not to ring, to arrive on Joanne's doorstep and shout, *Surprise!* was strong but Megan resisted, said her goodbyes to Beth and pressed another speed dial button. As predicted, Joanne dismissed her offer to pick her up and said she'd prefer to meet there. 'You sure?' Megan said, 'I could do a little detour and pick you up.'

'No, thanks, I'd prefer to drive,' Joanne said quickly. 'I'm planning to go shopping on the way home on Saturday.'

'Okay, in that case, I'll see you there.' Megan hung up and shook her head. She knew Joanne's address and had looked it up on Google Maps. It was a lovely house, on a delightful street, so it wasn't as though she were ashamed of it. There seemed to be no logical reason for her reluctance to invite her friends down. After all, Joanne had been in Megan and Trudy's apartment several times and had stayed in their spare room a couple of nights. And they'd both been in Beth's tiny house in South Croydon. Maybe it was something they could ask her when they were in Capel-le-Ferne. Megan knew Beth, in particular, hated the mystery of it all. It was strange too, because Joanne was one of the most honest, straightforward people she knew, so why this one oddity? Megan was still mulling over it when Trudy came into the living room.

'I'm heading off to work,' she said, wrapping a scarf around her neck. 'Meeting a new client.'

Megan stood and held out her arms, afraid for a terrifying moment that Trudy would step back, relieved when she moved forward into her embrace.

'I know you think I'm being unreasonable,' Trudy said, her breath warming Megan's cheek. 'But this has been so hard for me. I thought I knew you so well. When this dreadful lie is out in the open, I think the pain will ease and slowly, everything will heal.'

VALERIE KEOGH

'Yes, of course it will,' Megan said, breathing in her scent. She wished she wasn't leaving, that there was no need to, that she could stay there forever wrapped in her lover's arms. But she couldn't. She dropped a kiss on Trudy's cheek. 'Shall I book dinner in Ricardo's for tomorrow night?'

Pulling away, Trudy checked her watch. 'I'd better get going. You'll never get a reservation in Ricardo's at such short notice. I'll cook something, it'll give me something to do while I'm waiting for you to come home.' Then with a smile, she said, 'Good luck, my love. I'll see you tomorrow.'

Restless, Megan filled her time doing paperwork and answering emails. There was nothing that couldn't have waited but she had an hour to kill and wanted to keep busy. Finally, at ten, she switched off her laptop and put it away. In their bedroom, she opened the wardrobe and considered what clothes she should pack. Joanne would, as usual, be incredibly glamorous and expensively dressed. Beth would probably arrive in her workday uniform of dark jeans, shirt, and jacket, all of which would be inexpensive and well-worn and she'd change into something equally cheap for the evening. And despite it, she'd look absolutely gorgeous. Megan smiled. It wasn't fair but it was the way it was.

Dragging a small overnight case down from the top shelf, she filled it with underwear, swimsuit, gym clothes and a dress for dinner that Trudy said made her look stunning. Her eyes softened at the memory. Love was a wonderful liar. No matter what Megan wore, she knew she would never look that good, although she certainly looked a lot better than she had when she was younger. She'd learned to buy well-cut clothes that accentuated her good features and hid the bad. Now, short skirts showed off her slim legs and tailored jackets added a waist where there wasn't one. But no matter what she did, she'd still be a small, fairly unattractive woman and she frequently wondered what the slim beautiful Trudy saw in her.

Her bag packed, Megan double-checked what she'd put in, guessing she was taking far too much. She shut it, left it by the front door, and returned to the lounge to pull a blank sheet of paper from her briefcase. Picking up a pen, she chewed the end of it while she considered what to write. There had to be something profound and poetic that would fit the occasion, but if there were, it wasn't coming to her – she resorted, in the end, to a maudlin cliché she thought would make Trudy smile, scrawling, *I love you to the moon and back*, across the page in her usual loopy writing and propping it against her pillow.

Megan stood looking at the page for a moment. Telling her friends, the truth was going to be horrendous but, if she had any doubts, she only had to think of how much she loved Trudy to know she had no other choice.

11

The White Cliffs Boutique Hotel was in stark contrast to the beauty of the countryside that surrounded it. A single-storey white building, it was flat-roofed, jagged-edged, and desperately modern, trying too hard to stand out in scenery that was famously stunning.

Megan pulled into the first free parking bay in the car park and gazed at the hotel through her car window. It had looked better in the photographs. Getting out, she stood and admired the grounds which did, at least, live up to their depiction on the hotel's website. The clever use of a variety of palm trees, both in the ground and in huge pots, hinted at the sea just a mile away and tall grasses added movement, the winter sun highlighting their golden plumes as they swayed in the slight breeze. It was okay, Megan decided, taking out her case and walking the short distance to the entrance. Inside, they'd stuck to a contemporary look with a black and gold colour scheme that was almost too dramatic a contrast to the white exterior of the building. It took a few moments for her head, and her eyes, to adjust and then she smiled. It worked very well.

It was only one o'clock. She was the first of the three to arrive but she'd expected to be. Everything had to be perfect, and arriving early to ensure it was seemed like a good idea. The tall elegant receptionist who checked her in didn't seem in the slightest bit perturbed when Megan said she wanted to check her friends' rooms too. 'If you'll give me a moment,' she said pleasantly, 'I'll call my colleague to relieve me and take you along.'

Minutes later, she opened the door into the first of the three rooms. 'They're adjacent rooms,' she explained, as she walked across the floor to the window. 'Identically furnished, with the same view and each has a door onto the communal patio.'

'Excellent,' Megan said, staring out and noting the comfortable outdoor seating. Maybe they could sit outside later and have a drink. 'This is my room?' she asked, turning to the receptionist, giving a slight smile when she saw the nod. 'Okay, if I could have a quick look at the other two then?'

They were, as the receptionist had said, identical.

'That's fine,' Megan said as they walked back along the corridor. 'My friends should be here soon; would you please arrange for a bottle of Bollinger and three glasses to be sent to my room.'

The receptionist assured her that would be done and headed off leaving Megan to return to her room. She was pleased with it. It was both stylish and comfortable. Sitting on the king-sized bed, she bounced a little, pleased to feel how soft it was. She opened her suitcase, hung up her dress, placed the rest of the clothes she'd brought on one of the wardrobe shelves and took her toiletries through to the large en suite.

Unable to settle, she stood at the window and stared out at

the garden without really seeing it, restlessly checking her watch every few minutes. She hoped they'd be here soon; her head was spinning with anxiety. She'd planned what to say, gone over the where and the how in her head several times, but she couldn't anticipate how they'd receive it. Anger. Disbelief. Shock. All of that and more, she guessed.

Twenty years. It was a long time to carry a lie. She hoped Trudy was right and everything would be better when it was out. Megan ran a hand over her sleek bob. Better maybe, for Trudy, who only knew the story of the lie. Megan wasn't so sure about Joanne and Beth; they'd been there, had witnessed it, had held her while she'd howled her pain. How were they going to feel when she tried to explain that she had been crying for something different?

She headed back to the foyer and had a look around, peering into the restaurant and the bar. A gin and tonic would have been the perfect relaxant, but she was afraid if she started she wouldn't stop. It would be too easy then to chicken out of what she was going to do. What she *had* to do. Thinking of honest beautiful Trudy would keep her focused.

Restless and fidgety, Megan stayed in the foyer, sat into a large comfortable armchair and pulled out her mobile. She'd liked to have rung and spoken to Trudy to hear her voice, but Megan didn't want to hear the slight chill that had lingered despite her words of love. Instead, she sent a text. *Arrived safely, hotel is interestingly different, missing you already.*

There was a pile of newspapers on the table beside her. Picking one up, she scanned the headlines with little interest, her eyes constantly drawn to the door as more guests arrived. But it wasn't until nearly three thirty that she saw Joanne's elegant figure push through the door and glance around. Megan waved and stood as she approached, holding out her arms. Joanne dropped her suitcase and they met in a brief comfortable hug. 'A belated Happy New Year,' Megan said, standing back. 'It's been a while.'

'We lead busy lives.' Joanne looked towards the reception desk. 'I'll go and check in while it's quiet, drop my case in my room, and join you back here, shall I?'

'Yes, do.' Megan smiled at her and sat back into the armchair. 'We may as well wait here for Beth. I have a bottle of Bolly waiting on ice in my room for whenever she arrives.'

'My favourite, excellent. Hopefully, she won't get delayed. I'll be back in a minute.' Joanne picked up her case and walked with an elegant sway to the reception desk.

Megan, worried about Beth's no-show, had picked up her mobile to check for messages when Joanne returned almost fifteen minutes later looking elegant and incredibly sexy in black trousers, a cream silk shirt and, despite her height, sky-scrapingly high stilettos. She was the only woman, apart from Trudy, who made Megan's heart beat a little faster.

Joanne sat in the chair opposite, crossed one long leg over the other and looked at her watch. 'Beth's very late.'

'She definitely said she was coming, but I'm starting to worry. You know what her job's like. I'll give her a ring.' Megan looked at her mobile with a frown. Everything was set, she didn't want things to fall apart at this stage.

Joanne's chair faced the window, so she was first to see the familiar figure hurrying across from the car park. 'You can relax. Here she comes.'

Megan glanced up to see Beth pushing through the door. Megan dropped her mobile into her bag and stood to wave, seeing her friend immediately turn in her direction. A smile of pleasure flitted across Megan's face. It was going to be fine.

They exchanged hugs. 'I'm so sorry,' Beth said. 'Work was mayhem as usual.'

'You're here, that's the important thing. Now,' Megan indicated the reception desk, 'let's get you checked in.' Relief washed over her. Everything was going to be okay.

~

Once she had checked in, they followed Beth to her room to drop off a holdall so tiny that Megan wondered if it contained anything more than a change of underwear. They were all chatting together without saying much as they headed to Megan's room and the promised drink. The hotel had been efficient and very generous. A small table had been set with the champagne chilling nicely in an ice bucket, three champagne glasses and a small tray holding bowls of mixed olives and a variety of nuts.

'Very nice,' Beth said, pulling out one of the chairs and dropping onto it with a tired groan. 'Just what I needed.'

Neither Joanne nor Megan fell into the trap of asking her if she'd had a tough morning. They knew the answer from old, and neither wanted to listen to a catalogue of the awful abuses she'd had to deal with since they'd seen her last. It wasn't lack of interest, as such, more self-preservation. Some of the stories Beth had told them over the years were sordid beyond belief.

Picking up the champagne, Megan peeled off the foil, grasped the cork with the towel that had been left draped over it, and twisted the bottle. The cork came out with a satisfying pop. Filling the glasses, she returned the bottle to the ice bucket and, waiting until her friends had picked up their glasses, she raised hers in a toast. 'To friendship.'

Joanne and Beth chimed *to friendship* back and they clinked glasses, sipped the champagne and murmured appreciatively.

'You can't beat it,' Joanne said, 'the best bubbles in the world.'

Megan smiled but said nothing and the silence that followed grew uncomfortable.

Suddenly, Beth gave a dramatic sigh. 'Okay, when are you going to tell us what this is all about? It's not like you to be so mysterious.'

Megan held her glass to her lips. Maybe it would be easier to tell them now and get it over with. She looked at them over the rim. Such good-looking women, how did she ever end up being friends with them? She was willing to risk losing their friendship to save her relationship with Trudy, but it wasn't something she wanted to do. Would they forgive her for lying? No, she wouldn't tell them yet, it would be better to wait and spend some time together first, perhaps to remind them why they'd become friends in the first place. 'In good time,' she said finally, 'don't go all detective on me.'

Beth held out her empty glass. 'I *am* a detective; mysteries don't sit well with me.'

'Everything will be revealed soon,' Megan said, picking up the bottle, filling Beth's glass, and holding it out towards Joanne who looked the epitome of cool relaxation, legs crossed, silk blouse open just enough to show the lacy border of her bra. Megan filled her glass, topped up her own and set the empty bottle down. 'Maybe I should have asked for two bottles,' she said with a chuckle.

'I brought a bottle,' Beth said, surprising them. 'It's in the car, I'll go and get it and stick it into the ice to cool.' Putting down her glass, she headed out.

Megan felt Joanne's eyes on her and fiddled with the stem of her glass. She took another sip, waiting for her to say something.

'I do wish you'd tell us what this is all about,' Joanne said softly, a worried frown creasing her forehead. 'It's not like you to be so cagey.'

Megan felt a band of stress tighten around her head. Perhaps she should tell her, then tell Beth later. Perhaps, she shouldn't tell either of them. She was still trying to decide what to do when Beth's return made the decision for her. She gave Joanne a quick smile, and shook her head. No, she'd stick to her carefully laid plan.

Luckily, Beth's performance in opening the bottle lightened the mood. Megan and Joanne chuckling at her exaggerated antics. It was Cava, not champagne, Megan noticed, as the cork popped. She didn't care; if she had a choice, she'd prefer Prosecco any day but she knew Joanne preferred what she considered to be *the real thing*.

'I know, I know,' Beth said, holding the bottle out for Joanne to see. 'It's Cava, but this is nice, seriously.'

If Joanne had any reservations, she kept them to herself, and Megan noticed she didn't refuse the refill. Eyes were raised, however, when *she* refused another drink.

'Come on, lightweight,' Beth said, wiggling the bottle.

Megan would have liked nothing better than to get smashed and forget all about her dirty little secret but she shook her head. 'No thanks, I've had enough for the mo. When you're finished, we'll be heading out and I need to drive.' She smiled at their astonishment. 'Don't worry, I've dinner booked in the restaurant here for later, I'll have a few glasses of wine then.'

'How much later?' Beth asked. 'I haven't had any lunch.'

When Megan said the table was booked for nine, Beth groaned and reached a hand for one of the bowls of nuts. 'I suppose this will have to keep me going.'

A sudden squeal from Joanne made the other women jump.

'Bloody hell,' Beth said, brushing spilled Cava from one leg and wiping her hand on the other.

'Sorry,' Joanne said, grabbing a napkin from the tray and handing it to her before turning her attention back to Megan. 'I suddenly remembered. Show us,' she said, holding out her hand.

Confused, Megan looked from Joanne to Beth, blinking rapidly. 'Show you what?'

'The ring!'

Megan had been so stressed about her strained relationship with Trudy and this meeting that she'd forgotten her two friends hadn't seen her engagement ring. She gave a gurgle of laughter and held her left hand forward before sliding it off her finger to allow them to try it on, and ooh and ahh over how lovely it was. They demanded to know the details of the wedding, both looking astounded when she had to admit that, as yet, there were none to share.

'It's early days,' she explained. Later, of course, they'd know the truth.

'We'll be your bridesmaids,' Joanne insisted, and for the next few minutes the discussion was on possible venues and what they would all wear.

Listening to them talk, enjoying their enthusiasm, Megan felt the bitter bite of regret. If only everything could stay like this.

The conversation drifted from weddings and venues to gossip about mutual friends as they worked their way through the bottle of Cava. Megan watched its level drop slowly, wanting to ask them to drink faster, knowing she wouldn't. She tried to keep up with the conversation, but kept slipping out of it into the one she'd rehearsed in her head so many times over the last few hours.

At last, the bottle was empty. As they drained the final drop from their glasses, she stood so abruptly their eyebrows shot up and she watched as they exchanged concerned looks.

'You'll know it all soon,' she said but there was a quaver in her voice and she saw Beth and Joanne's keen eyes search her face as if clues to what was going on were written there. 'You'll need your coats,' she said, and looked down at the shoes Joanne was wearing. 'Have you anything flatter? We'll be walking for about fifteen minutes.'

'I'd hope to go to the gym tomorrow so I have trainers with me, I'll change into them,' Joanne said. 'I wish you'd tell us what the hell's going on though. This is starting to freak me out a little.'

'Soon,' Megan said again, her voice a little firmer. She had to hold it together for a while longer.

'Okay,' Joanne said, lifting her hands in defeat. 'I'll go and change my shoes, and my trousers as well, otherwise they'll be trailing in the mud.'

Ten minutes later, they were crossing the foyer. Megan, trying to physically and mentally prepare herself for what lay ahead, ignored the worried glances that passed between her friends, 'It's only a short drive,' she said as they reached her car.

Joanne jumped into the front seat where there was more space for her long legs and Beth climbed in behind. It was a mere ten-minute drive to the pub. Joanne and Beth, chatting about a mutual friend recently engaged to a man neither of them liked, looked out the window as the car pulled into the car park. They stopped speaking mid-sentence, their eyes opening in shocked surprise and then they spoke at the same time.

'Isn't this the place...?'

'Isn't this where...?'

Neither finished their sentence, waiting for Megan to enlighten them.

'Yes, it is,' she said, opening the door and getting out. She shut the door and stayed leaning against it for a moment, hearing the muttered whispers of her friends who hadn't moved.

'Yes,' she said almost to herself, as she stared across at the pub. 'This was where it all started.'

She waited until they got out, and then, hooking her arms through theirs, she dragged them reluctantly with her across the small car park.

Reaching the pub, she released their arms, grabbed the cold metal handle and pulled the door open. 'After you,' she said, waiting until they passed through before taking a deep breath, and following them through the door and back twenty years.

12

Joanne felt her breath catch as they walked inside, almost overwhelmed by echoes of the past. Twenty years; she would have expected the place to have changed a little and she felt an irrational stirring of resentment that it looked exactly the same, that fateful night hadn't left its mark on it the way it had done on her.

It was an old coaching house whose owner obviously relished its history. Moments from its past were captured with drawings and photographs hanging on the uneven whitewashed walls. There were images of the old carriages and suitably dressed travellers as well as big draft horses and the more refined carriage horses. The windows were small, set deep into the thick walls so that the fading light outside barely penetrated. There were a few lamps dotted about but they provided little in the way of functional light and seemed to have been positioned simply to make the multitude of horse brasses that edged the beams criss-crossing the roof space gleam and shine. Joanne had never seen so many in one place and wasn't sure she wanted to again.

'I remembered it as being amazingly atmospheric,' Beth said, not making any attempt to disguise her disappointment.

Joanne, having swallowed her resentment, looked around with dismay at the worn, uncomfortable-looking seats, the chipped and scratched Formica tables and the pervading air of neglect. Had it been the same back then or had they seen it through different, more innocent, eyes? 'I think our standards have changed,' she said nodding towards one of many vacant tables. 'That looks about the best.'

There were only five other people in the pub, two couples sitting over their drinks and one elderly man propping up the bar. Apart from a first curious look, nobody paid them any attention.

'It doesn't look as if it's a student stomping ground anymore,' Joanne said with a wry smile, eying the rather grubby seat with disfavour before sitting.

'They probably head into Dover.' Beth shuffled in her seat. 'Not sure I blame them.'

Megan sat and then immediately stood. 'I'll get us some drinks. What'll you have?'

Joanne sensed the enthusiasm in Megan's voice was forced, the smile that went with it false and awkward. 'If we must stay, I'll have a G&T please.'

'I like trying local bitters,' Beth said, looking towards the bar to study the pumps. 'I'll try a pint of Red Fox.'

As soon as Megan left to get the drinks, Joanne turned to Beth, 'This is getting creepy. Have you any idea what's going on?'

Beth shook her head. 'Not a clue. She's being very odd and, to be honest, I could have done without all this cloak and dagger stuff. I've got enough to deal with.'

Surprised at the note of defeat in her voice, Joanne studied Beth more closely. She was always pale, but today her pallor was more noticeable and her eyes were red-rimmed. Unusually, Beth wouldn't meet her eyes, as if she were afraid they might give something away. It had been a while since they'd met; they were getting older and time moved past with a swiftness that occasionally startled Joanne. It had been November sometime, or was it October? A few months ago anyway; she wasn't sure what was going on in Beth's life anymore. 'Are you okay?'

'Oh, just work, a difficult case came in last week, sometimes it's hard to let it go,' Beth said, slipping off her coat and letting it hang on the chair behind her.

But Joanne noticed she still didn't meet her eyes. 'How's Graham?'

'Never better.'

The blunt non-committal response was a clear indicator that something was wrong and Joanne knew whatever it was, it was personal not work-related, not entirely anyway. Beth, unlike her, had never learned to completely separate her personal and her work life. Joanne had met Graham numerous times over the years. He was a nice guy, one of the good ones. She wanted to ask Beth if there was something wrong between them, but if there was, who was Joanne to give relationship advice? She wasn't the person, it wasn't the time, and certainly, this wasn't the right place.

Megan returned with three glasses awkwardly held in her hands, giving Joanne a grateful nod as she reached up to take them from her.

There was a long embarrassing silence as each picked up their drink. It would have been nice to have made a toast, to drink to happy memories and times gone by, but not there, not in that place. Joanne took a mouthful of her G&T, regretting not having asked for a double, bitterly sorry that she'd ever agreed to come. As soon as Megan had mentioned Capel-le-Ferne, Joanne should have made an excuse. What had happened that night, couldn't unhappen.

Joanne took another swallow of her drink and looked at Megan. Of the three of them, she'd changed the most and was hardly recognisable as the student who'd dropped that tray of food in the university restaurant, a memory that made Joanne smile.

However, it wasn't the three years in university that had changed Megan. The same awkward woman had come to Capel-le-Ferne twenty years ago, but although she'd come through that traumatic ordeal so well, with such incredible bravery that Joanne was full of admiration for her, she'd been a different woman when she'd left. Joanne had been haunted by that night for a long time. It had taken many months for the horror of it all to fade, for her to be able to put the memory of Megan's distress and desolation in the past. But she'd never forgotten.

Joanne had done things and made choices based on what had happened that terrible night. Now, looking across the table to where Megan sat, pale and weary, Joanne knew, given the same circumstances, she'd make the same choices again.

13

Megan put down her mineral water and took a deep breath. It caught halfway on a sob that had her friends leaning towards her with worried eyes. She held up a hand, gave them a reassuring smile and waited until they sat back before speaking. 'It was different the last time we were here; it was buzzing with local people and those young and very handsome students. I remember, when we walked in, every man turned and looked the two of you over with appreciation. You both preened... it was quite amusing really.' Her smile was dreamy, lost in the past, although her voice said she'd been anything but amused.

Joanne gave an uneasy laugh. 'Preened? Really?'

Megan reached over and patted her arm. 'It wasn't deliberate, just the automatic reaction of someone who knows how good they look.' She gave a slight shrug, picked up her glass with a trembling hand and took a sip of water before continuing. 'I tried not to let it bother me, you know, but I was a big ugly lump, there was no denying it.'

An uncomfortable few seconds passed before she continued. 'It didn't bother me in school, I always felt I made up for it by being more intelligent and smarter than everyone else.' She shrugged, a weary defeated rise and fall of her shoulders. 'It wasn't until I met you two that I realised what an absolute horror I was.' She looked from one to the other. 'Remember the day we met?'

'You dropped your tray in the restaurant,' Beth said with a smile of reminiscence. 'Food and drink went flying everywhere and caused a huge commotion.'

'I managed to get half a dozen people upset and I was so mortified I couldn't pick everything up fast enough. Then you two got up from a nearby table and helped me.'

Joanne smiled. 'You looked so woebegone, and people were being so mean, how could we not?'

Megan, returned the smile briefly and played with her glass before continuing. 'Meeting people like you wasn't something I'd expected. It wasn't something I'd wanted, but you know what you're both like.' Her smile was genuine, warm. 'Irresistible forces, both of you; before I was even aware of what was happening, I'd been swept along on a wave that just kept rolling.' Her smile faded and a sad expression flitted across her face. 'But being friends with you was a double-edged sword.'

'I don't understand,' Joanne said. 'I thought you liked hanging around with us.'

Megan gave a frustrated shake of her head. 'I'm not explaining myself very well.'

To her surprise, Beth reached over and put a hand on her arm. 'Actually, I think I understand. You liked being with us but maybe we made you feel a little...' She hesitated. 'I can't think of any word other than inadequate.'

'Inadequate?' Megan looked at her. 'That's a nice word for it but it's not quite right.' She wasn't sure if she could explain how she'd felt. 'When it was just the three of us, it was fine. We'd laugh and joke and, although I was aware how gorgeous you both were, I never felt in any way different when I was with you, neither of you ever made me feel bad about myself. But when we went out it was another matter. I could see the sideways glances people gave as they wondered why two good-looking popular students wanted to be friends with someone so short, fat and ugly.'

'I'm sure they didn't think that,' Joanne hurried to say. 'You were always so hard on yourself. We never considered you ugly.'

'Short, fat and ugly,' Megan insisted. 'You were more honest back then, Jo. Remember you told me I should get my teeth straightened and have laser surgery on my eyes?'

Joanne's cheeks reddened. 'I don't remember saying anything like that. I'm sorry, if I did, it was unforgiveable of me.'

Megan gave a short laugh. 'You really don't remember?' When Joanne shook her head, Megan shrugged. 'Well, you did, and you were right.' She took another sip. 'I got both done after we parted that summer. I persuaded my parents to pay for it as a graduation present.'

Beth chimed in. 'Yes, and although we spoke on the phone, we didn't meet up for several months afterwards and by then you'd lost loads of weight too. I remember barely recognising you when you walked into the restaurant.'

'Your reaction was perfect,' Megan said with a laugh. 'I swear your jaw dropped open.' She looked from one to the other. 'I'll never be a good-looking woman, but I'm happy in my skin now. That's what was important to me, not the weight loss, as such, but being happy with my shape, with the face that looks at me in the mirror. Back then...' She sighed. 'When you invited me to come away for the night to celebrate our graduation, I was going to refuse at first, like I always had. Remember those weekends you two went away together? You'd tell me stories of everything you'd got up to: the men, the drinking, the fun you had while I was slogging over my books.'

Their eyes were fixed on her so intently, listening to every word she said, more importantly, caring about what she said. She'd made the mistake of taking their friendship for granted and now, when she was in danger of losing it, she realised how very precious it was. Now it was too late, it was time to move on with her story.

'Girly nights away really weren't something I was keen on anyway. I'd absolutely no interest in men and hadn't, at that stage, really thought much about being attracted to women. But I'd become so fond of you as friends, and I knew I was going to miss you both desperately, so when you asked, this time I thought, why not.' She ran a hand over her hair, playing for time as she tried to get her story out in a way they'd understand. 'It was fun at first,' she continued, 'fun while we were in the bunga- low, the three of us, chatting like we always did, just being friends. But then we came here.' She looked around the room, her eyes losing focus as they drifted back to that night.

'We'd had a lot of wine before we left the bungalow, from what I can remember,' Joanne said. 'I know I was fairly drunk.'

'We all were,' Megan agreed. 'I wasn't used to drinking, but when we came in here I sobered up pretty quickly. That gang of students was around us like bees to a honeypot or, should I say, they were around you two. I was edged to the side of the group until, before I knew what was happening, I was staring at their tall broad backs. It was almost as if they'd deliberately closed ranks to keep me out.'

Beth shuffled in her chair. 'We were only out for a bit of fun, Megan.'

'Neither of you even noticed I wasn't with you,' Megan said quietly, as if Beth hadn't spoken. 'I was going to leave and go back to the bungalow but I felt so... hurt and disappointed, I suppose.' She sipped her water and then nodded towards a corner of the bar. 'I drifted down there, trying not to look as miserable as I felt. Obviously, I wasn't doing a very good job of it because a second later there was a man beside me, asking if I was okay.' Closing her eyes for a moment, she swallowed. 'He wasn't bad-looking, pleasant to chat to but not very bright, and he'd absolutely no sense of humour. I watched you both laughing and flirting and I remember feeling suddenly so terribly angry.'

'With us?' Beth said, thinking back to that night.

'With you, with me.' Megan lifted her hand in a vague gesture of hopelessness. 'Mostly with myself. For having come along in the first place, and for feeling so damn envious of you both. I watched you flirt and chat with those students, watched as they all but drooled over you both, and I wondered what it must be like to be so admired and swooned over, to be the centre of attention.'

'Is that why you agreed to go with him?' Joanne leaned forward and rested her hand on Megan's arm.

She put her hand on top of it and kept it there as she continued her story. 'When he said he was leaving, I asked him if he could drop me off on the way but he didn't have a car with him. He asked me where we were staying and, when I told him, he said he passed by it, if I wanted to walk with him.' She took her hand back and held it to her trembling mouth for a moment before nodding to their almost-empty glasses. 'Finish your drinks, we have one more place to go.' Their startled looks would have amused her had the circumstances been different. But they weren't. Coming back here, it was worse than Megan expected but, she had to hold it together for a little while longer.

They finished their drinks in silence. Megan was first to stand, pulling on the jacket she'd hung on the back of the chair. With a final look around, she walked towards the exit, hearing her friends behind her, muttering to each other in worried tones. Pushing the door open, Megan stepped out into the night and held it open for them. 'It'll all be clear soon. We're going to walk for a little way, okay?'

'This is getting seriously weird,' Beth said, shoving her hands into her coat pockets.

'It's not far,' Megan said. She led the way, keeping to the side of the road. In a few hundred yards, the light from the pub's brightly lit car park faded and, with the moon obscured by heavy cloud, they walked in almost darkness for a few minutes until a dip in the road ahead allowed them to see the lights of Capel-le-Ferne. The bungalow they'd stayed in that night was the third in the first row of homes they would come to.

'We're going to the bungalow,' Joanne said, catching up with Megan and linking her arm through hers while Beth continued to walk behind.

'Yes,' Megan said, the warmth of the body beside her giving her some comfort. It would all be over soon; they'd know the worst about her, and they'd understand. And forgive? She wasn't sure.

They reached the bungalow a minute later. The gate was shut; one car parked in the driveway indicating someone lived there but the windows were dark and there was no sign of life. Megan stopped. Pulling away from Joanne, she moved to the gate and leaned on it to stare at the unremarkable bungalow, hearing the restless shuffling footsteps of her two friends behind, one of them, Beth she guessed, sighing loudly.

Megan turned. 'I haven't gone crazy, honestly. It seemed easier, to bring you back here to tell you something I should have told you both a long time ago, something I need to tell you now.' She saw their puzzled expressions and hoped they wouldn't turn to disgust. She wished she could change her mind, even now, to forget about it. But she remembered Trudy's look of disappointment. She was right, it had to end.

14

'That night,' Megan said slowly, her voice soft and low, her eyes on the ground between them, 'we were chatting as we walked along. Once, when I stumbled, he caught my arm to steady me and then, when we lost the light from the car park, he held my hand for a few feet. Only for a few feet, but it felt... nice.' Megan gulped. 'When we got here, I asked him to come in–'

'What?' Beth interrupted her. 'You said he'd dragged you inside.'

'Please, let me tell it.' Megan looked up to see Beth shrug. '*I* asked him inside,' she repeated, laying heavy emphasis on the I, wanting to make it absolutely clear. '*I* pushed my breasts against his arm and asked him to come inside.' She wrapped her arms around herself, not so much for comfort as to stop herself falling apart. 'I suppose I was lucky he didn't laugh,' she said, her voice laced with bitterness. 'But he did smile. He smiled, and said he wasn't interested, that he was a married man and didn't cheat on his wife. And he walked away. She took a deep shaky breath. 'He walked away and I went inside alone.'

'And then he came back?' Joanne asked.

94

Megan looked at Joanne's puzzled face. She was such an honest woman, what was she going to make of her lies? 'No, he didn't come back. I went inside and took a bottle of whiskey from the cabinet in the lounge, poured myself a glass and downed it. When it was finished, I poured another. After that–'

'He came back then?'

Megan shook her head and continued in a harsh grating whisper. 'He didn't come back. He *never* came back. I'd almost begged him to fuck me, but I was so ugly, so undesirable, that even when I handed it to him on a plate, he wasn't interested.' Panting, she swallowed and said quietly, 'I didn't know I was capable of such anger. I felt rejected by everyone, by you, by that sad creep I'd thrown myself at. After the whiskey, I started to cry, becoming hysterical and the anger...' She squeezed her eyes shut, her mouth twisting in a terrible grimace.

It was a few seconds before she spoke again, her voice thick with emotion. 'It was as if the anger had consumed me. I became this growling snarling animal, pulling at my clothes, tearing my dress. I hit myself, dug my nails into my skin and tried to scratch my ugly face off. I was screaming as I threw myself against the walls and banged my head on the floor. Absolute and utter self-loathing. I was eaten up by it and then, when I was at my worst, you came home.' She took a shuddering breath. 'You came home and jumped to the wrong conclusion.'

'What?' Beth said, moving closer until Megan could smell her perfume. 'Wait a minute! Are you telling us that you weren't raped?'

'No,' Joanne said, softly. 'You were, you're just trying to block it out or something.'

'I wasn't raped,' Megan said firmly, each word loud and clear. 'If I hadn't been so drunk and so full of that dreadful anger, I would have told you, but then...' She let her breath out in a long slow sigh filled with regret. 'Then... you were both hovering around me, being so kind, so attentive, so *nice* to me. For a moment, *I* was the centre of attention. Ugly undesirable me. And, I loved it.' She waited for a comment and, when none came, she said, 'I lapped it all up and then, well, then it was too late to tell you the truth.'

'Bloody hell!' Beth shouted, the words bitten out with such anger that spittle landed on Megan's cheek. 'I don't believe this! All these years, you've let us think you'd been raped, and now you're telling us it was all a big lie.' Beth gave Megan one last glare before turning away and walking to the far side of the road to stand visibly shaking in the semi-darkness. Megan could hear Beth muttering to herself.

Even in the dim light that filtered across from the bungalows on either side, Megan could see Joanne had grown pale. 'I'm sorry,' Megan said, knowing what an empty useless word it was, but it was all she had.

'Sorry?' Joanne whispered.

Beth turned and walked back to join her, continuing to glare at Megan. 'That was why you insisted we didn't report it to the police. All your crap about wanting to concentrate on your law career, not wanting to be that woman who'd been raped, it was all a load of baloney.'

'I would never have let it go that far,' Megan said. 'If you'd insisted that I had to report it, I'd have had no option but to confess, but you seemed to understand so I knew eventually it would be forgotten about.'

'Forgotten about?' Joanne whispered.

Beth turned to Joanne and glared at her. 'Will you stop parroting what she says, for God's sake!'

'I'm just stunned,' Joanne said, wiping a hand over her eyes.

'We're both stunned,' Beth said, looking back at Megan. 'How can you have lived with that lie all these years? And why tell us now? Why didn't you bloody well keep it to yourself? Wouldn't it have been better?'

Much better. Megan should have borne the burden of living the lie quietly, as she'd always planned to do. But like all good plans, it depended on everyone playing their part. 'Really, Beth! *You* broke your promise and told Trudy I'd been raped, remember? I know,' she held her hands up, 'you were drunk and you assumed I'd told her. I hadn't, of course, and never intended to, but your intoxicated, toxic whispers, caught me off-guard and I'd no time to think of the best thing to do.'

Megan sighed heavily. 'Stupidly, I decided it was easier to continue the lie than to admit the truth. But then Trudy proposed to me. It should have been the happiest moment of my life. The woman I adore, asked me to marry her.' Megan sniffed, and looked at Beth's closed, angry face silently pleading with her to understand. 'She asked me to marry her, and spoke about how honest and pure our relationship was, how much she trusted and respected me. I listened to her words and the lie seemed to jump up and punch me in the gut.'

A car driving by slowed as it passed, the driver peering at them as if unsure whether he should stop. Beth waved at it impatiently, and it kept going. 'We should go back,' she said.

'Wait!' Megan said, reaching a hand out to her. 'You have to understand, I had to tell Trudy the truth, I couldn't marry her until I had. There was a moment when I didn't think she'd forgive me, that my honesty about that stupid lie had destroyed everything. But she said if I were honest with you two as well, she'd try to put it behind us.'

'I still can't believe you made it all up.' Joanne's voice was ragged with disbelief.

Tears fell down Megan's cheeks. 'I didn't... or at least I hadn't planned to. It hadn't even entered my head, but when you both came in and assumed...' She turned from them, hanging her head and resting her hands on the rough brick garden wall. 'Do you know what the worst part is–'

'You mean there's something worse than lying about being raped?' Beth's voice was scathing

There was silence for a moment, broken only by the eerie screech of an owl in the distance. Nobody moved for what felt like hours until finally, Megan spoke, her voice trembling. 'The worst part, is that for a few minutes I was pleased that you thought I'd been raped... that you'd think a *man* would want me, even in such a violent, brutal way.'

Beth swore softly. 'What?'

'Oh, I know now how stupid it was to think that way, but back then I knew nothing.' There was an edge of desperation in Megan's voice. 'I was sexually ignorant. Still a virgin. Totally confused about my sexuality, and convinced I was so unbearably ugly that nobody would ever want to be with me and then, there you were, thinking that this man had wanted me. And for one second, and I know this sounds hard to believe, but it made me feel better about myself, as if I was just like you two with all your men-troubles and woes.'

'That's ridiculous!' Beth snapped. 'Rape isn't about desire, it's about power and control. You know that. You knew it back then, you were never stupid, Megan. Or,' she sneered, 'I thought you weren't, now I'm not so sure. This is all so... warped.'

Megan turned away from Beth's condemning eyes. This was so much worse than she'd expected. Joanne had stepped away from the light to hover at the edge of the darkness on the other side of the road. 'Jo?' Megan begged, desperate for a crumb of understanding.

'Warped,' Joanne echoed Beth's word.

'Oh, for fuck's sake,' Beth said, turning away from them both. 'I don't believe any of this! This has to be the craziest thing I've ever heard, and I'm a bloody police officer, I've heard crazy in many forms.' When nobody spoke, Beth continued. 'Do you know what? I don't want to hear another word of your sob story, Megan. I'm starving. All I've had to eat all bloody day are blasted nuts, so I'm heading back for that dinner we were promised and I'm going to get very, very drunk.' She took a few steps before she stopped and shouted, 'Come on. I'm damned if I'm walking to the hotel.'

Nothing was said as the three did the short walk back to the car. Megan slid into the driver's seat, not surprised when the others both sat in the back. In silence, she drove to the hotel.

~

'We can go straight in to dinner, unless you want to change?' Megan said, parking in the same space she'd left earlier.

Beth gave an unamused snort of laughter. 'Seriously? You really think we're going to dress up, sit and make casual conversation over dinner after what we've just heard?'

Without another word, they walked from the car park.

The hotel's restaurant was off the foyer. Leading the way, Megan stopped at the door and gave the maître d' her name.

'A table for three,' he said, checking the reservation.

'Yes,' Megan said and looked around. Beth was behind her, glaring at her with hard narrowed eyes. It was a look she guessed Beth usually reserved for the thugs she met in the course of her job, one that was both condemning and unforgiving. A glance over her shoulder showed no sign of Joanne.

Megan waited until they were sitting at the table before asking, 'Is she coming back?'

'I doubt it,' Beth said, picking up the menu. 'You know what she's like. This has hit her hard. You heard her repeating what you said like a blasted parrot. Shock, is my guess.'

'And you?' Megan asked, not bothering to hide the note of

desperation in her voice. 'Do you think you'll ever be able to forgive me?' She held her breath as Beth kept her eyes down, focused on a menu Megan was sure she wasn't reading. 'Please, Beth.'

That brought Beth's attention to her but her eyes were cold. 'Forgive? I don't know, to be honest. It's going to take time to understand what you did and all the...' her mouth twisted in a grimace, '...consequences.'

'I'm so sorry,' Megan said, wearily. 'Sorry for misleading you both in the first place, sorry I didn't bury the secret and keep my mouth shut.'

'That might have been the wisest course of action, honesty is a dangerous blade to wave about.'

Megan swallowed. A dangerous blade? Yes, it was proving to be that. She wondered if Joanne would ever speak to her again. Honesty... it was supposed to have been a good thing. How terribly naïve she'd been; she'd waved that damn blade around and lanced the deeply hidden festering boil that was her secret, allowing the poisonous crap to leak out and destroy everyone around her.

Her shoulders slumped as she felt the weight of what she'd done pressing her down. She should have kept her mouth shut. It was all too late. She had to hope for forgiveness from her friends, and from Trudy. Thinking about her fiancée caused Megan a jolt of pain, anguish twisting her face. What if she didn't? What if her damn stupid, self-indulgent honesty had spoiled everything permanently?

15

B eth watched Megan's torment, resisting the temptation to offer comfort. Telling the truth had been an unbelievably stupid thing to have done, almost as incredible as her lie all those years ago. Beth still couldn't quite get her head around that and refused to think of the implications. Her brain had enough to cope with. There'd be time to consider everything later.

When the waiter returned, Beth insisted they order dinner, too hungry to allow Megan's dramatic revelation delay them any longer. Joanne, she guessed, wouldn't be joining them. Beth glanced at the menu and ordered the roast lamb, ordering the same for Megan when she looked blankly at the waiter.

'And a bottle of Chardonnay,' Beth said, handing the waiter the menu.

They sat silently as they waited for their meal. Megan, Beth supposed, had run out of words to apologise or to justify her actions and since the only words she could think to say were variations on, *you stupid fucking idiot*, she said nothing.

The wine arrived almost immediately, Beth nodding as the waiter showed her the label, resisting the temptation to tell him to get a move on, save all the palaver and pour the damn stuff. She gulped a mouthful when he'd gone, and then another, emptying the glass and refilling it.

Finally, into their uncomfortable silence, the food came. The roast lamb on large white plates, the vegetables in individual crescent-shaped dishes. It all looked very nice but as soon as it came, her appetite deserted her. She forced down a few mouthfuls, refusing to look across the table or to acknowledge that Megan hadn't moved, her meal sitting untouched.

Beth ate a little more before pushing the plate away. She picked up her wine glass, sat back and stared across the table with little sympathy, taking in the trembling lower lip, the furrowed forehead, and tear-filled eyes of her friend. It was hard to believe Megan had lied all those years ago. Beth remembered the terrible feeling of helplessness when she'd seen her poor abused body. It wasn't something she'd ever forgotten. And now, they were to believe that all that awful damage had been self-inflicted. That Beth and Joanne had jumped to the same wrong conclusion. Even with the confession still ringing in her ears, Beth found it hard to believe.

Putting her glass down, she asked, 'Are you sure?'

Megan couldn't hide the tremble in her voice. 'Sure that I wasn't raped, you mean? It's hardly something I'm going to lie about.'

'It wasn't something I thought you'd lie about twenty years ago either. And please,' she said, holding up her hand, 'don't give me that crap about it being our fault, that we'd jumped to the wrong conclusion and you'd gone along with it. That's nonsense.'

'I hadn't planned it; I didn't do any of it deliberately. I was just so angry and very drunk. And then it all snowballed.'

Draining her glass, Beth picked up the wine bottle and refilled it. Alcohol probably wouldn't help but it might soften the edges of what felt like a nightmare. 'You should eat something,' she said, noticing Megan still hadn't touched her meal.

Megan picked up her cutlery with little enthusiasm and after a couple of mouthfuls, she pushed the plate away and reached for her wine glass. 'I hope Joanne got something to eat,' she said quietly.

Feeling a little light-headed from all the alcohol, Beth shut her eyes. Maybe she should go to bed; she'd wake up in the morning and find this was all a bad dream.

She opened her eyes to see Megan staring at her and shook her head. Not a bad dream, a waking nightmare. 'Seriously, this confession was the stupidest idea, I don't know what possessed you.' Or maybe she did. She knew how much Megan loved Trudy. Would Beth do the same to get Graham back? Even confess all she'd done? She gulped some wine. *All she'd done.* She tried not to think about it and, Megan, she guessed, had no idea the can of worms she'd opened.

Megan drained her glass of wine with one swallow. 'So, what now?'

Beth frowned at her. What now? Was she supposed to know? Was she supposed to sweep up the mess – Megan's mess – and make everything better? She had her own problems with Graham to deal with. And it was going to take a while for Megan's confession to sink in, longer to think it through, and a long, long time to come to terms with it. 'I don't know,' she admitted. 'I'm still trying to process it.'

'Joanne seemed to take it very badly.'

A gross understatement, she had taken it very badly indeed. She'd looked shocked, stunned even. But then she'd always been the more honest of the three of them, the kind of person who'd check her change and if a penny over, bring it back. 'It's going to take time,' Beth said, wishing she could think of something more profound to say.

When they'd finished the wine, Beth suggested they go and knock on Joanne's door. 'Maybe she'll speak to us now.' It was worth a shot. She was worried about how awful Joanne had looked. If nothing else, they could check that she was okay.

They knocked and waited. When there was no answer, they tried again. Beth held her cheek close to the door. 'Joanne, come on, let me in.' When there was still no answer, her brow creased in concern. 'I don't like this,' she said, almost to herself. 'Wait here, Megan. I'll go and get someone to let us in. I'll tell them we're concerned about our friend.'

She hurried to the reception, the receptionist looking up at her approach with a puzzled smile. 'Is everything okay?'

Beth, with years of training behind her, managed to control her voice. 'Joanne Marsden, my friend, she had some bad news earlier and went to her room. We've been knocking on her door but there's no answer and we're a bit worried.'

The receptionist's expression went from puzzled to concerned in a blink. 'What room number?'

'Six,' Beth said, squeezing her hands together. To her surprise, the receptionist's expression cleared.

'Room six?' Her eyes turned to the computer screen in front of her and she tapped a few keys with her long manicured fingernails before looking back to Beth. 'Ms Marsden checked out about thirty minutes ago. She said an urgent matter had come up and she needed to go home.'

Stunned, Beth wanted to scream at the receptionist, to reach across the desk, grab her by the neck and shake her until her eyes popped. Instead, she shut her own eyes briefly and took a deep breath. It wasn't the receptionist's fault. She wasn't to know that Joanne had had far too much to drink and shouldn't be driving anywhere, wasn't to know how badly she'd taken Megan's stupid, unnecessary, unfuckingbelievable news. For a moment, Beth was unable to move, as if her feet were stuck to the floor.

'Are you all right?' the receptionist asked.

All right? No, she bloody well wasn't all right! It was a mess; every fucking thing was a mess. 'Yes,' Beth said, with a nod, 'thank you.' She moved stiffly away, having to concentrate hard to put one foot in front of the other, feeling the receptionist's suddenly curious eyes watching her, seeing the door just ahead, inches, miles. On the other side, she leaned against the wall for a few seconds, armpits sticky, forehead damp. She wiped her eyes with the sleeve of her shirt and took deep breaths, trying to get her thoughts in order.

When she got back to Joanne's room, a few seconds later, Megan was leaning against the door, her cheek resting against it, her eyes tightly shut. Maybe she was apologising, begging Joanne's forgiveness for the lies, for the shocking deceit. Beth couldn't help her lip curling. It was going to take a lot of that before this was resolved. 'She's gone,' she said bluntly. 'She checked out half an hour ago.'

'Gone?' Megan opened her eyes wide. 'Oh no!' Blood seemed to drain from her face, she held shaking hands up to it, red varnished nails stark against her skin. 'She's had too much to drink to drive safely.'

Beth had thought exactly the same thing, but there wasn't much they could do about it except to hope that Joanne got home without crashing, or worse, killing someone. 'The shock probably sobered her up,' Beth said and then regretted the words when she saw Megan's horrified face. 'There's no point in worrying. I'll text her, tell her to let us know she got home safely.'

Megan started to cry. 'If anything happens to her.'

The temptation to say that it would be all her fault was brushed aside. Joanne's decision to drive under the influence was hers alone. It was far too easy to blame others. Megan was trying to blame them for assuming she'd been raped, for putting the crazy idea into her head in the first place but they'd all made their own choices. One thing was certain, the honesty about what had happened that night twenty years ago was stopping here.

Some secrets were better being kept.

16

Beth and Megan had breakfast together the next morning. Beth had wanted to leave earlier, to get away from Megan's pleading eyes and sad desperation, and would have done if she hadn't knocked at Beth's door at eight thirty.

'I heard your shower running,' Megan said, explaining her arrival.

Beth, one hand on the door, glared at her, but one look at Megan's pale face and the dark shadows under her eyes that said she'd not slept well, if at all, and Beth couldn't bring herself to slam the door in her face. She, however, had taken a couple of sleeping pills and slept like the dead. It was the only way she got through a lot of her nights. It was the only way she'd slept since Graham had left.

The dining room was already busy with a continuous movement of people between their seats and the breakfast buffet. Beth and Megan were shown to a table for two overlooking a garden that probably looked pretty in the sunshine, but in the gloom of a thundery sky there was something chilling about the imposing palm trees and the spiky leaved cordylines.

'Creepy,' Beth said, moving to sit with her back to it.

The waiter brought them the cafetière of coffee they'd requested and left them to help themselves. Beth went to the buffet, returning with a single croissant, and sat nibbling it as Megan reluctantly went up and filled a bowl with cereal.

Neither of them finished what they'd chosen. Instead, they drank cup after cup of coffee and sat staring into space. The original plan had been that they'd use the spa facilities for a few hours and leave after a late lunch. There would have been time to chat and catch up on their very different lives and somewhere during the morning, Beth had planned to break the news about Graham. Now she wanted to get away as fast as she could, leave Capel-le-Ferne and never look back. 'I'm heading off straight after breakfast,' she said, pouring more coffee from a second pot the waiter had brought.

Megan looked up and blinked slowly. 'Yes, I suppose that's for the best.' She put her coffee down, the cup rattling on the saucer. 'I thought I might go home via Royal Tunbridge Wells and–'

'No,' Beth interrupted her without apology. 'Absolutely not. You need to give her some space.' When it looked as if Megan was going to argue the point, Beth shook her head. 'Please, for Joanne's sake, leave it for a few days.' Beth ran a hand over her hair. 'I tell you what, if we don't hear from her by tonight, I'll drive down tomorrow and check on her, okay?'

With reluctance, Megan said, 'Okay, if you think it's for the best.'

What would have been for the best, would have been for her to have kept her mouth shut on her nasty little secret, but there was no point in rehashing that now.

As soon as breakfast was over, they left, meeting in reception a few minutes later. 'I'll pay for the dinner and drinks,' Beth said, as they headed towards the desk.

'No, that's okay, I'll get it,' Megan said, taking out her wallet.

Beth didn't argue, handing the receptionist her key card and, with a promise to let Megan know if Joanne got in contact, she headed off, checking her phone as she walked. No message from her, and although she really wasn't expecting one, her heart ached when she saw there were none from Graham.

She drove home without stopping, keeping the radio blaring to try to drown the thoughts whirling around her head. It didn't work and by the time she reached home, her head was pounding from the effort as much as from the noise. Graham hadn't answered her text. She'd no idea where he was staying, but if there was some tiny part of her that hoped he'd have returned while she was away, it died a quick death when she pushed open the front door. It was too quiet. A deadly, lonely silence that told her the house was empty.

It took her only a few seconds to realise that while she had been away, Graham had called in, and the few things he'd left behind were gone. She walked from room to room, a heavy weight in her chest as she took note of everything he'd taken. The few books that were his, a couple of CDs, an old sweatshirt hanging on the back of a kitchen chair. He'd taken the lot. But what made her cry out, what made her howl, a sad pathetic sound of loss and despair, was when she saw what he *hadn't* taken. There were four framed photographs of the two of them on the bookshelf in the sitting room, smiling photographs taken on holidays over the years. Happy shots of a happy couple. Four of them. They were still there. He hadn't even wanted to take one.

It was that, more than anything else, that told her he wasn't coming back. And once again, he'd not bothered to leave a note, his actions speaking for themselves. They'd need to have a conversation, eventually, about the house, but it wouldn't be done in the middle of their pain. *Their pain*, because, even though he was the instigator, she knew he would be hurting as much as her.

Swallowing the lump in her throat, she returned to the kitchen and sat. The champagne was still where he'd put it, listing sadly in a bowl of water. She supposed she should empty it but she didn't move. There were other practicalities she'd have to consider, but right now all she wanted to do was weep. In less than a week, she'd lost Graham and all trust in one of her best friends.

Beth was still sitting twenty minutes later when her mobile chirped. The time would come, she knew, when she wouldn't hope that it was Graham. But it hadn't come yet, and she grabbed it and stared at the screen, swallowing her disappointment when she saw it was Joanne. Beth was tempted to ignore it, unsure if she was able to talk to her just then. But, with a deep breath, she pressed the key to answer. Maybe someone else's misery would be the perfect antidote. 'Hi, Joanne. Are you okay?'

'Fine,' the answer came, barely above a whisper. 'I'm sorry for going off without telling you last night, I needed to get away.'

Beth heard the strain in Joanne's voice. 'That's okay, don't worry about it, it was a weird day.'

'Yes.'

She waited for more, holding the phone tightly to her ear. Thinking she'd been cut off, Beth called, 'Joanne?'

'Yes.'

Bloody hell. Why had she answered the damn phone? 'Megan was terribly worried about you,' Beth said, trying not to let her irritation show. 'She wanted to call at your house on the way back this morning but I persuaded her to give you some space.'

'Thank you.'

'It's going to take time for us to come to terms with what she told us, Jo. I think she's hoping we'll forgive her.'

'I'm sure she is.'

There was no inflection in the words, just a sad monotone. Beth, tired of the one-way conversation, decided she'd had enough. 'Anyway, good to hear you're okay. I was heading out. Do you want me to let Megan know?'

'Please. And thanks. Talk soon.'

Joanne hung up before Beth had a chance to say goodbye, leaving her looking at the phone with growing irritation. Megan, she knew, would be anxiously waiting for news but Beth couldn't cope with another laboured conversation. Instead, she sent a short text. *Joanne rang, she's fine.* Pressing send, Beth switched off her phone.

The silence of the house was uncomfortable, almost unnerving, and the rest of the day stretched drearily before her. Graham had been part of her life for so long, she couldn't remember how she'd filled the weekends before him, but anything was preferable to moping around the house feeling sorry for herself.

Running upstairs, she stuffed her gym gear into a bag and, an hour later, she was working up a sweat running on the treadmill. She went straight from it to the weight machines, trying to lose herself in physical exertion. Pushing herself, she deliberately overdid it to cause pain in the hope that it would consume the ache that had settled in her chest.

She stayed until the gym shut at nine and then, reluctantly, drove home. It crossed her mind to call around to one of their friends and see if they knew where Graham was. But what if he were there? Most of their friends, if she were honest, were his, not hers. Megan and Joanne were the only two who were just hers. And if she did go around, and they didn't know where he was, or worse, knew but wouldn't tell her, what then? She'd look sad and pathetic and she didn't want that. It was going to take time but she had to face the truth. It was over, she had to let him go.

She did a detour and stopped at a row of shops. In the off licence, she chose a bottle of wine, red, since Graham would only ever drink white, grabbing the pitiful feeling of satisfaction with both hands and, as it quickly faded, she picked up a bottle of whiskey to add to her purchases. The Indian restaurant next door caught her eye. She stood for a moment reading their take-away menu, thinking she should eat something. Nothing appealed. Heartache was a great appetite suppressant.

Unusually, she managed to get parking right outside their house and was immediately sorry she had. The dark windows screamed *nobody's home*. There was a timer somewhere, she'd find it and plug one of the lamps into it. It would make coming home late a little easier. But for now, she pushed open the door and quickly reached for the light switch.

In the kitchen, knowing she should eat something before she started to drink, she opened the fridge, her eyes lighting on a chunk of cheese; she picked it up and dropped it quickly with a loud *yuk* when she saw it was fuzzy with mould. The only other thing in the fridge, apart from milk and butter, was an opened jar of olives. She emptied some into a bowl, took it, a wine glass and a small tumbler through to the sitting room, put them on a table and headed upstairs to change.

She hadn't bothered to shower after her workout and she couldn't be bothered doing so now either. Instead, she ignored the acrid smell of sweat, dropped her clothes on the floor, pulled on a robe and headed downstairs. She couldn't resist turning on her phone and checking for messages, throwing it across the sofa when it told her what it had told her before. There was no message from Graham. There was one from Megan, but Beth couldn't bring herself to open it.

Picking up the wine, she twisted the cap and then put it down and picked up the whiskey. She opened it, poured a large one and took a mouthful, feeling the pleasurable burn as it went down. With each sip, she could feel the edges of everything that hurt fuzzing and getting softer so she sipped until the glass was empty. She might have felt a little better except for the silence, it was like a heavy blanket, pressing her down. Music was her first choice as an antidote but when she looked at what was available, she couldn't find anything that didn't remind her of Graham. Instead, she switched on the TV and, immediately, the room was filled with sound. It was some reality programme; she hated them but the voices were loud and cheerful so she left it on for company. She finished the whiskey, debated having more, but poured a glass of wine instead and sat back to sip it and eat the olives.

It was impossible to forget about Graham, but thinking about Megan and her shocking deception helped push him to the back of her mind – for the moment at least. In her job, she'd met countless liars and heard innumerable lies, but this? This was different. Who'd have guessed Megan could be such a good actress? Beth would never have thought her capable of such deception.

She poured another glass of wine and rested her head back, closing her eyes and letting the sound of shouting and laughter drift from the TV to surround her. But the noise couldn't drown out the voices in her head, the ones that were telling her that thanks to Megan's revelation, her own life was now based on a lie. It had always been in the back of her mind to join the police after finishing her degree in criminology, but it was precisely because of what had happened to Megan that she had chosen the career path she was on. What she had seen that night had haunted her for a long time. She'd decided then, she was going to do whatever she could to make sure that violent men were held accountable for what they did to their victims.

Choosing to work for the Rape and Serious Sexual Offences Unit was the result. She was good at what she did, and over the years she'd helped put some sick sons-of-bitches away. But Megan's deception was going to haunt her, in the same way as her desolate expression had done for so many years. Because now, it looked as though Beth had made her choice based on a lie. If that had been the only one, it wouldn't be so bad, but she'd made others over the years, all with the same aim in mind, to make the guilty pay.

The memory of them standing in that damn bungalow, their hands clasped, making a promise to keep what happened a secret, had never faded. It was a terrible shame she hadn't remembered the promise when she had stupidly told Trudy.

'I don't know how you do the job you do,' Trudy had said, putting a sympathetic hand on her arm.

Perhaps, if she hadn't looked across the room and seen Megan, she would have brushed Trudy's concern off with her usual bravado. Instead, stupidly, she'd said, 'I do it for women like Megan.'

She could have stopped when she saw Trudy's blank look. Was it the alcohol that loosened her tongue, or her belief that Trudy should know what Megan had been through that made her break her word and tell her?

If Beth had kept her mouth shut that night, Megan wouldn't have had to come clean about her lie, and none of them would know the truth.

Beth's hand tightened on the stem of the wine glass as her face hardened. It would have been much better all around.

17

Megan waited to see if Beth would answer her text. When she didn't, she was tempted to ring her but then, with a grunt of frustration, she threw her phone aside. The earlier text had said Joanne was fine, Megan should probably settle for that.

She'd arrived home from Capel-le-Ferne just after twelve and had hoped to find Trudy at home but the apartment was empty. She wasn't expected until late afternoon so, although disappointed, Megan wasn't entirely surprised. Trudy would be either meeting one of her many friends for lunch or shopping for the dinner she'd promised to cook. The thought made Megan smile; she loved to eat out, but a candlelit meal here with the lights of London as a backdrop and the woman she loved cooking was far preferable. It would be perfect; things would be the way they used to be and the ice that had crept into Trudy's voice would thaw.

Her bag unpacked, Megan made herself a mug of tea and sat on the sofa to await her return while her mind dwelled on the previous evening's disastrous outcome. She'd known her friends would be surprised and shocked, but she'd not anticipated the violence of their reaction nor their expression of absolute horror and revulsion. And she certainly hadn't expected Joanne to leave the way she had.

Megan should be feeling relieved that, after all these years, it was out in the open. Trudy would be happy she'd come clean, and they could move on. But Megan couldn't get Joanne's wide-eyed look of shock out of her head. Maybe, she should have ignored Beth and gone to see her on the way home, but it might have made things worse, especially in view of Joanne's reluctance to invite them into her house. For the moment, Megan would do as she'd been advised, and give her time.

She'd known it was going to be a risk telling them the truth, and she'd accepted that she might lose their friendship as a result. But she hadn't really thought it would come to that and, now that it had, she realised she couldn't bear to lose them. They, with their advice, support and encouragement had made her the woman she was today, a woman that someone like Trudy could love.

Thoughts kept spinning around Megan's head as the afternoon drifted on. She tried reading, picking up a book she'd started the previous week, only to throw it aside, minutes later, when she found herself staring at the pages without seeing the words. At four, restless and edgy, she made a mug of camomile tea in the hope that it would soothe her racing brain, and stood sipping it as she looked out the window. The light was fading over a view she never tired of, the bustling heart of a city she loved, and usually it soothed whatever ailed. But not today.

It wasn't until nearly six that she heard a key in the door and turning, the empty mug still held in her hand, she watched as the woman she loved came in. Megan's eyes softened automatically. Trudy had a rare timeless beauty; high cheekbones, slightly pointed chin, perfect mouth, and creamy skin. Megan had met her at an art exhibition she'd been looking forward to for weeks, but afterwards, trying to remember the artwork, the only thing she could recall was Trudy's beautiful face. She'd been introduced by a mutual friend, but had been struck dumb by an instant attraction and only managed a pathetic, squeaky *hello* before she'd been swallowed up by the crowd that surrounded them.

For the rest of the evening, fascinated by her, Megan had watched as Trudy moved around the gallery, stopping to speak to various people, using her slim hands to make a point, or throwing back her head as she laughed. Love at first sight, she'd said, much later, but then it was just an overwhelming awe that robbed Megan of courage and she'd left without speaking to her. Unable to get her out of her mind, she'd gone to every art exhibition in London over the next month hoping to see her again.

Finally, as she was about to give up, she walked into a new gallery in Camden Town and saw Trudy standing in front of a large painting. Heart beating with excitement, this time she didn't hesitate and pushed her way rudely through the crowded room to get to Trudy's side and stood barely able to breathe, staring at the painting and desperately trying to think of something witty, clever, or at least not completely stupid to say. 'It's a little Monet meets Jack Vettriano, isn't it.'

Trudy had turned with a smile of amusement. 'Do you know I was thinking exactly the same thing. How strange!'

They'd continued around the gallery together and to her surprise, amazement and absolute joy, that was all it took. They'd chatted, and afterwards, had gone for a drink to a nearby pub that was so busy they were crushed together. They'd stood and drunk their trendy gin and tonics surrounded by loud voices and laughter, managing only a disjointed conversation, heads close together, Trudy's spicy exotic scent tickling Megan's nose.

When Trudy mentioned she hadn't had time to eat, they wandered out in search of food, finding a perfect little Italian restaurant where they sat in the window overlooking a small courtyard garden strung with solar lights. It was pretty and romantic but Megan had eyes only for the captivating woman opposite. Later, reluctant to say goodbye, she'd suggested a walk along the Thames Embankment. And somewhere along that magical walk, with the lights sparkling in the water, and her heart thumping, she'd dared to reach for Trudy's hand. When she didn't pull away, when instead Megan felt Trudy's long fingers curl around her hand and give a little squeeze, Megan knew she was, for the first time in her life, in love.

If there were still moments when she couldn't believe her luck, times when she caught their joint reflection in a window and cringed at the question of what such a beauty was doing with such a beast, she tried not to let it show. She loved Trudy; Trudy loved her. She couldn't imagine living without her.

'Hi,' she said, putting her empty mug down on the coffee table and walking across the room. She reached out for her, taken aback when Trudy stepped away. 'It's all good,' Megan said quickly, trying to sound far more positive than she felt. It wasn't necessary to give her the details of what Beth and Joanne had said or how they'd taken her disclosure, Trudy just needed to know they'd been told, that her deception was no longer a secret. 'I told them everything, they were surprised, of course,' she said, blinking as Joanne's horrified expression popped into her head, 'but I think they'll be okay, eventually.'

Trudy said nothing, passing Megan by without a glance.

'Honestly,' Megan tried again, managing to drag a smile into place, 'it's done.' And then, because she was suddenly frightened of Trudy's tight closed look, she added, 'They were okay about it, really.'

'Really?' Trudy plumped up the cushion that Megan had been sitting against and returned it to its place, keeping her eyes averted. 'They didn't mind that you'd lied to them?' Her voice was cold.

Megan felt something tear inside and searched for the right words to say, words to make everything better because suddenly she knew there was something terribly wrong. 'They were upset but they understood,' she said finally, willing now to lie, to do or say anything as long as it would remove that look from her lover's face.

But Trudy continued to move around the apartment, moving ornaments, straightening picture frames, never once looking across to where Megan stood, rigid, her eyes filling, her heart aching as if it knew what was coming and was getting ready to break. 'You said, if I told them the truth, that we'd be able to move forward.'

'Did I?' Trudy picked up a picture frame that held a photograph of the two of them outside the Taj Mahal. They were in front of the seat where Princess Diana had sat for that iconic photograph many years before. Afraid of tempting fate, they had refused to sit, standing instead with their arms around each other, beaming for the camera. They'd been so very much in love. Trudy stood looking at it for a moment and then, without warning, she threw it at Megan.

She ducked automatically and yelled out from shock as the frame smashed against the wall behind, pieces of wood and shards of glass crashing to the floor. 'Trudy!' Megan said, looking at the smashed frame in horror.

'Shocked you, did I?' Trudy stood with her arms folded across her chest, her face screwed up in anger, glaring at her.

'But the frame can be picked up, it might even be possible to fix it, and the glass can be replaced. It can all look as good as new.'

There was silence for a moment, broken only by their heaving breaths.

Trudy crossed to the window, stared out for a moment and then turned. 'Trust is a different matter, Megan. You break that and it never, ever, goes back together in the same way. Okay, you can try to fix it with glue, and it might even last for a while, but it's never as strong and finally, without a doubt, it will fall apart.' She turned back to stare out the window. 'It was Beth who told me about the rape,' she said, 'not you–'

'Yes,' Megan said, moving towards her, stopping at Trudy's raised hand. Her left hand. With a sinking feeling, Megan noticed she wasn't wearing her ring.

'And if she hadn't told me,' Trudy said coldly, 'the lie would have continued and I'd never have known a thing about it.' When she turned around again, her look of contempt made Megan gasp. 'So how many other secrets are there in your life that I don't know about? Secrets that might come out when one or another of your friends imbibes too much?'

Megan took a step towards her, a hand reaching out, pleading. 'There's nothing, I swear to you!'

'But how do I know you're telling me the truth?' Trudy's voice was so quiet and cold that Megan shivered and dropped her hand. 'How will I ever know you're telling me the truth again? And if I can't trust you,' flint eyes swept over her, 'we have nothing.'

Shock rocked Megan; swaying, she reached a trembling hand out to grab the back of a chair. She'd felt something tear inside, rip her apart. The pain was agonising. 'No,' she moaned. 'I love you. This is crazy, we can work things out.'

'It's over.' Trudy crossed her arms again and, lifting her chin, she looked down her nose at her as if Megan were some particularly nasty bug. 'You've destroyed it.'

'We can talk about this,' she pleaded, taking an unsteady step closer, reaching both hands out, almost begging her to take them. 'I promise you, there are no other secrets.'

'How could I ever be sure?' Trudy shook her head before taking a step away. 'I never could, could I? You can stay until Friday but then I'd like you to move out, please. I'll stay with Vikki until you've gone.' Trudy turned to walk away, looking back to say, with a cutting finality, 'Make sure you take everything; I won't want to see you again.'

It couldn't be true. Megan hurried after her and grabbed her by the arm. 'I love you. We can get through this, maybe go for counselling or something... I'll do whatever you want. Anything, you want.'

Trudy's eyes dropped to her hand. For the briefest of moments, Megan thought she was going to put her hand over it, was going to soften and say of course she didn't mean it, that she was just angry and disappointed but that she loved her too much to want her to go. But her relief was short-lived as Trudy raised her head and glared at her. 'Take your hand off me. All I want, is for you to leave me alone, okay? I thought we had something special; something pure and good–'

'We have,' Megan cried, tears rolling down her cheeks. 'We still have. This was something that happened twenty years ago, for pity's sake. I'm not the person I was then. I was young and mixed up and confused. I made a mistake, a stupid mistake.'

'A mistake? Is that what you're calling it now? It was deceit, a lie,' Trudy sneered, 'and everything you are, is built on that. Everything you are, all that you have become is predicated on that one awful unforgiveable lie. I don't know who you are anymore. And I don't want to.'

The contempt in Trudy's voice made Megan squirm and the

pain inside reached a crescendo as she felt her heart shatter into a million painful pieces. 'But I love you.'

'That's your problem.' Trudy's voice was cold and sharp.

Megan wrapped her arms around herself tightly, holding herself together as the world crashed and burned around her. 'But where will I go?' she said, knowing how pathetic those words sounded as she looked around the apartment she'd called home for the last eight years.

Trudy stopped with her hand on the front door. She didn't turn around and when she spoke, her voice was no longer cold and hard, instead, and so much worse, she sounded sad and weary. 'That too is your problem, and nothing to do with me. I really don't care where you go, just be sure to be gone by Friday.'

Megan would have preferred if Trudy had slammed the door, would have been happy at any sign of anger that would eventually dissipate but the door was closed in her usual calm controlled way. No anger, just calm determination. She wasn't sure there was a way to fight that.

It was several minutes before she could move, and when she did it was with difficulty, barely making it to the sofa before collapsing. The pain had settled to an agonising burning in her chest and in contrast, everything else felt numb.

A dangerous blade to wave around... How right Beth had been. How could Megan have known the destructive power of the truth, that it could destroy... had destroyed... her life with Trudy... How could Megan live without her?

Did she want to?

18

On Sunday morning, Beth woke with a groan and a pounding head. She pulled the duvet up to shield herself from the light that was driving daggers into her eyes. It's likely she'd have stayed there the whole day if the doorbell hadn't chimed, the sound reverberating through the house and hammering on her aching skull. Pulling the pillow around her ears, she tried to ignore it but, when it rang again and again, she groaned, dragged herself from the bed, threw on a robe, and went to answer it.

She was immediately sorry she had when she saw Megan standing on the doorstep. Her first thought was to ask her to go away, to beg for solitude in her misery, but something in what she saw made her change her mind. Unlike her, Megan was one of those women who would never leave home without perfectly applied make-up and without looking impeccably dressed, so her pale bare face, mismatched trousers and jacket, and a shirt with the buttons incorrectly fastened rang a loud warning bell.

'You look terrible,' Beth said, turning and heading to the kitchen, leaving Megan to follow. 'What are you doing here? I thought you and Trudy always went out for brunch on a Sunday morning?'

Ignoring her questions, Megan perched on the edge of a chair. 'To be exact, it's the afternoon,' she said, eyeing Beth's robe with a raised eyebrow. 'I hope I haven't interrupted something.'

Beth shook her head, immediately regretted the action when everything swam. She couldn't remember how much whiskey she'd downed the night before, or how much wine. The bottles were still in the sitting room, she wasn't sure she wanted to look. She filled the kettle. 'Would you like some coffee?'

'Sure,' Megan said, taking off her jacket and throwing it onto another chair.

'Is instant okay? I have a fancy all-singing-and-dancing machine but I couldn't bear the noise this morning.'

'Instant is fine. I thought you looked a bit under the weather. Were you two out on the town?'

Beth said nothing until she put coffee in front of Megan and sat, both hands wrapped around her mug. For a second, she was tempted to lie, to say that yes, they'd had a brilliant night wining and dining and that Graham was lying curled up in their bed waiting for her return. She could feel her heart squeeze on the wish that she could say just that. Instead, she swallowed noisily and shook her head. 'No, we weren't,' she said, taking a deep breath to steady herself before she put it into words, the first step in accepting it was over. She took a sip of her coffee and put the mug down. 'We've split up.'

Having taken a mouthful of coffee, Megan spluttered and coughed. 'What? What did you say?'

Maybe if Beth kept saying it, it would become easier to bear, easier to believe. 'We've split up.'

'You can't be serious.' Megan's eyes opened wide in disbelief. 'You two have been together forever.'

Forever. The word made Beth cringe. 'We're not together

anymore,' she said sharply. She'd thought she was hiding her grief and pain well, but she guessed she was fooling no one when Megan stood and moved across to grab her in a hug.

'I'm so sorry,' she said. 'And on top of that you had all my shit to deal with.'

Beth had considered telling her friends that the break-up had been her idea, that she'd thrown him out but, wrapped in Megan's arms, she found she couldn't tell that lie. Instead, she told the unvarnished and painful truth. 'He left without a word, without explanation. I came home and he was gone.'

The arms tightened around her. 'He'll come back, you two are good together.'

'He came while I was away and took the rest of his stuff,' Beth snuffled into Megan's shoulder, feeling like a child. 'He hasn't answered my texts, I've no idea where he is or who he's staying with.'

With a final squeeze, Megan let her go, sat and picked up her coffee. 'Did you have a row about something?'

'I wish!' She did wish it were that simple. A row, with each of them shouting, raised voices, cross words. A big fuss and then sweet make-up sex. The usual, not this terrible emptiness. 'You know how erratic my hours are. I'm so often late but, Thursday before last, Graham asked me to come home on time, he made me promise and stupidly, so stupidly because I know what my job is like, I did.'

Beth's sigh ended on a hint of a sob. 'But I really meant to, and would have done if something hadn't come up that I couldn't get out of. When I got home, hours late, I saw he'd cooked this big dinner. The table was set with candles, and flowers, that bottle of champagne,' she waved towards where it still sat, like a pathetic reminder of a forgotten party, 'was sitting in a bowl of half-melted ice.' She smiled sadly at her friend's gasp before continuing. 'I thought he was upstairs, annoyed with me. But he was gone and he'd taken most of his stuff.'

'Oh no!' Megan said, her face collapsing in sadness.

'It's hard to blame him really, you know. He'd gone to so much trouble and I hadn't given him a thought. I should at least have called to let him know I was running late.' She shrugged wearily. 'If I could have left work, I would have done, but there was a young girl, only fourteen, she'd been sexually assaulted by a gang of boys. I couldn't find an advocate available so I needed to stay with her until we could contact her family. I spent two hours with her, churning out all the good advice we're taught to give.'

'But Graham's being so unfair!' Megan reached across the table to her. 'He knows what your job's like, that you can't drop things and scarper when you want. You were a copper when you met, after all. It's not like you suddenly changed jobs. It's easy for him with his personal training business to suit himself.'

Beth put her hand over Megan's. 'He's complained before about my blinkered approach to life, that all I see and think about is my job. We've argued about it a lot. I don't know, maybe he was right, maybe I give too much and should have found a better balance.' She pulled a sheet of paper towel from a roll and blew her nose. 'Anyway, it's over, I need to accept it and as a start, I really need to get rid of that,' she said, nodding to the champagne and the bowl of water. She stood, grabbed a towel and reached for the bottle, lifting it by the neck so it dripped water into the bowl.

'We could drink it, of course, do you fancy a glass? We could toast the end of my relationship.' She could hear the sad bitterness in her voice. 'Sorry, I'm just trying to make light of the situation, I suppose.'

She dried the bottle, put it on the counter and had half-turned away to pick up the bowl of water when something caught her eye. The foil covering the champagne cork had been torn and pressed back, the edges no longer meeting. Curious she looked closer, pushing the tear apart with a fingernail. What she saw made her reel with shock and gut-wrenching pain. There, on the top of the cork, anchored in place by the foil, was a ring. She took it out. 'Oh no,' she whispered, looking at the simple solitaire. 'Oh, Megan, look!' She held it towards her friend who stared at it with such sorrow in her eyes that she felt hers fill with tears. 'The stupid man was going to propose.'

'Oh, Beth,' Megan said, 'there must be something you can do.'

'I've tried texting him but he doesn't answer.' She saw Megan frown. 'What?'

'Why a Thursday? Seriously? He knows what your job's like, Beth. For something this special, why couldn't he have waited until the weekend when you were sure to be free?'

Beth looked at the ring, sparkling in the light, shut her eyes briefly and groaned. Of course! She hadn't thought of it at the time, too caught up in work, in the things that were important to *her*. He had always been the more romantic half, the one who remembered anniversaries and birthdays without being reminded. In fact, he usually reminded her. This year, he hadn't; he'd laid on a surprise instead. Tilting the ring to make it sparkle even more, she explained, 'We met on a Thursday; we would have been together eight years, give or take a day or three. I suppose that was why.'

Megan reached out and took her hand in hers. 'Oh, Beth,' she said again, in a voice laced with sadness.

'That's why he made me promise,' Beth gave a sad smile. 'I'd only been half listening to him, I was thinking about work and he'd been annoyed and said again how important it was that I be home on time. I thought he was just fussing.'

The ring was beautiful. It was tempting to try it on, to see if it fitted and how it would look but, she didn't. It would fit, he'd have made sure, the same way as he'd chosen the most perfect ring, one single diamond, classy and strong. She put it carefully down on the counter beside the bottle and turned back to Megan. 'Enough about me, what brings you here on a Sunday afternoon? You're usually out having a long leisurely lunch. But here you are. I'm guessing there's a reason.'

Megan looked as if she wanted to continue the conversation, to discuss what to do about Beth and Graham but she must have seen the shuttered look that descended on Beth's face because, instead, she said, 'We met a group of friends. I pleaded a headache and came away early.'

Beth looked at her and frowned. No make-up, and looking like she'd dressed in the dark. It was obvious she was lying. But why? Beth stood, went to the window and stared out at the tiny courtyard garden where the previous summer's flowers lay brown and withered in the ceramic pots she'd bought the year before. Her head was churning. Graham's departure, the proposal he would have made on that fateful Thursday, and Megan's revelation all spun out of control. Beth couldn't handle anything else. Whatever else was troubling her friend, right at that moment, Beth didn't want to know.

'I was worried about Joanne,' Megan said. 'I didn't think I had to worry about you, but now...'

'You don't need to worry about me, I'll live,' Beth said shortly, turning around to look at Megan. 'Joanne said she was okay. Your...' Beth searched for the right word, 'your deception has hit her hard, just give her time.' *And me... give me time!* Megan was behaving as if her confession had no lasting impact whatsoever on her. Beth swallowed. It was all too much. Running a hand over her unbrushed hair, she gave a loud sigh, hoping Megan would get the hint, and leave, irritated when she just shook her head slowly.

'You don't think I should go down there?'

'No, I don't,' Beth said, trying to keep her temper. It had always been a bit of a joke between the friends, that Megan didn't know when to give up. It didn't seem quite so funny now. 'I think,' Beth said firmly, 'that you'd be better off letting her come to terms with it in her own time.'

'But she will?'

'I don't know that, do I?' Beth's voice rose as irritation took over. She wanted Megan to leave, she had enough angst in her head without adding more. 'You must have realised your truth would have implications.' When Megan continued to sit, showing no signs of wanting to leave, Beth said, 'Listen, leave Joanne to me. I'll give her a buzz during the week and suggest meeting up. I'll let you know what she says. Okay?' Beth willed Megan to nod and leave.

It seemed to work. 'If you think that's for the best.' Megan stood and reached for her jacket. 'Okay, I suppose I'd better get home anyway.'

At last! When she'd gone, Beth shut the door and turned the key in the lock. Nobody else was getting in today. She ignored the tiny voice that said nobody else would want to call around now that Graham was gone. It had been his friends who'd popped in without warning, rarely hers. She frowned as she realised that Megan had never really said why she'd called around. Was it simply her concern for Joanne that caused her stricken look and unkempt appearance? That lie about leaving Trudy with friends because she had a headache, what was that all about? Beth probably should have been a good friend and asked her what was wrong. Because something obviously was. The next day, if she felt up to it, she'd give her a ring, talk to her then and find out what was going on. For now, she needed some time to think about healing herself.

19

There didn't seem to be any point in getting dressed. Instead, Beth lounged around in her robe and watched a series of movies without noticing when one ended and the next began. Her hangover had cleared but it had left her feeling queasy. Self-inflicted punishment, just like the aches and pains in her legs and back from the excesses in the gym. At one stage that day, she fell asleep on the couch and woke feeling disorientated.

For a moment, she was so sure she could hear Graham's voice and his deep earthy laugh, she swung her feet to the floor and stood, ready to rush into his arms. When the silence hit her, the almost unbearable weight of her loss pressed her back onto the sofa. She blinked away tears and took some comfort in that *almost*; her inner core was strong, she'd get through this.

No alcohol, and an early night, meant she felt a little better when she woke the next morning. But not a lot, her heart still ached, and when she went into the kitchen and saw that ring, that beautiful ring that she would never wear, her eyes again filled with tears. Why had he left it? He could have returned it, and she'd never have known he was going to propose. It had been left to hurt her, and it had; but she knew Graham, there wasn't a mean bone in his body, he must be hurting a lot to deliberately cause her so much pain. That's what their relationship had descended to, a spiral of hurt and be hurt. There was no recovery from that.

At least it was Monday and the empty lonely weekend was over. It was her habit to go into the station early, to get ahead of the day and check out any reports that had come in through the night. She waved to various people who were heading off shift or others who had also drifted in early, sat at her desk and switched on her desktop computer.

While it powered up, she headed to get coffee and sat sipping it while she flicked through some paperwork with one hand. There was nothing that needed to be done urgently, a few memos, most of which she read without much interest, a couple that had her raise an eyebrow in surprise and one that made her shake her head in disgust. Finishing the last one, she tossed it on top of the others and put down her empty mug. Turning to her computer, she tapped in her password. *Access Denied.*

Blinking, she tried again, tapping each letter and number of her password slowly. *Access Denied.*

There were often problems with the old computers, staff were constantly complaining about them and she'd had the odd issue herself, but this particular problem hadn't happened to her before. Hoping that whatever was wrong was confined to her computer, she moved to a neighbouring desk, waited impatiently for it to power up and tapped in her password again, staring at the screen in disbelief when once again, it said, *Access Denied*.

Feeling annoyed, she looked around the room. There were a few other early birds at their desks, but all were staring in concentration at their screens, their fingers tapping away. She was the only one doing nothing. For a brief second, she thought about asking one of them for their password, but using someone else's was against departmental regulations and there was nobody in the room she was friendly enough with to ask to break the rules.

With a grunt of exasperation, she returned to her desk and sat. It was eight forty-five. The IT department didn't open till nine unless it was an emergency and although it was irritating, it wasn't that. She'd just have to wait.

She had another mug of coffee, the fingers of one hand restlessly tapping the desk.

As soon as it hit nine, she reached for the phone, hesitating when she saw her immediate superior, Chief Inspector Dowling, enter the room and head in her direction. She had an easy-going professional relationship with him based on mutual respect and, typically, her dealings with him were without problem. Today, however, his usually affable face was set in grim lines and when his eyes, cold and unfriendly, turned on her without any relaxation in those lines, she knew with a sinking feeling that there was trouble.

He approached her desk and stood looking down at her. 'I need you to come with me,' he said without any prelude. His shuttered expression didn't invite question.

Startled, Beth opened and shut her mouth before standing awkwardly and grabbing her jacket from the back of the chair. She pulled it on, brushing her hands nervously over the sleeves and then, unable to stop herself, she blurted out, 'Is there a problem?'

'All in good time,' he said, turning to leave.

She followed; her forehead creased. Her password failing and now this. What the hell was going on?

The station was a warren of corridors, the original building having been extended numerous times. The chief inspector walked at a brisk pace and never looked back, assuming she was following as ordered. They stopped outside an interview room on the second floor, a room Beth had never had reason to enter. It was rarely used except for the odd training course and – a wave of fear washed over her – whenever officers from the Professional Standards department needed to attend.

Chief Inspector Dowling rapped sharply on the door before pushing it open. He finally turned to look at Beth with an expression of distaste but said nothing, merely indicating with a nod that she precede him into the room. Beth had confronted any number of knife and fist-wielding thugs in her time as a police officer but she couldn't ever remember feeling the level of terror that hit her as she entered. It took every ounce of physical strength to make her legs move, one step at a time, every ounce of inner strength to keep her chin in the air and to stop that give-away tremor from appearing on her lips.

It was a small room, dominated by a long table in the centre. There were four chairs on the far side of it and one on the nearest side. Once Dowling took his seat, all four chairs were filled. Nervously, she looked at the others, the thin, almost emaciated, figure of Deputy Assistant Commissioner Benton, the stocky Chief Superintendent Youlden, a man she'd never cared for, and the unknown fourth, a slim serious-looking woman who stared at her with curiosity. All the men wore crisp long-sleeved white shirts with their rank badges on their epaulettes, and black ties. The woman was in civilian dress but her jacket was smart, her shirt collar perfectly ironed, the top two buttons open to show a fine gold chain around her neck. Beth, feeling every crease in her cheap navy Primark jacket, resisted the temptation to close it over a shirt she knew had an old stain on the front.

'Sit down, please, Detective Inspector Anderson,' Benton said.

Sitting, Beth kept both feet on the ground and rested her hands, one on top of the other, palm upward, on her lap. It was important to present the right appearance, to look calm and in control; it was half the battle. Her insides, meanwhile, had turned to jelly, and although she tried not to, she kept sucking her lower lip between her teeth in a nervous habit she'd had since childhood. She looked across the table and forced herself to meet their eyes.

Benton adjusted heavy-rimmed spectacles on his bony nose. 'You will know everyone here, of course, apart from Detective Inspector Ling.' He indicated the woman sitting on his right. 'DI Ling is with the Professional Standards Body.'

It was almost a relief to have it out in the open. Beth released her lower lip and took a deep breath. She was under investigation.

'This is a preliminary meeting, DI Anderson,' Benton continued, 'to inform you that there have been a number of allegations made about your conduct.' He shuffled some pages on the desk in front of him before selecting one, settling his spectacles again and reading from it. 'The allegations are that you did, on at least two occasions, pervert the course of justice by providing victims with information to assist their cases.'

With difficulty, Beth kept her expression carefully neutral. He didn't ask if the allegations were true, that was for the investigation to decide. But they were; of course they were; she had helped when she could. Otherwise, half the bastards she'd arrested would have got off and their victims denied justice. Beth kept her eyes fixed on Benton as he outlined what would happen.

'You are suspended with immediate effect, pending investigation. Depending on the outcome of said investigation, we will reconvene in a week for either a misconduct meeting or a disciplinary hearing. You are advised to contact your local Fed rep.' He looked to the woman beside him. 'Is there anything you want to add?'

Detective Inspector Ling, despite a surname that hinted at oriental heritage, was a pale-skinned red-haired woman with hazel eyes. Cold hazel eyes that looked Beth over as if she were some form of repugnant pond life. 'These are extremely serious allegations, DI Anderson,' Ling said with a deep voice at odds with her slim frame. 'The Crown Prosecution Service has indicated that it may put a number of convictions in jeopardy. If the allegations are proven, they will, they say, push for a custodial sentence for this offence. In view of that, I have had no option but to report the matter to the Independent Office for Police Conduct. They have indicated they are willing to run a managed investigation which allows me to continue under their direction.' She looked at Benton. 'I'm assuming you are satisfied with that, sir?'

He, as much as any of the others, knew her question was a formality; he had no power to dictate to the IOPC how they did their job. 'Perfectly,' he said with a slight smile in her direction before looking back at Beth. 'DI Anderson, you are not to speak to other officers about this matter. Collect your belongings and leave the premises immediately. It is possible you are already aware that your password no longer works. All rights and privileges attendant to your position are also suspended pending the investigation.'

Beth wanted to ask if that meant she couldn't use her police pass for the local gym but she thought they might think the question was frivolous so kept her mouth shut. It was the only privilege she could think of. Maybe she'd been missing out.

'Do you have any questions?' Benton asked finally.

She couldn't think of one. No doubt she would have some later when the numbness of shock had worn off but now, in a weedy voice she barely recognised as her own, she said, 'No, sir.'

'Fine, in that case this preliminary meeting is adjourned and will reconvene in one week. Your Fed rep will advise you what form the next meeting will take.' He dropped his eyes to the papers on the desk, sorting them into one neat pile. DI Ling spoke to Chief Inspector Dowling who sat to her right.

It was a few seconds before Beth realised she'd been dismissed. Feeling a flush of colour on her cheeks, she stood and turned for the door. Her legs were trembling. She willed them to keep going. Making it to the door, she reached for the handle, her sweaty palm sliding on the metal. God, what if she couldn't get out? How much more mortification could she take? She quickly wiped her hand on the sleeve of her jacket and tried again. This time, the handle moved, the door opened, and she was out, standing in the corridor, a sick feeling in her stomach, her head swimming. She waited, trying to regain some equilibrium before moving away.

She was under investigation.

20

Beth kept her head down as she returned to the squad room. It was busy, officers milling about, on their computers, on the phone, gossiping, complaining. Forcing herself to take her time, she picked up her bag and keys and walked calmly to the door. She chanced a look around when she got there; nobody was looking in her direction.

The few people she passed in the corridors and stairway as she left greeted her with the same casualness as usual. Word hadn't got out yet. But it would. Within a few hours, everyone would know she'd been suspended. Worse, everyone would speculate as to why. Conclusions would be reached, some might even be right, most would be way off the mark.

~

Sitting in her car, she realised she was trembling too much to drive. She'd liked to have gone into a pub and drunk her way into oblivion, but she needed to ring her Fed rep and he or she mightn't be impressed if she couldn't string two words together. Instead, she got out and headed towards a local café, changing her mind at the last moment and walking on. The place was too popular with staff from the station, she was bound to see someone she knew. She kept walking, feeling the shock fade with every step so that ten minutes later when she saw a café she'd never tried before, she was feeling a little calmer.

Ordering a double espresso, she took it to a seat as far from the window as she could, sat and took out her mobile. Who to ring? Graham would have been the first name on the list. In truth, he still was. Maybe he'd be pleased she was suspended, and he would come back. It was her job that had been a problem for him. She could ring the gym where he worked, ask to speak to him, tell him she'd been suspended… *suspended*… She suddenly felt sick, holding her hand to her mouth, she gulped. After a few seconds, she swallowed and sat back.

No, she wasn't going to ring Graham and have him return out of a sense of pity. Because, he would, she knew he would. He knew how much her job meant to her; he knew how devastated she'd be. He'd come back and she'd never know if he was going to stay. Worse, he'd ask if the allegations were true and she'd have to admit they were, and be forced to tell him she was facing a custodial sentence. *A custodial sentence*. He'd be horrified, shocked, disappointed. *Appalled*. What she had done, what they suspected she had done, it would appal him, and he'd leave her anyway. Better not to tell him yet. She'd have to eventually, would certainly have to if she got sent down, he'd have to sort out the house and the finances.

Smiling at how prosaic her thoughts had turned, she finished her coffee, feeling a little stronger. It would have been nice to just sit there, drink coffee, maybe have a slice of cake or a sandwich, pretend it was an ordinary day. It would have been nice. But it was impossible. She picked up her phone and scrawled through her contacts for a number she thought she'd never have to use, and with a quick look around to make sure there was nobody she knew within eavesdropping distance, she dialled the Police Federation.

She gave the person who answered a quick synopsis of her situation and was then put on hold for so long she was about to hang up in frustration when a deep voice with a pronounced Welsh lilt spoke.

'Is that DI Anderson?'

What? Did he think she'd given the phone to someone else because she'd been kept waiting? She shut her eyes briefly and took a calming breath. It wasn't his fault she was in this fucking mess, after all. 'Yes,' she said and waited.

'It sounds like you're in a spot of trouble.'

A spot of trouble? Her fingers tightened on the phone as she tried to think of something cutting to say but, instead, she laughed, a short humourless sound that was quickly over. Maybe he was right and she was getting upset for no reason. Although he didn't know the details as yet, calling it a spot of trouble put it into perspective; it would be sorted and things would return to normal. They were only trying to scare her with their talk of a custodial sentence. More likely, she'd be ordered to follow some pathetic improvement plan for a few months. It would be irritating and embarrassing but she'd do anything to stay in her job, losing it didn't bear thinking about.

'Yes,' she said, 'you could say that.'

'My name is, Medwyn Kendrick, I'll be your Fed rep. It sounds like you're in a public place so best not to discuss anything now. But the sooner I can hear what the allegations against you are, the sooner I can start the ball rolling to get it all sorted, okay?'

'Okay,' Beth said, feeling relieved. 'I was heading home but I can come into your office if you want.'

'It's easier if I come to your place,' he said, and without waiting for her agreement asked for her postcode and house number. 'I'll be there in an hour.' Again without waiting for a yay or nay, he hung up.

Beth pocketed her phone and checked her watch. If she left straight away, she'd make it just in time.

As it turned out, she was quicker than she'd expected and pushed open her front door with twenty minutes to spare. Restless, she made coffee and stood staring out of the sitting-room window with a mug in her hand. She watched a car pass by about ten minutes later and knew straight away it was him. He was in luck and found parking a hundred yards up the street. She craned her neck to see him but it was a few minutes before the car door opened and he got out, an overstuffed briefcase under one arm.

Kendrick was a small stocky man with a shock of thick black hair and, she noted, when she opened her front door, startlingly blue eyes. 'Hi,' she said, standing back and waving him in, directing him towards the open kitchen door. 'Would you like some coffee or tea?'

'Coffee, black, three sugars.' He moved into the dining area, put the well-worn bulging briefcase on the floor, took off his jacket, hung it on the back of a chair, and sat at the table, looking around with assessing eyes.

Beth wondered, gritting her teeth, if he were calculating how much everything cost to see if she was living beyond a copper's salary. Perhaps she should point out her seven-year-old rusty Suzuki and the threadbare carpet in the sitting room. He was on her side, she reminded herself as she made the coffee. Putting a mug in front of him, she took the chair opposite and waited to hear what he had to say.

'Okay,' Kendrick said, pulling a blank A4 pad from his briefcase and squaring it up on the table in front of him. He tapped a pen on the empty page. 'First, tell me everything you can remember about the meeting this morning. Who was there and what was said?'

It wasn't difficult, the meeting and every word was etched in Beth's mind. Without hesitating, she gave an accurate account of everything that had occurred, from the moment she had arrived at the station, the names of those present at the meeting and what each had said.

'There were four people at it?' He raised an eyebrow when she muttered *yes*.

Beth felt fear clutching her insides when she saw his worried expression. 'That's bad, is it?'

Kendrick tapped the pad with the end of his pen. 'There's no point in my prettying things up to make you feel better,' he said quietly. 'It's important for you to know exactly what's going on so that you can make the correct decision if needed, okay?'

She licked her lips. 'Okay.'

'Three senior officers plus someone from Professional Standards at a preliminary meeting tells me this is serious, DI Anderson.' His blue eyes bored into hers. 'Why don't you tell me exactly what you did. And please,' he added, keeping his eyes locked on hers, 'if you want me to do the best for you, tell me absolutely everything.'

Beth hugged her coffee mug to her chest and tried to put her thoughts in order. Where to start? She wondered what he would say if she said she needed to go back twenty years, to the lie that had persuaded her that this was a worthy career choice.

'I'm on your side, remember,' he said, when she hadn't spoken for a few minutes. 'Whatever you tell me, I'll do the best I can to support you and get you through this.'

Putting the mug down, Beth crossed her arms. 'Okay. They

seem to think I gave some of the victims information about their alleged attackers.'

He looked at his notes. 'On at least two occasions? Is that correct?'

She shrugged one shoulder. 'That's what they said.'

'And did you?'

'I wouldn't be the only–'

He held up his hand, interrupting her. 'You're the only one under investigation. It won't help your case if you say you broke regulations because others did, DI Anderson.'

'It's Beth,' she said tiredly. 'Okay, yes, I did give a couple of women some information that would have helped make their cases stronger.'

'How many times?'

She shrugged, both shoulders this time, as if shifting the weight of the accusations. 'I don't know.'

'More than the twice they inferred?'

When he continued to stare, his blue eyes unblinking as he waited for her to answer, she sat back and met his gaze. 'Okay, several times. It's difficult to say because sometimes it was just a suggestion rather than anything specific.'

'What kind of suggestion? Give me one example, so I can see what we're dealing with.'

She took a breath to calm her nerves. 'Last week before a court case, I was speaking to the victim. She was worried that if they asked her how she was so sure the accused was the assailant she wouldn't be able to say. I reminded her of a comment she'd made about his rather protuberant brown eyes.'

'And that was it?'

'It was enough.'

'And where did you speak to her precisely?'

Her hesitation was clear and it spoke volumes. She guessed there was no point in lying. 'I called around to her house.'

'Did you log this visit?' Kendrick asked, scribbling a note on his pad. 'You didn't,' he said when she stayed silent. 'Where else did you give these suggestions?'

'After they'd given their statement.'

He frowned. 'But that would be on record.'

'I'd wait until we left the room.'

Kendrick tapped the pad again. 'There's no CCTV in the corridor outside?'

Beth shook her head.

He frowned. 'So far, I haven't heard anything that would justify the level of seriousness they're approaching this with, which leads me to believe that either they're losing the plot or you're not telling me everything.' Once again, Kendrick fixed her with his eyes until she lowered hers and looked away. 'Tell me what you're leaving out, Beth. Prepared, I'm better able to fight your corner.'

Standing abruptly, she went to the sitting room and returned moments later with the half-full whiskey bottle. She waved it at him, unsurprised when he shook his head. Pouring a large measure for herself, she sat and took a mouthful. 'Do you know how many sexual predators get off because of lack of evidence?'

'Too many,' he guessed.

She raised her glass in a toast to his correct answer. 'Way too many. They leave a trail of devastated victims, their families, friends, loved ones. With no evidence, our hands are tied.'

Kendrick looked at her for a moment, then shut his eyes and dropped his pen. 'You planted evidence?'

She waited a beat before nodding slowly. 'Only when I was one hundred per cent sure we had the right man.'

'And you think that vindicates your actions?' He rubbed a hand over his chin. 'That's why they were out in force, why the Professional Standards officer felt she had to inform the IOPC.

It's mandatory when the case might result in a criminal prosecution.'

Criminal prosecution? She gulped. Maybe they weren't using scare tactics after all. 'You think it'll come to that?'

'If they can prove you planted evidence that resulted in prosecution, I'm positive it will. But they have to prove it.' For a few seconds neither of them spoke, and then he picked up the pen he'd dropped and put it in his pocket. 'With your permission, I'll speak to one of our retained solicitors.' He waited for her nod before continuing. 'They might be able to save you from a prison sentence,' he said slowly, 'but I'm afraid you're going to have to accept the truth. Your police career is over.'

He stood and looked down at her. 'If anyone contacts you, refer them to me. Do not, under any circumstance, engage them in conversation, do you understand?' He didn't wait for an answer, packing the pad back into his briefcase and fastening it with a snap. 'I'll be in touch,' he said and let himself out.

21

Beth didn't move from the table for a long time. It was tempting to drink the remainder of the whiskey but she knew getting drunk wasn't the answer. Problem was, she didn't think there were any answers to her growing list of dilemmas. A glance at the kitchen clock startled her. It was only one o'clock. A lot had happened in such a short space of time.

What was she going to do now?

As if on cue, her phone chirped. It was tempting to ignore it, there was nobody she wanted to speak to, nobody who would understand. When it stopped, she let out the breath she'd been holding and swore softly when it rang again.

Picking it up, she saw DS Kadam's name. Beth hesitated before answering. Was she ringing with sympathy or reproach, to commiserate or condemn? After her meeting with Kendrick, Beth didn't think she was ready for either, but maybe it was time to start facing up to the reality of her situation. She slid her thumb across the phone to answer. 'Hi,' she said and waited.

'Beth, I've just heard.' Sunita Kadam's voice was barely above a whisper. 'I'm so sorry. If there's anything I can do...'

Beth took a deep breath before replying. 'Thank you, but it's okay. My Fed rep was just here. Thank you for ringing but it would be better if you didn't ring again.' She was about to hang up when she heard a quickly whispered, *Wait!*

She heard louder voices and then Sunita's quiet whisper again. 'I thought you should know that Arthur Lewis is dead.'

'What!' Beth gripped her phone tighter, holding it closer to her ear. 'How? When?'

'Last night. Neighbours heard screams and rang the police. When they arrived, they found the front door open, Lewis lying on the floor in a pool of blood and a man standing over him.'

Beth didn't have to ask who it was. A leaden weight seemed to have become lodged in her chest.

Sunita was oblivious and continued in the same whisper. 'It's Bruno Forest, Beth. Lydia's father. He killed him.'

She wanted to hang up, switch off her phone and hide. If they found out she'd given him Lewis' address there was a long list of charges they could throw at her. A custodial sentence would be a given. 'Okay,' she said, 'thanks for letting me know, Sunita. I appreciate it.' Beth waited a beat before adding, 'If you could let me know what happens, I'd be extremely grateful.' She listened to Sunita's emphatic assurances before saying goodbye and hanging up.

Would Forest tell them where he'd got the information that led him to Lewis? She remembered the devastated man's grip on the piece of paper she'd given him as he'd walked away. He probably wouldn't. Despite the force's best efforts, it was easy enough to get a copy of the list of registered sex offenders so maybe they wouldn't even ask him. It's not as if his guilt was being disputed after all. She'd feel sorry for the man, if she didn't need all her pity for herself.

When the phone chirped, she swore softly. She should have switched the damn thing off. Seeing Megan's name on the screen, she swore again, loudly this time. There was no point in not answering, she would just keep ringing. 'Hi.'

'Beth, thank God.' Megan's voice was strained and tight. 'I know you'll think I'm being silly and dramatic, and I know with Graham's leaving you have enough to worry about, but there's something not right about Joanne.'

A wave of irritation washed over Beth. She wanted to say she had enough to worry about, more than enough. To scream that she might lose her career because she'd been stupid. She wanted to blame Megan for that lie all those years ago, for putting her on a path that could only ever have ended one way. She wanted to but she didn't blame her, not really. Megan might have put her on the path, but Beth had followed it of her own accord and she'd known, hadn't she, that she might get caught someday. Every time she took a risk, she knew there was a chance that it could be the end for her. Before she'd met Graham, there'd been a few anxious moments that had come to nothing. She'd put an escape plan in place, just in case, but as her relationship with him had grown and she realised how much more she had to lose, she'd been more careful.

But she hadn't stopped. She'd thought it was worth it, to prevent men like Matt Peters doing what he'd done to Megan. Except, he hadn't done anything, had he. And if Beth told Megan about the allegations against her, she knew her friend would be stunned and horrified, and would agree with Kendrick that her career was over – worse, as a crown prosecutor, she would probably agree that she should go to prison. So, she kept her mouth shut about her own troubles and asked, 'What do you mean?'

'I rang her first thing this morning. I had to ring a few times before she answered but when she did, she said something really strange.'

Beth heard the gulp down the line and hugged the phone

closer to her ear. So many strange things had happened recently, she may as well listen to one more. 'What did she say?'

Megan's voice was ragged and cracked, her words fading so Beth struggled to hear. 'Joanne said that she wasn't sure she could live with the secret anymore. I assumed she was talking about mine and told her it was okay, that it was all out in the open. That's when she said it.' There was another louder gulp before Megan continued. 'She said, that it wasn't my secret she couldn't live with, it was hers. And she hung up.'

Beth frowned. For a change, Megan wasn't exaggerating. That was an odd thing for Joanne to say.

Megan sounded worried. 'I think I should drive down and check on her.'

'No, don't,' Beth said quickly, 'leave it to me. I'm actually on a day off and have nothing planned for the rest of the day. I'll drive down and see what's up with her.'

A loud sigh came down the line. 'Oh, thank you, that's a huge load off my mind. I've got a tonne of cases on my desk and could ill afford to take the time off. You'll ring me and let me know she's okay as soon as you get there, won't you?'

Reassuring Megan that she'd keep her informed, Beth hung up and sat tapping the phone against her chin. Driving to Royal Tunbridge Wells certainly beat sitting around all afternoon wondering what she was going to do. She quickly changed from her work clothes to comfortable stretchy jeans, a cotton sweater and a warm showerproof jacket. Slipping her feet into flat red pumps, she grabbed her keys and purse and was ready to go, remembering at the last second to look for Joanne's address.

Beth found her address book after an exhaustive search where she opened and closed almost every possible drawer in the house, finally finding it underneath a pile of newspapers she'd never had time to read. She put the postcode in the satnav, noted the expected arrival time and pulled out onto the road. She should be there in two hours.

It was good to be doing something rather than sitting at home worrying about her job or thinking about Graham. Unfortunately, an accident on the M25 meant the traffic ground to a halt, the delay giving her too much time to think and nowhere to go to get away from her thoughts. She banged the steering wheel in frustration, sorry she'd ever suggested this wild-goose chase.

Over two hours later she was finally on the A21 where the traffic was moving a little faster, and it was almost three and a half hours after leaving London before she arrived outside Joanne's house.

She'd looked at the house on Google Maps when her friend had bought it several years before but the reality was far better than the street view footage had indicated. It was a mid-terrace three-storey Victorian house with all that you'd expect from that era; a fanlight over the door, a nice bay window on the ground floor and sash windows on the floors above. Each house on the terrace was painted a different colour. Joanne's was a pale yellow with the woodwork, including the front door, startlingly white.

It was bigger in reality too, and Beth, who liked to think she was fairly knowledgeable about the property market, frowned. There wouldn't be any change from a million pounds when you bought a house like this. Maybe Joanne had bought when the market was in a slump but it would never have been cheap. Money wasn't something they'd ever discussed, each of them successful in their own way, all of them financially secure. Now, looking up at the very lovely house, Beth wondered how successful Joanne's business was.

There was enough room beside Joanne's car at the front of the house to squeeze in Beth's Suzuki. The Mondeo was parked at an angle and it took a little negotiating and twisting to get out without hitting it with her door. Beth stretched and looked around. It was a lovely day, and in the sunshine, the windows of the house sparkled and the gloss white paint shone. It was a very well-maintained and exceedingly pretty house, but there were interior shutters on each window and they were all closed, giving the house, despite its lovely exterior, a blind unwelcoming look. Beth hoped it would be more welcoming inside – assuming Joanne let her in.

Beth approached the front door and saw a shiny brass bell set to one side. She pressed it once, heard it chime within and waited, her head cocked, listening for any sound of movement from inside. Hearing nothing, she pressed the bell again, holding her finger on it for longer and once again, waited.

Ten minutes later, she was still standing on the doorstep. Maybe Joanne had gone away, taken a taxi to the train station or to an airport. She could be sunning herself on a beach somewhere. But Beth remembered what Joanne had said to Megan, and her mouth tightened. She'd been a police officer for too long to ignore her instinct. Something wasn't right.

She pulled her mobile from her back pocket and dialled Joanne's number. No answer. She tapped it against the palm of her hand for a few seconds and dialled again, waited for the opportunity and left a message. 'Joanne, it's Beth. I'm on your doorstep. Let me in. You have ten minutes to think about it. If you don't answer, or at least ring me back, I'm going to contact the police and tell them I suspect something untoward has occurred and get them to batter your door down, okay? And, Joanne,' she added, 'you know me; I mean what I say.'

Beth turned and sat on the concrete step, lifting her face to the sun, enjoying the warmth, wishing it would make its way to her insides where a chill had settled when Graham had left. After seeing that damn ring, she wasn't sure it would ever thaw.

Every now and then, she leaned back and listened at the door. There was no sound. She had meant what she'd said, but she wasn't sure what the reaction would be if she contacted the local nick. Would word about her suspension have leaked and spread this far? She could, of course, contact them without mentioning who she was, say she was a concerned member of the public. But she knew what would happen – they'd come around, see the shut-up house, see no reason to be concerned, and leave.

She was still worrying about what to do when she heard the distinct sound of movement from behind her and jumped to her feet. The sound stopped. Bending, she pushed open the letterbox and shouted, 'Joanne!' In the following silence, Beth was sure she heard shuffling. 'Joanne, for God's sake, open the damn door!'

Beth straightened when she heard the clicking sound as a key turned in the lock. The door opened, so slowly that her breath caught and, for a second, she didn't recognise the woman who peered around the edge. Beth's breath came out in a rush of air. 'Joanne?'

It was the smile she recognised. A smile in a face that looked gaunt and haunted, dark circles hinting at little sleep, hair that hung lank to her shoulders. The clothes she was wearing were the same ones she had on when Beth had last seen her in Capel-le-Ferne and a foetid smell wafted from her. It stank of despair.

'Oh, Joanne,' Beth said, stepping into the house and kicking the door shut behind her. Despite the off-putting smell, Beth engulfed her in a hug and held her quivering body tightly. She didn't know what was going on but, in all the years she'd known her, she'd never seen her like this. What was this secret that she had told Megan she couldn't live with?

What on earth could this gentle honest woman have done?

22

J oanne hadn't wanted to answer the door. She didn't want to see anyone, couldn't bear to see her friends. But she knew Beth meant what she said, and facing her was preferable to facing the police. Joanne stood, arms hanging by her side, accepting, but incapable, of returning the hug that engulfed her. 'You shouldn't have come,' she said, eventually, grateful for the concern but really wishing Beth wasn't there and desperately wondering how she could get rid of her, and how soon.

'We were worried about you,' Beth said, leaning back to look at her. 'You said something to Megan about being unable to live with a secret. What's that all about, Jo?'

Joanne tried to laugh it off. 'Is that what she told you? Gosh, you should know better than to listen to her. She's still trying to turn everything around onto us, blaming us for jumping to the wrong conclusion that night. I was referring to her secret, her revelation, that was all.' She pulled away from Beth's arms and waved to the first door that led off the hallway. 'Come in, have a seat.'

It was a spacious bright room with high ceilings and

windows to two sides. An opulently ornate fireplace was flanked by two shallow shelved alcoves displaying ornaments, books and a couple of photographs in silver frames. There was no wood by the fire, no coal scuttle, nothing to indicate a fire had ever been lit in the grate and the room was decidedly chilly.

Joanne waved Beth to the sofa that stretched along one wall while she took one of the two single sofas, sitting on the edge as if waiting to get up. 'Would you like a tea or coffee?' She didn't want to offer, forcing herself to follow the rules of polite behaviour when all she wanted to do was scream at her, tell her to go away and leave her alone. To her relief, Beth declined her offer with a gruff *no* before fixing her with a worried look.

'What's going on, Joanne?'

Joanne pushed lank locks of hair behind her ears and sat back, crossing her knees, trying to look relaxed. 'Going on? Nothing's going on, detective.' Joanne gave what, even to her ears, sounded like a false laugh. 'I will admit, I found Megan's deception a little difficult to take, but that's all. She can't be surprised that I was a little cool with her, surely.' Joanne lifted her arm and pointedly looked at her watch. 'Now, I'm really sorry, and I do hope you didn't come all this way just to see me, but I have to go and have a shower and get ready, I've an appointment in about an hour.'

Joanne watched a mix of emotions cross Beth's face. She guessed she didn't believe her but there wasn't a lot she could say. Megan's earlier phone call had caught her in a weak moment, she'd never have said anything otherwise and she certainly wasn't going to say anything to Beth who was a police officer after all. Wouldn't Beth be obliged to act if Joanne confessed to a crime? She squeezed her eyes shut. A crime. It *had* been a crime, hadn't it? She couldn't get it out of her head. Nor could she forget the choices she'd made as a consequence.

Opening her eyes, she saw Beth's puzzled frown, her sharp

eyes fixed on Joanne, searching for the truth. 'You never could tell a lie, Jo. I'm not leaving until you tell me what's going on.'

This time, her laughter was genuine. 'You're not questioning one of your creepy sexual predators now, you know! I've told you. There's nothing going on. You know what Megan's like.' Joanne stood. 'Now, I don't mean to be rude, but I really do need to go and get ready.' She looked down at her clothes and shook her head. 'I threw on any old thing this morning, I've been gardening that's why it took me so long to answer the front door.' It took every particle of the little energy she had left to make her voice sound calm and reasonable. She gazed at her friend from beneath her lashes. Beth wasn't a fool. Had Joanne managed to convince her that everything was okay?

'If you're sure.' Beth stood and looked at her as if searching for the truth in Joanne's pale blue eyes.

'I'm sure,' she said, keeping her eyes steady, resisting the temptation to look away. Any wavering might make Beth think again. 'Tell Megan she must have caught me at a bad moment. Sorry you made the long drive for nothing.' Joanne moved towards the door as she spoke, willing Beth to follow without further questions, needing her to be gone.

As she watched Beth climb into her car, Joanne stood at the door, waiting for her to reverse from the drive, standing with a raised hand and an inane smile until, finally, the car was gone from sight. Releasing the sob she'd been holding in, she shut the door and collapsed back against it, her eyes resuming the stricken look they'd held since Megan's revelation. It was a look she'd struggled successfully to hide from Beth and she was surprised she'd got away with it, but she'd seen something in her old friend's eyes that told her Beth had troubles of her own.

Vaguely, Joanne wondered what they were. In another time, she'd have asked, but now, her own secret was consuming her. Holding on to the banisters, she trudged upstairs to the small back room where she'd been working when she heard first the doorbell and then her phone ring.

When she'd returned from Capel-le-Ferne, after a drive she'd no recollection of, she wasn't sure what she was going to do. She'd sat on the sofa for the rest of that night, going over and over what Megan had told them, heart thumping and head spinning, trying to make sense of it all. When morning had finally come, she'd gone upstairs to the small room that she normally used to store her vast amount of clothes and had moved the hanging racks, the stacks of clothes and shoes into the spare bedroom, leaving the room empty.

The wall-to-wall wardrobes in her bedroom had top shelves she seldom used. They were a place for storing rarely worn clothes or outdated clothes she couldn't bring herself to throw away. They were also a good place to hide secrets. Dragging a chair nearer, she'd stood on it and slid her hand under the clothes to search for the heavy-duty brown envelope she'd hidden there many years before. Her fingers had closed over it and pulled it out.

She'd held it to her chest as she swayed to the beat of exhaustion, gripping the wardrobe door to stop herself falling and then she'd slipped down to sit on the chair. The envelope was still clutched to her chest. After several minutes staring blankly, she'd opened the flap and taken out the contents – two press clippings, yellowed with age, she'd cut from newspapers twenty years before. She wasn't sure how long she'd sat there looking at them, hours maybe. At some point, she'd started to cry, and small wet spots peppered the paper where her tears had fallen. Carefully, she'd patted them dry.

She hadn't changed her clothes; her hair had fallen down

from the neat chignon she'd had it in the previous day, and the tears had made her expertly applied eye make-up run. But she didn't care, and at nine o'clock she'd headed out to a local newsagent that provided a photocopying service. The shop had just opened and was empty when she'd arrived. She'd handed the two press cuttings to the acne-skinned young man behind the counter who had eyed her with curiosity but said nothing.

'Can you photocopy each of these so that they fit onto an A4 page?' she asked him.

'Sure,' he said, taking the cuttings.

'I'll want five hundred of each.' It was a guess; she wasn't really sure how many she'd need in total but a thousand seemed like a good amount.

He showed no surprise, as if being asked for such large amounts was an everyday occurrence, simply saying, 'That'll take a while, and if another customer comes in for a quick job, I'll have to interrupt it.'

'Fine,' she said, and seconds later the photocopier was starting on the first of the two cuttings, clunking as it scanned and then swishing as it sent the first copy sliding out.

'I'll need some kind of glue too,' she'd said. 'Enough to stick them all onto a wall.'

She watched him amble across the shop and stand in front of a small display, his head slightly tilted as if weighing up the options before selecting an item and peering at the printed instructions. As if satisfied with what he read, he picked up three more. He returned and dropped all four tubes of glue on the counter in front of her. 'This'll do the job.'

Joanne waited while he served other customers who drifted in, and returned to the photocopier to replenish the paper before starting to copy the second newspaper cutting. It took longer than she'd expected, almost forty-five minutes to do the thousand copies she'd requested. She stood watching them as they were delivered, the soft swish almost hypnotic, her head bobbing as tiredness swept over her. The assistant offered her the seat from behind the counter but she smiled and declined. Finally, there was silence; her copies were ready.

The stack of A4 pages were put on the counter beside the tubes of glue. 'And here are the original press cuttings,' the assistant said, putting them on top of the stack. 'That'll be one hundred and eight pounds and twenty-eight p.' And then, perhaps because he'd had time to consider, he asked, 'Are you okay?'

If she told him what she'd done, this young man whose life lay ahead of him full of rosy hope and exciting promise, would his concern turn to abhorrence, disgust, fear? 'Thank you, I will be,' she said, handing over her credit card to pay.

'Have you a bag?' he asked, waiting until she whispered *no* before reaching under the counter to pull out a battered cardboard box. 'This should do,' he said. He slipped the copies into it, folded the top down and pushed it across the counter.

She took hold, held it against her chest, gave him a nod of thanks and left without another word.

Back home in the small bedroom, she'd started straight away. The glue came with a roller-ball applicator and was easy to use. She rolled it over the back of an A4 page and placed it on the wall, beginning in one corner, placing each neatly beside the other. When tears blinded her she stopped, but only for long enough to dry her eyes on the sleeve of the cream silk blouse that was now streaked with multicoloured stains. When exhaustion overtook her, she'd curled up on the floor, but she couldn't sleep and, minutes later, got up and started again, her fingers trembling as they worked.

The ceiling and the upper part of the ten-foot high walls had been the most difficult to do. She stood on a bedroom chair, but still couldn't reach. Of course, she didn't have a ladder and cursed herself for this oversight, wondering if she should go and try to source one. But she was so tired, any delay was unacceptable. In desperation, she'd dragged a low table up the stairs from the lounge and placed the chair on top of that, climbing up awkwardly, balancing precariously as she applied a couple of sheets, getting down to move the chair slightly and go through it all again. Twice she'd fallen, lying shaken on the floor, until she was sure she could move and then climbed back up. It was a slow, painful process, but she knew she had to finish it before she could carry out the second part of her plan.

Beth's visit had interrupted her work. Joanne was still amazed she'd managed to fool a woman who was usually wise to every ruse. Once again, she wondered what was troubling her friend before brushing thoughts of her aside. She needed to get on. There was still half of one wall to do, another couple of hours should do it. She picked up the next photocopy, applied glue to the back and, carefully making sure there were no gaps, stuck it to the wall.

She'd planned to finish it that night, but it was taking longer than she'd expected. Probably because, every now and then, she would pause and stand, staring. Sometimes, she wasn't sure how long she'd been standing: minutes, hours? She hadn't eaten or drunk since Friday and it was having an effect; every time she bent down and stood up, she felt dizzy. But there was no point in eating or drinking. After all, she wasn't going to die of starvation or thirst.

Her head had started to ache early that morning and Beth's stress-inducing visit hadn't helped. Now, it wasn't so much an ache as a hideous pounding as if her head was going to explode. It made every task, every movement difficult.

Looking around the almost-finished room, she felt the hundreds of eyes on her, condemning, judging. Eyes that looked at her and asked why? Soon, she wouldn't have to look at them, wouldn't have to suffer the excruciating guilt that was corroding her. A small section of the wall was still to be done but her hands were trembling so much there was more glue on them than on the paper. Scrunching up a ruined sheet, she threw it to one side with a sob of distress. She'd have a rest and start again when she was able.

But first, before she closed her eyes, she needed to prepare for the final step. Holding tightly to the banisters, she headed down to the kitchen.

It took her a few minutes to choose the right knife; she needed it to be sharp enough to cut through skin and muscle. She wasn't a masochist; it needed to be quick. Unable to decide, she took two from the drawer, headed back upstairs, and laid them together on the table she'd pushed to the side.

With the eyes in every photocopy staring at her, she curled up in the middle of the floor, her cheek resting on her joined hands. Exhausted, her head still pounding, she shut her eyes.

Soon, it would be over.

23

Beth was annoyed. She'd listened to Megan and come on this stupid waste-of-time journey. Okay, Joanne looked a mess but maybe that was the way she liked to be when she was in the comfort of her own home. Maybe that's why she never invited them to stay. Beth brushed away the niggling feeling that something wasn't quite right and concentrated on the road back to London and her own problems.

The drive back, despite steadily moving traffic, seemed interminable, and she was in a foul mood by the time she reached the city. The continuous chirping of her phone telling her she had a message didn't help. She'd checked the first time, the vague hope still lingering that it might be Graham. Instead, every single time, it was Megan. After the fourth message, Beth grabbed her phone, pressed the off button and tried to relax. But that was a fool's game, there were too many thoughts spinning in her head.

Home held no promise of comfort either. The light was fading, night would have fallen before she got there and, despite the timer she'd attached to one of the lamps, the house would be cold, unwelcoming and very, very quiet. Home, it didn't seem to merit that word anymore.

Almost without thinking, she indicated to take the turn for Megan's apartment. Maybe talking to her would take her mind off her problems. At least she could tackle her about the stupid mission she'd sent her on.

She knew the code to the apartment block's underground parking. There weren't designated visitor spaces available, usually she left her small car directly behind Megan's and Trudy's and, so far, there'd been no complaint. Today, however, she was surprised to see Trudy's space empty, an unusual enough occurrence to make Beth frown. She'd often wondered why the woman kept a car as she never seemed to use it. Apparently there was an exception to everything.

A different code was required to access the lift that would take Beth to the top floor. To her annoyance, she couldn't remember it and spent fruitless minutes trying various combinations before, softly swearing under her breath, she took out her phone and switched it on. 'It's me. I'm in your garage. What's the code? I can't remember it.' Beth had to wait until Megan had gushed out words of relief at hearing from her before she gave her the code. 'Four, five, three, two, of course, okay, I'll see you in a sec.' She pocketed her phone, pressed the numbers and waited for the door to open.

Megan was waiting in the doorway of her apartment when she stepped out of the lift. Although she was dressed immaculately in a fitted black skirt and loose grey jumper, she didn't look well. She was too pale and her eyes were red-rimmed as if she'd been weeping all day. Beth regretted she hadn't gone straight home; she could have drowned her sorrows in the rest of the whiskey. Now it looked as if she'd have to listen to Megan's continued attempts to justify her actions in Capel-le-Ferne.

Stepping out of the lift, the doors immediately slid closed

behind Beth, giving her no choice but to move forward and walk across the hall to her friend. 'You look like shit, Megan, if you don't mind me saying so,' Beth said, her eyes narrowing at her friend's obvious distress.

Suddenly, the absent car made sense and she groaned. 'Oh, no!' Reaching out a hand, she grabbed her arm. 'Not you and Trudy?'

Megan snuffled and put her hand over Beth's for a moment before stepping back and waving her in. 'I'm afraid so. I didn't want to tell you when I found out about you and Graham splitting. I thought you had enough on your plate.'

'But why? What happened?' Beth said, watching as Megan vanished into the kitchen, returning moments later with a bottle of wine and two glasses.

'Sit,' Megan said, opening the wine.

Beth sat on the sofa and took the glass that was handed to her, raising an eyebrow as her friend downed half a glass in one gulp. 'Steady on, you'll make yourself sick. Sit down, tell me what happened.'

Megan sat, fiddled with the stem of the glass, and took another mouthful of wine. 'Trudy said she couldn't forgive my deception, that she no longer trusted me, couldn't see that we had any future.' Megan gave Beth a wry smile. 'She's given me till Friday to move out.'

Beth opened her mouth to speak, and shut it again. It was thanks to her drunken prattling that Trudy had found out about that stupid lie in the first place. 'I'm so sorry,' she said, feeling as if everything she thought she knew and could trust in her world was falling apart. Trudy and Megan, they'd been solid. 'Maybe she just needs time?' Beth tried to read her friend's expression. What she saw there didn't look too hopeful.

Megan shook her head and gave a sad laugh. 'I only told her the truth about what I'd done because she'd been going on about how pure and honest our relationship was. I didn't want to marry her with that lie on my conscience. I thought being honest was best, but what was it you said about honesty, Beth, that it was a dangerous blade to wave about? How right you were.' The sob sounded as if it came from Megan's broken heart.

Beth put her glass down, took the one from Megan's hand and pulled her into a hug, holding her tightly while she sobbed uncontrollably. Beth guessed she should be trotting out the old faithful platitudes, the lie that it would all be okay, that she was better off without her, that there were plenty more people out there to love. The lies she'd been telling herself since Graham left. Lies. It wouldn't ever be okay, neither of them was better off without the one they loved and she knew, for Megan as much as for her, there was nobody else out there.

Soon both were sobbing, a deep heart-broken sound that echoed around the apartment.

They were exhausted by the time the crying stopped. Arms still wrapped around each other, they rested back against the sofa without a word and stayed there for a long time, each deep in thought of what they had lost.

'Where are you going to go?' Beth asked finally, pulling away and reaching into her pocket for a tissue to wipe her eyes and nose.

Megan, snuffling, shook her head. 'I don't know, I'll have to find somewhere to rent, I suppose. Trudy was quite clear; Friday at the latest.'

'You're welcome to move in with me, if it would help,' Beth said with a quick grin. 'I know it'll be a huge comedown from this.' She waved her hand around at the spacious elegant room with the stunning city views. 'But it will allow you to take your time and find something decent rather than grabbing the first place you see.'

'Thank you,' Megan said, sounding genuinely grateful.

'The offer is there, if you need it.' Beth reached for her glass. She had never given any thought to their living arrangements. If she had, she'd have assumed the apartment belonged to both of them. 'You never contributed to the mortgage?' she asked quietly.

Megan shook her head and picked up her glass. 'Trudy bought the apartment just before we met. She'd won a very prestigious architect's award where the first prize was a large amount of cash that she used as a deposit. The award also led to some very lucrative jobs and, sensibly, she paid money off the mortgage each time.' Megan sighed. 'When I moved in, I did suggest that I pay towards it, but she said no and that was that. She continued to pay off the mortgage with any spare cash. Meanwhile, we used my money for holidays, nights out etc.' Megan's laugh was sardonic. 'What a fool I was, eh?'

'Couldn't you argue that since your contribution to the lifestyle you both enjoyed allowed her to reduce the mortgage, that you were, in effect, paying some of it?'

'I was the one who liked the nice holidays, the five-star hotels, the fine dining. Trudy could get any number of people to say she'd have been just as happy with a weekend in Margate.' Megan shrugged. 'It's true actually, she wasn't wild about travelling but came with me to keep me happy. It never entered my head to worry about the future. I thought that was sorted.'

Beth was mentally congratulating herself that at least her home was secure when the crashing truth hit her. Secure? Yes, she could just about pay the mortgage single-handed but that depended on her police salary. What would happen if she lost her job? Worse, if she ended up in prison? Despite the gloomy look on her Fed rep's face, she didn't think that would happen.

So, okay, she could afford to pay the mortgage, but what she hadn't considered was that Graham might want his share of the house. Might? Of course he would. He'd meet someone else, want to start a life with them. The thought made her stomach heave.

What was she going to do? They'd paid over three hundred thousand for the house but prices had risen, she guessed the market price now would be nearer six. She'd no savings, and no bank in its right mind would allow her to borrow what she'd need. There would be no option but to sell, pay off their joint mortgage, and divide the profit. All she could hope to get for the money she'd have, was a small one-bedded flat much further from the station. She'd have to hope that Graham gave her time to get everything sorted.

She finished her wine, holding her hand over the glass when Megan gestured to the bottle. 'No thanks, I really can't afford another hangover. I'd quite like some coffee but don't get up,' Beth hurried to say as her friend stirred. 'I can get it myself. Would you like one?'

'No, I think I'll stick to the wine, thanks.'

Beth watched Megan as she waited for the kettle to boil. She'd soon discover the oblivion wine gave didn't last, she thought, spooning coffee into a mug. She carried it to the window to stare out over the twinkling city lights. They looked so cheery, so full of promise. It was all a lie, a deception. In the morning, they'd fade and be gone like her dwindling hope that Graham would come home. She turned back to look at Megan slouched on the sofa, her glass held in her two hands, eyes unfocused.

'I hadn't planned to call in, you know,' she said as she pulled a small leather chair over and sat facing her. 'I'd gone down to check on Joanne, as I'd promised.'

Megan's blank staring eyes blinked as if to bring herself back from wherever she'd drifted. 'Sorry,' she said, lifting a hand to rub her eyes. 'What were you saying?'

'I saw Joanne,' Beth said more bluntly. Despite her woes, Megan *had* sent her on that waste-of-time journey to Tunbridge Wells.

'Oh yes, Joanne.' Megan's expression continued blank and distant for a moment before she set down the wine and straightened herself in the seat. 'Is she all right? She sounded so odd on the phone and there was that thing about her having a secret... It all sounded so unlike her.'

'I think you just caught her at a bad time,' Beth said, repeating what Joanne had said to her. 'You must have misunderstood. It was your secret she said she was referring to.'

Megan frowned and then, slowly, shook her head. 'No... no, it wasn't. That wasn't what she said.'

Beth ran a hand over her head. A headache was brewing; migraine, she could feel the soft throb that she knew would build to a crescendo and leave her crippled. It would be best to get home before it got worse. 'It doesn't really matter, does it. Listen, I'd better head off.'

'No wait,' Megan said hurriedly, 'I can prove it.' Getting to her feet, she headed to the kitchen, returning seconds later with her mobile phone in her hand, frowning as she looked at it. 'I only have one phone for both work and personal use. It's important for me to have a record of my business calls.'

Beth watched her and waited.

'So many people swear they said x whereas they actually said y so I've always recorded my calls for security. I tell people that when they ring.' She raised an eyebrow. 'It's surprising how many people hang up, you know. Anyway, I keep the business ones and delete the personal ones.' She tapped a key. 'I haven't had a chance to delete Joanne's call as yet so you can hear exactly what she said, listen.'

Seconds later, the room filled with Joanne's voice, sounding as Beth had never heard it before, eerily empty and cold. It was a voice that answered questions in a dead monotone. Finally, barely audible, she said, *It's not your secret I can't live with, Megan, it's mine.* And then she hung up.

In the silence that followed, they stared at each other. Megan had been right, there was something wrong here. There'd been something so profoundly unnerving about the way Joanne spoke. Thinking back to her visit that morning, Beth knew she'd ignored the blatant hints because she hadn't wanted to see them. Hadn't wanted more heartache. She'd visited, wasn't that enough? Now, she knew it wasn't. A good friend, one who wasn't wrapped up in her own problems, would have seen through Joanne's patent attempt to appear perfectly normal, and refused to leave until she had told her what was really going on. There was only one thing to do.

Only one thing she *could* do. She had to go back.

24

Megan insisted they wait until morning. 'You've had a glass of wine and you look wretched, Beth. Sleep for a few hours and we'll head down together.' It took a lot of persuading but eventually she managed to coax her to stay and take the spare bedroom. 'I can lend you pyjamas, if you'd like, and there's spare toothbrushes and moisturiser etc. in the bathroom cabinet. Trudy liked to be prepared for unexpected visitors.'

'Thanks,' Beth said, standing up and stretching tiredly. 'I think, I'll take you up on it. To be honest, it beats going home to an empty house. I'll say yes to the toothbrush but no to the pjs.'

Megan could tell from her friend's tight-lipped expression that something was bothering her. 'What is it?' she asked, the alcohol making her brave. Whatever it was that Beth was reluctant to say, she knew it wasn't something good. She tipped the remainder of the wine in the glass into her mouth, and reached for the bottle. 'Tell me, I'm a big girl, I can take it.' She was lying, she really wasn't sure she could take much more but she was a good liar, hadn't she already proven that?

'Okay,' Beth said, looking down at her feet. 'I don't think you should come with me tomorrow.'

Megan didn't know what she'd been expecting, but not this rejection. 'Why?' she managed, unable to prevent the tremor in the one word.

'Because whatever's wrong with Jo, it started the night you made your confession. She's not been the same since.' Beth's shrug was apologetic. 'I'm afraid if you come, you might make things worse.'

Megan stood speechless as she watched Beth turn and walk from the room. It wasn't until she heard the sound of the spare bedroom shutting that she moved, anger flashing through her. She put the wine bottle down and threw her empty glass across the room, taking a measure of satisfaction in the crash as it hit the wall and smashed into tiny pieces. She wasn't sure who she was angry with. With Beth for laying all the blame on a lie that was never meant to harm, with Trudy for leaving her, or with the world in general for shifting precariously under her feet.

Megan rubbed a hand over her forehead. For the first time in her life, she had no future planned, nothing to look forward to, just a vast emptiness that made her head ache and sent ice sliding down her spine. She was genuinely worried about Joanne, of course she was, but she hadn't really wanted to traipse down to Royal Tunbridge Wells to be blamed and berated, nor did she really want to know Joanne's secret. She'd learned, too late as it happened, that secrets should stay just that.

With enough woes of her own to occupy her, the offer to go with Beth was made on the spur of the moment, in a spirit of camaraderie and out of concern for Joanne. Reality had kicked in almost before the words were said; she was due in the Magistrate's Court at nine and the CPS wouldn't take kindly to her ringing so late with some made-up excuse. Still, Beth's rejection cut deeply.

She was slightly surprised that the ordinarily astute Beth had been so easily fooled by whatever performance Joanne had put on. Or maybe she shouldn't have been; after all, if Megan couldn't think straight since Trudy had left, maybe it was the same for Beth. They were both suffering.

Frowning, Megan thought about what Beth had said... that whatever was wrong with Joanne began the night Megan had told them about her deception. A coincidence, wasn't it? Whatever Joanne had done, whatever secret she was talking about couldn't possibly be anything to do with her, could it? Maybe it was just that her honesty had forced Joanne to confront something *she'd* done in the past. Megan nodded. That would be it. Hardly her fault then, was it? Everything couldn't be laid on her and that stupid, thoughtless, spur-of-the-moment decision she'd made twenty years earlier.

Tears gathered and trickled, ignored, down her cheeks. One thing could be laid firmly at her feet, the destruction of her relationship with Trudy. It would be nice to believe that it was Beth's fault for telling her in the first place, to shift blame in her direction, but that was a fool's game. The fault was hers, just hers. Accepting that didn't make it any easier. It didn't make the pain any easier to bear. It didn't make that bleak empty future any easier to face.

Wearily, drying her eyes, she stood up, feeling a weakness that was partially due to the alcohol, and partly due to the desolation that came over her in waves. She stood a moment in the hallway wondering if she should go and speak to Beth and tell her she was right, that for the moment she'd leave Joanne to her. But there was no light showing from underneath the door and when she pressed her ear to it there was no sound to be heard. She moved away. It would be unkind to disturb her; she'd been exhausted and probably fell asleep immediately. There'd be time to talk in the morning.

Shutting her bedroom door quietly, Megan leaned against it for a moment before turning to look at the bed she had shared with Trudy for so many years. How could it have ended the way it did? Was it right that she should be paying so much for one stupid mistake? She would never have thought Trudy could be so coldly unforgiving, or maybe she'd never really known her at all.

Despite her exhaustion, despite the wine, Megan knew she'd never get to sleep with so much churning in her head. Trudy took sleeping tablets on occasion, the packet kept on a shelf in the bathroom cabinet. Taking it out, Megan pressed one from the foil and then pressed a second, avoiding the face that looked back at her from the cabinet mirror. She didn't want to see the pain in her eyes, didn't want to see the sad droop of her mouth. She didn't want to see, feel or think, and hoped the two pills would give her some much-needed, if temporary, oblivion.

Too exhausted to undress, she lay down on Trudy's side of the bed and buried her nose in her pillow. With every breath, she came to her; that spicy exotic perfume she favoured, the vanilla body lotion she always used. Suddenly frantic to be closer to her, Megan pushed back the duvet, kicked off her shoes and crawled underneath. There was more of her there. Megan breathed her in and curled into the duvet to surround herself in the scent of the only woman she'd ever loved.

Eventually, gratefully, she fell into a deep medicated sleep.

Sometime during the night, she must have overheated and thrown off her clothes. When she woke, the first thing she saw was her skirt and shirt in a heap on the floor. She groaned and turned onto her back, resting a hand over her eyes as sunlight filtered through the fine gauze voile. She'd forgotten to close the heavy curtains. It had always been the last thing Trudy did at night. She hated bright mornings and would be awake with the first ray of sunshine if the room weren't in complete darkness. Megan felt tears gather. Everything was changing and every change was painful.

The apartment was quiet. She wondered, vaguely, what time it was. She tended to wake automatically around seven and never bothered with an alarm. Beth, she guessed, was probably still asleep. Turning again, Megan wiped her eyes, lifted her head to look at the clock on the bedside table and blinked with shock when she saw the time. Nine thirty! She'd missed her nine o'clock appearance at the court. There would be hell to pay.

A wave of nausea hit her. Swinging her feet hurriedly to the floor, she stumbled to the bathroom and hung her head over the toilet as her stomach spasmed and a stream of fluid gushed from her mouth. The rancid taste of old wine made her retch again.

When she was sure she'd finished, she went to the wash handbasin and turned on the taps to rinse her mouth and throw some water on her face. A glance in the mirror told her she looked as bad as she felt. With a hand on the wall to steady her, she went to the lounge to get her phone. 'I'm really sorry,' she said when it was answered. 'I've been sick all night, and then fell asleep just when I'd planned to ring. Food poisoning, I think,' she added when asked what was wrong. 'I'll be back as soon as I can.'

The Criminal Prosecution Service secretary was always a bit cool so Megan ignored the less-than-friendly advice to see a doctor and hung up. She stood with the phone in her hand for a few seconds before returning to her room, grabbing a robe from the back of the door and crossing to the spare bedroom. She tapped gently, listened, and knocked a little louder.

Finally, she opened the door slowly and peered around its edge. The bed was empty. 'Beth?' she called, going inside and moving across the room to the door of the en suite. It too was empty. She had gone.

The silence of the apartment seemed to taunt her.

Only when the quiet was broken by the sound of her sobs did Megan finally move.

25

Usually, Beth could get to sleep easily, but not that night. She always carried medication for migraine and took two pills, feeling relief within the hour, but still she couldn't switch off and lay for another hour, tossing and turning. She'd have liked a cup of tea but, now and then, the sound of movement indicated Megan was still awake. If Beth went to the kitchen, Megan might join her, and they'd end up having one of those conversations that went around in circles. Yes, Beth shouldn't have told Trudy something she'd sworn to keep secret, but Megan shouldn't have lied in the first place. Playing the blame game was exhausting and nobody ever won.

Instead, Beth lay thinking about Graham, wondering where he was, what he was doing, and who he was doing it with. If there wasn't someone already, there soon would be. He was a man who liked female company, who preferred to be in a relationship. He'd told her once after walking through the front door that he loved having someone to come home to, and they'd hugged. The memory made her heart ache. An incredibly handsome man, with those brown eyes and that mop of shaggy blond hair, she guessed Graham – her Graham whom she still loved – wouldn't be on his own for long.

The only way to stop thinking about him was to force her thoughts to the more seriously pressing matter of her suspension. The risks she'd taken over the years had seemed worth it. Now, she didn't know. How many of those men she'd planted evidence on, or helped put away, were as innocent as that poor fool in Capel-le-Ferne?

A noise outside her door made her hold her breath. Then she heard the distinct sound of the bedroom door opposite opening and closing. She stayed an hour longer, alternating trying to get to sleep with churning troubling thoughts over in her head. Finally, she threw the duvet back and got up.

A few minutes later, dressed and carrying her shoes, Beth slipped from the apartment, closing the front door softly behind her.

It was still night, but in London it was never really dark. She pulled her car out onto the night-time quiet road, thought about heading home for a change of clothes and maybe some breakfast but then decided to take the road that would eventually lead her back to Royal Tunbridge Wells.

It was, of course, far too early to descend on Joanne. Instead, Beth stopped at the first service station she came to and sat with the other night owls: the truck drivers, taxi drivers, shift-workers and the people who had nowhere else to go, sipping strong coffee and waiting restlessly for the night to end.

At eight, she decided it was time to leave. There was only so much bad coffee she could drink and only so long she could ignore the leering eyes of the truck driver who'd been staring at her for the last twenty minutes, his hand moving over the obvious bulge in his crotch. Fat and sweaty, she could have easily thrown him to the floor but that would have brought the security guard she could see walking up and down outside to the scene. It wasn't worth it.

～

Back on the road, the traffic was heavy but moving. She tuned the radio to a music channel and increased the volume to drown her thoughts, lowering it down quickly as she turned onto Joanne's quiet residential road. It was almost nine as she parked beside Joanne's car. Getting out, Beth looked around. There were cars pulling out of driveways and parking spaces, people going about their business, living their normal everyday lives. She looked at Joanne's house. It looked pretty normal too but Beth knew something odd was going on inside.

Joanne's car didn't appear to have been moved. It didn't prove anything, she could have ordered a taxi to take her to the appointment she'd mentioned. Beth stood back and looked up at the house. There was no light creeping around the edges of the shuttered windows. Maybe Joanne was still asleep.

Beth pressed the doorbell, waited a few minutes and pressed again. When there was still no response, frustrated, Beth decided to get some breakfast and come back later. The food at the service station had been unappetising and she hadn't eaten anything the day before. No wonder she was feeling weary, weak and out of sorts. After something to eat, she'd be better able to think and decide what to do.

Leaving her car where it was, she walked down Grove Hill Road. It was a lovely morning, the houses she passed were architecturally striking enough to command her attention but try as she might, her attention drifted, her thoughts focusing on Joanne. At the roundabout, unsure of which direction to go, she chose to turn right along Mount Pleasant Road. There was a mix of houses and high-end independent shops just opening their door for business. Her eyes drifted over the windows of a butcher's, an artisan bakery, and what looked like an extremely pricey clothes shop. Finally, after another five minutes' walk, she reached what she was looking for and pushed open the door into a warm cosy café.

This early, there were only a couple of customers, eyes glued to newspapers, or mobiles, free hands lifting food or drink. Nobody was speaking although the café wasn't quiet thanks to background music that came from speakers set high on the walls. Elevator music, Graham always called it, and he'd go and ask for something different to be played. She almost smiled at the memory, dismissing it and him to concentrate on the young man behind the counter who was waiting impatiently.

Behind him, on the wall, a white board was scrawled with curly, almost illegible writing showing the morning's menu. She gave it a cursory glance and took out her purse. 'I'll have the scrambled eggs on toast, please, and a large coffee.'

He didn't bother writing her order down. 'Take a seat and I'll bring it over when it's ready.'

Beth took a table in the bay window overlooking the street, pulling out a chair and sitting with a weary grunt. Her eyes felt gritty from tiredness. She hoped the coffee and food would make her feel a little more human. But she had no appetite and when both came, she picked up the fork listlessly. With effort, she forced herself to eat almost half the scrambled egg before giving up and pushing the plate away. There was no problem, however, in finishing the coffee, it was excellent, and when she finished the first, she went up and ordered another, hoping the caffeine would help to keep her awake.

Lingering over the second coffee, she glanced around as the café filled with people and enough chatter to drown out the music. When she found herself staring with a twinge of jealousy at a loved-up couple at another table, she knew it was time to move.

～

It was just after ten when she stood outside Joanne's house again but if she'd hoped to see a sign of life, she was disappointed. Nothing had changed. With little enthusiasm and less hope, Beth pressed the doorbell, letting it ring for a long time before removing her finger. Taking out her mobile, she left the same message as she had the previous day, hoping to get the same positive response. 'You have ten minutes to open the door, Joanne, or I'm ringing the police.'

Beth waited for a few minutes, staring at the house as if expecting to see some indication of Joanne's presence before swearing softly and getting back into her car. It was as easy to wait there as to stand or sit on the doorstep, and certainly a lot warmer. She propped her mobile on the dashboard, adjusted the seat back a little and sat staring at the front door, willing it to open. Despite the amount of coffee she'd had, a wave of tiredness washed over her. Perhaps, feeling this tired, sitting down hadn't been such a good idea. She'd shut her eyes for a few minutes to rest them.

The knock on the car door that woke her was so loud Beth jerked upward and banged her knee hard on the steering wheel. 'Ouch, damn it,' she said, grabbing her knee before looking out the window. Expecting to see Joanne, Beth groaned when she saw who was staring through the window. Megan! What the hell was she doing here? Still rubbing her knee, there was nothing Beth could do but open the door. 'Hi,' Beth said, getting out, putting her foot gingerly to the ground. It felt like her knee was broken, but she guessed it wasn't. She glared at Megan. 'I thought we'd agreed you were going to stay at home?'

'No, we didn't agree. You made a statement and walked away without discussing it, as if I were a not-very-bright junior member of your team.' Megan's voice was sharp with annoyance. 'And if you'd bothered to wake me before you left, Beth, I wouldn't bloody well be here either. I had a case in the Magistrate's Court at nine and I missed it. Do you have any idea how detrimental that is to my career?'

Beth raised an eyebrow. 'How on earth can I be responsible for you not waking on time? That's a stretch by anyone's standards. What time is it anyway?' She reached into the car to pick up her phone as she spoke and checked the screen, blinking in disbelief when she saw it was midday. 'I fell asleep,' she said, almost to herself. She looked at Megan's worried face. 'I rang the doorbell and waited. When Joanne didn't answer, I did what I did yesterday, left a message saying I'd give her ten minutes before ringing the police. I sat in the car to wait... that was just after ten o'clock.'

Megan turned to the house. 'Maybe she's not here. She may have taken a train somewhere.'

'I thought the same yesterday but she was here.' The two hours' sleep had done Beth good. She felt much better, more able to think logically. 'Let's try the doorbell again. Maybe she did come out, saw me asleep, and decided to leave me alone.' Beth didn't really believe what she was saying, but trying the doorbell again would do no harm and would give her time to think about what they should do next.

They waited several minutes on the doorstep, ringing the bell for a long time, shouting through the letterbox when they got no reply. Beth rang Joanne's mobile again and left the same message and they waited, without a word, as the minutes ticked by.

26

When it was obvious that either Joanne wasn't there or wasn't going to answer, Megan looked at Beth and said, 'What do we do now?'

Beth tapped the phone against her chin. The threat to ring the police was made in earnest, but she couldn't bring herself to take that drastic step. After all, it might be that Joanne's appointment required her to stay overnight somewhere. Maybe she had taken a train. Without answering Megan's question, Beth walked out to the footpath and checked up and down the street. 'Come on,' she said and started walking, leaving Megan to catch up. 'I think there might be a laneway behind these houses,' Beth said, as Megan fell into step beside her. 'It's worth having a look.'

Beth was pleased to see she was right. At the end of the terrace, there was a narrow laneway. Dark and damp, it didn't appear enticing but it might give them the access they needed. With a jerk of her head at Megan to follow, she started down it. The laneway ran straight ahead, past another row of terraced houses behind and out onto a parallel road. But as she'd hoped, between the back gardens of the two terraces, another lane ran perpendicularly to give access. It wasn't wide enough for vehicles and with weeds and moss making it slippery underfoot, it looked as if it were rarely used by pedestrians either.

They walked into it, Beth's eyes on the houses, Megan's on the ground, her leather-soled court shoes unsuitable for the slippery surface, raising her head only when she heard Beth say, 'This is it.'

'Are you sure?' she asked, peering at the building, the upper floors just visible over the shoulder-high wall. 'They all look the same from this side.' The terrace, multicoloured in the front, was uniformly grey behind.

'I counted the windows.' Beth reached for the handle of a wooden gate and pushed, half-expecting it to be locked, but the gate opened immediately without a creak or squeak. The small garden it opened into gave lie to Joanne's story that she'd been doing gardening the day before. There was nothing to garden; the entire area was laid with huge square paving stones, no gaps left to plant trees or flowers. Nor were there potted plants to soften the area or justify Joanne's claim.

'How awfully sterile,' Megan said as she and Beth looked around. 'A shame too. It could be made quite homely with a few pots and some nice furniture.'

Ignoring her, Beth walked up to the back door and tried the handle. This time she was met with resistance and peered in through the glass-panelled door to the very small room beyond. A utility room, she guessed, pulling back and crossing to the window. Unlike the windows to the front, there were no shutters to impede the view.

'The kitchen,' Megan said coming up beside her to look through the window. 'How are we going to get in?'

Beth tried the windows. They were old, aluminium framed, with two opening windows on either side of a fixed pane. She cupped her hands to the glass, examined the side of one of the opening windows and gave it a firm push. There was definite movement. Turning, her eyes searched the garden. There was nothing there she could use. 'Wait here,' she said, 'I need to get something from the car.'

Minutes later, Beth returned with a crowbar held discreetly by her side. When she came through the gate, she waved it in satisfaction. 'Always a handy thing to carry in your car boot.' She searched closely around the window frame. As far as she could see, it wasn't alarmed. There could, of course, be sensors inside. 'If I say run,' she said, turning to look at Megan, 'run back to your car and get inside. I'll follow, okay?'

She waited until Megan agreed before turning back to the window. Inserting the crowbar, she levered it gently back and forth. It was surprisingly easy and didn't take long to prise the window open. She stood with her head cocked as she listened for any alarm but there was nothing audible. It didn't mean there wasn't an inaudible one notifying an alarm company or the local police station but she'd worry about that if and when it became a problem.

Dropping the crowbar to the ground, Beth gave Megan a satisfied grin and with little effort clambered up and slipped through the window. It opened onto the kitchen sink that was thankfully empty and she stepped lightly from it to the floor. She stood and listened for a moment but if Joanne was somewhere, she was keeping quiet.

A narrow-eyed glance around the window and the corners of the room told Beth there were no alarms to worry about. She'd definitely have to have a word with her friend about security. The door to the utility room was unlocked and she went through, nodding in satisfaction to see the key in the back door. Through the glass panel Beth could see Megan looking nervously around and quickly opened the door for her.

'Thank goodness,' Megan said, hurrying inside. 'I could hear people next door, and I was afraid they'd look over the fence and ask what I was doing.'

Back in the kitchen, Beth reached over and shut the window, pushing the handle down to lock it. It wasn't very secure but it would suffice. She turned to see Megan standing in the middle of the room with wide eyes and a jaw-dropped mouth.

'Look at this place,' she said. 'It's like a laboratory.'

Beth had to agree. Glossy white cupboard doors, white stone countertops, white backsplash. Even the floor was covered in shiny white tiles. The room was pristine, not a speck of dust, not a single crumb marred the shiny glaring whiteness. She remembered the lounge; it too had been white. But they weren't there to discuss Joanne's decorating foibles. 'Let's find out if Joanne is actually here,' Beth said.

Megan couldn't let it go though. As they went through into the hall, she commented on the glossy white painted woodwork and couldn't resist peeking into the lounge, pushing the door open with the vague excuse that Joanne might be inside. 'Oh, my word,' Megan said in a loud whisper, 'this is beyond bizarre!'

Beth remembered being surprised by the all-white décor but she'd been too engrossed in Joanne's appearance to give it more than a passing thought. But after the all-white kitchen, she had to admit Megan was right. This was a little bizarre. They stood in the open doorway and scrutinised the room. Woodwork, carpet, sofa, light shades, even the few ornaments – were all startlingly white. The only colour in the room came from the spines of the books on the bookshelves and a few photographs in silver frames.

'This is creepy,' Megan said.

'Come on,' Beth said, taking Megan by the elbow and pulling her out. 'Let's go upstairs.'

The stairs, unusually, were uncarpeted, painted instead in a whitewash reminiscent of a Scandinavian-type décor Beth had seen in style magazines. Had there been colour elsewhere, it might have looked good but the unrelenting white was eerie. They stood a moment in the hallway, glancing up. 'Joanne?' Beth called, waiting a second before starting up the stairs.

Megan's leather heels on the wood knocked with every footstep, even Beth's flat synthetic-soled pumps made a sound. Surely, Beth thought, if Joanne were here, she'd have come out to investigate by now. Perhaps, after all, she was away.

The first door off the landing led into a large bright front bedroom. A king-sized bed faced the window, a locker on each side, a large wardrobe against the far wall. Here the colour choice continued; glossy white furniture, thick white carpet and crisp white duvet cover.

'It's just too weird.' Megan's voice was still an unsteady whisper, her eyes wide in what Beth guessed was the same horrified amazement she felt.

The next door led into a small bathroom where the all-white glossy décor made it look cold and clinical. Even the soap was white. Beth frowned. There was something very wrong with this level of obsession. How had they never seen this? In all the years they'd known Joanne there'd never been the slightest hint. It was no wonder that she'd never invited them there. Beth doubted if she'd ever invited anyone. How could she possibly explain this?

Megan pushed open the door of the next room and gasped. Beth peered over her shoulder. There was a bed against the wall covered in a white spread. Piles of clothes had been left untidily on top and were spilling over onto the floor. Freestanding clothes rails, hung with what looked like hundreds of dresses, trousers and blouses, had been pushed into the middle of the room. At the bottom, shoes of every colour and heel type, lay willy-nilly as if thrown there from the doorway. After the constant white, the array of colour in the room was almost shocking. 'She always did like her clothes,' Megan said, shutting the door and following Beth to the last door.

By this stage, convinced that Joanne had gone away, Beth was annoyed with herself for having bothered to come, and irritated with Megan for putting the idea into her head. Beth pushed open the last door with little enthusiasm, turning to say to her that they were wasting their time. 'This is a–'

But Megan's sudden and complete look of horror made Beth shut her mouth and turn. What she saw sent the floor heaving under her feet, managing to stay upright only by tightening her grip on the doorknob. As the door swung open fully under her weight, she sagged against it. 'What the fuck?'

The room was in semi-darkness, the one window papered over, the only light coming from the open door in which they stood. Unable to move, Beth held on to the door, Megan clinging to her arm. As their eyes adjusted to the light, they could see better the carnage within, the streaks of dark red on the white carpet and on Joanne's cream shirt. She lay, half lying, half sitting, on the floor, shoulders leaning against the wall, head slumped forward.

'She has to be dead,' Beth said in a whisper. 'So much blood, she can't be alive.' Light caught the long-bladed knife that hung loosely from Joanne's right hand. 'Oh, Joanne,' Beth whispered, a lump in her throat. 'Why didn't you talk to us?' Taking a steadying breath, she took a step forward, holding a hand out to stop Megan from following. 'Stay here,' she ordered. 'The police won't like us traipsing over a crime scene.' They wouldn't appreciate her walking over it either, but she needed to make sure there was nothing they could do for Joanne before ringing the police.

Beth was only one step into the room, her eyes fixed on Joanne's blood-smeared body when she saw movement. Had she imagined it? Then she saw it again, the slightest rise and fall of Joanne's chest. 'Oh my God, she's breathing! She's alive. Megan, call an ambulance,' Beth said, rushing to Joanne's side, uncaring of her footsteps in the blood-soaked carpet, and dropping to her knees to check her pulse.

'No,' the voice was barely a whisper but they heard it. And then it came again, stronger, firmer as Joanne lifted her head and looked at them, ravaged eyes in a ghostly face. 'No, no ambulance. There's really no need.' She lifted her arms, the knife hanging loosely from one hand. Joanne's hands were streaked with blood, her wrist and forearms criss-crossed with red lines but, up closer, Beth saw what she meant. There were multiple superficial lacerations to both arms with some deeper damage to the left but none looked bad enough to cause major concern. Blood was oozing and dribbling from their edges, not pumping.

Letting the knife fall, Joanne brushed the blood away and wiped it on her shirt. She laughed pitifully as she watched bubbles of red rise again from the cuts. 'I couldn't do it,' she said. 'No matter how hard I tried, I couldn't do it. I tried my left arm and then, when I couldn't slice deeply enough, I tried my right.'

Kneeling beside her, Beth reached out and smoothed a limp lock of hair from Joanne's face. 'Oh, Joanne,' she said softly. 'Why didn't you tell me things were so bad?' Concentrating on her, she didn't hear Megan coming in behind and stop a few feet away. It was her moaned *oh no* that brought Beth's head up. Turning, she saw Megan, her eyes fixed, not on the shocking sight of their blood-streaked friend, but on the walls of the room. Beth followed her gaze and stood slowly, frowning as she tried to understand what she was seeing.

'It's Matt Peters,' Megan said.

Beth heard the strain in Megan's voice and saw her look of anguish. It took Beth a few seconds to place the name. She shut her eyes in disbelief before opening them and moving closer to look at the A4 pages that were plastered over every surface. 'Matt Peters? Are you sure?' she asked, squinting to read the small print, unable to in the dim light. But she could tell they were photocopies of newspaper articles, two different articles, each with the same photo of a smiling man. Every inch of the room, even the window, was plastered with the pages. Following Megan's shocked eyes, Beth glanced upward, almost not believing what she was seeing. Joanne had covered the ceiling too.

Moving to the wall near the door where there was more light, Megan read the text. 'This one says he went missing.' She turned and stared at Joanne with wide shocked eyes. 'Not very long after–'

'After you accused him of raping you,' Joanne interrupted, her voice tired and weary.

Megan shook her head. 'I never accused him–'

'Sins of omission,' Beth said. 'You didn't deny it when we jumped to the wrong conclusion, did you?'

'You let us believe he raped you,' Joanne said. 'The torn clothes, bruises, scratches. What were we supposed to believe? Why would we have thought you were deceiving us?' Groaning, Joanne shuffled up to lean her back against the wall, holding both arms across her lap. 'I felt guilty for neglecting you that night, more than guilty when I saw your devastated face, your battered and bruised body. How could I sit back and do nothing?'

The blood drained from Megan's cheeks as the words sunk in.

Beth stood, and moving to the doorway, she felt around under the sheets of paper for the light switch. But if she'd hoped that light might take away some of the horror of the situation, she was wrong – instead it emphasised it; Matt Peters' handsome face surrounding the bloody mess of Joanne's slumped body.

'Oh God, Joanne,' Megan said, her voice cracking, 'what did you do?'

27

B eth felt like the world was splintering under her feet, one wrong step and it could fall apart. She wanted to get out of the room, away from all the damn staring eyes but first they had to take care of Joanne. Putting a hand on Megan's shoulder, she said, 'Listen, this isn't the time for explanations or recrimina- tions. We need to clean Joanne and get some dressings on those cuts, okay?'

Megan looked like she was going to argue but instead, she looked to the door. 'I'll go and get a bowl of hot water.'

A bowl of hot water? Beth wanted to snap that Joanne wasn't bloody well pregnant but shut her mouth on the words and let Megan go. As soon as she heard her footsteps on the stairway, she reached a hand down to Joanne. 'You think you can stand if I help you?' She waited patiently for a hint that she was able to move and when she saw the almost imperceptible nod, took a bloody hand in hers, reached down to put a supportive arm around her back and with a grunt, helped Joanne to her feet. When she swayed, Beth was forced to compensate, shifting her weight, holding her body closer. A nauseating combination of smells wafted from Joanne. A noxious mix of blood and body odour that made Beth gag. She swallowed. 'Let's try to get into the bathroom, Jo,' Beth said.

It took a couple of minutes to go the short distance. Beth crooned encouraging nonsensical words every time Joanne slumped, struggling to keep her balance as she led her forward. The bathroom door was open, Beth pushed her through and used her hip to manoeuvre her down onto the toilet seat. The shower, Beth was relieved to see, was modern and spacious with an inbuilt bench to sit on. She switched on the water, adjusted the temperature, left it running, and turned back to Joanne. Her breath caught; in the light of the bedroom, Joanne had looked shocking. In the glaringly bright whiteness of the bathroom, there was a nightmarish zombie-like quality to her blood-streaked body, the matted ropes of hair, the pale dirt-streaked face.

Beth gazed down at her bloodstained hands. Her life was already a nightmare before she came there. Now it was like she was living in a horror film. Leaning over her friend, she started the difficult job of gently removing the stained clothes. 'Move your arm, Jo,' she said patiently, moving it herself when there was no reaction. It was awkward, exhausting but, finally, it was done. 'Okay, my friend, let's get you into the shower.'

Putting an arm around Joanne's naked waist, Beth took a deep breath and helped her to her feet. 'Well done,' she encouraged, pressing her forward and helping her to negotiate the step into the shower. The water quickly soaked both of them, blood-stained water hitting the glossy white tiles and filling the shower tray. Beth was struggling to keep her balance as she tried to persuade Joanne to lower herself to the bench when Megan came in, a bowl of hot water in her hands, looking pathetic.

'Help me,' Beth said sharply, afraid Joanne was going to slip and fall. Megan dropped the bowl of water into the sink, the water sloshing over the side to drench the floor even more. With

Beth holding one arm, Megan took the other and, between them, they persuaded Joanne to sit.

Water running down her face and dripping from her hair, Beth spluttered, 'Get some clean clothes for her while I shower the blood away, and see if you can find something to use as dressings. Tear some clothes if you have to. Hurry!'

Beth used half a bottle of shower gel to wash Joanne's matted hair and filthy body, using a separate shower attachment to hose the debris away. Once most of the blood was washed away, she was pleased to see that the damage wasn't as bad as she had first thought. Some of the lacerations on Joanne's arms were deep and were still oozing blood. Without being sutured, they were going to leave some interesting scars that Joanne would find difficult to explain, but none were serious enough to be worried about.

Switching off the water, Beth grabbed one of the big white bath towels that lay across the towel rail and wrapped it around her friend's shoulders. Grabbing a second, she rubbed her hair, and wrapped a towel around her head. 'You're going to be okay,' Beth said repeatedly, soothingly, as she worked, wishing the dead look in Joanne's eyes would go away.

Megan returned with her hands full. 'I guessed pyjamas would be easiest,' she said, handing her a soft pink cotton top and bottoms. 'They're stretchy and the arms are fairly wide. And I thought we could wrap these around her arms.' She unfolded two crisp white pillowcases.

'Good,' Beth said with an approving nod. She put the pyjamas on the towel rail and, taking the first pillowcase, wrapped it around Joanne's right arm, tucking the end in to keep it in place and then repeated with the other on the left. It wasn't ideal, but it was the best she could do.

It took several minutes to get Joanne dry and into the pyjamas, every action, every movement a struggle as she seemed unable to understand what they wanted her to do. The makeshift dressings around her arms came undone while they tried to get the pyjama top on and needed to be redone.

By the time they were finished, Beth and Megan were exhausted and their clothes bloodstained and wet. 'Are there more pyjamas?' Beth asked. When Megan nodded, she said, 'Get a pair for both of us. We'll get Joanne downstairs and then we can take turns to shower and change, okay?'

Thirty minutes later, dressed in pyjamas, the three of them were sitting in the lounge, Beth and Megan in the single armchairs, Joanne in the middle of the sofa opposite.

Beth, shocked and exhausted, was unable to get her thoughts past what they'd witnessed. She turned to speak to Megan, but her stunned eyes and tightly shut mouth told Beth she was having the same struggle.

Nobody spoke for a long time.

When Beth saw the dead look in Joanne's eyes replaced by desolation, she crossed the room to sit beside her. She checked her arms, pleased to see that most of the bleeding had stopped, only a slight ooze from some of the deeper cuts showing through the white cotton.

'I'm going to check to see if there's anything to eat in that sterile-looking kitchen of yours,' Beth said, tucking the pillow-cases in more securely. She wasn't feeling hungry, but she guessed Joanne hadn't eaten since before Capel-le-Ferne and hoped she might be tempted if food was prepared for them all.

There was nothing of any use in the fridge; some milk that made her grimace when she sniffed it, some limp lettuce and hairy tomatoes. She had more luck in a freezer stocked full with ready meals. Taking out three lasagnes, she looked at the instructions and placed them, criss-crossed, one on top of the other, into the microwave.

Fifteen minutes later, Beth returned to the lounge with a tray holding the hot food, cutlery and three plates.

It looked as if neither Megan nor Joanne had moved or spoken since she left. She put the tray down on the coffee table and glanced from one to the other. 'Before we talk about anything,' she ordered, 'we're going to have something to eat, okay?' She dished up the lasagne and handed it out, refusing to take no for an answer. 'You need to eat,' she said to Joanne, settling the empty tray on a pillow on her lap, putting the plate on top and a fork between her fingers. 'Can you manage or would you like me to feed you?'

'I can manage,' Joanne said, proving the point by lifting a forkful of lasagne to her mouth.

But none of them ate much. They pushed the food around, an expectant silence lying heavily between them. Beth wasn't surprised when Megan put hers down, barely touched, and fixed her eyes on Joanne. 'Tell me,' she said. 'What did you do?'

Beth paused with food halfway to her mouth. Joanne, who was making a feeble attempt to eat, dropped her fork and pushed the cushion off her lap, sending the tray tilting, the plate sliding and a splash of red sauce shooting across the white fabric of the sofa. It was the same shade of red as the blood that seeped through the pillowcases wrapped around Joanne's arms. Beth gulped and her appetite, small as it was, vanished.

Joanne kept her eyes averted as she spoke to Megan, her voice a dead monotone. 'As I said, we'd all gone to Capel-le-Ferne in separate cars, because we were heading to different places afterwards.' She waited a few seconds as if to let them all drift back in their heads to that day, twenty years before. 'Beth and I were concerned about you driving home to Wales on your own after your... *ordeal*.' She laughed, a short bitter sound. 'Of course, now we know the ugly truth, you weren't being brave at all, you were being deceitful.'

Joanne's eyes lost focus as she went back to that night, unable to understand why neither she nor Beth had seen the lie. She shifted her gaze to where Megan was sitting, transfixed, tears rolling down her cheeks; she would have thought her incapable of such deception. But she knew better now. She and Beth had been spectacularly fooled. Joanne spoke again in the same slow monotone. 'You didn't want to tell the police and you made *us* promise not to.' Turning her head slowly, she fixed Megan with a piercing look. 'But I couldn't let it go. I had to make sure he was punished.'

What little colour had been in Megan's cheeks leeched away.

'I could do with a drink,' Joanne said to Beth, tilting her head to a small cupboard under the window. 'You'll find some brandy in there, would you mind?' She waited while Beth found the bottle and three shot glasses, filled them and handed them around. She lifted the glass with difficulty and took a mouthful, coughing as the alcohol hit the back of her throat. 'I didn't go home that morning as I'd planned to do,' she continued then. 'Instead, I waited in my car until the pub opened and asked the barman where Matt Peters lived.' She raised her glass to take another sip. 'I made up some ridiculous story about having promised to give him something, I needn't have bothered, the barman told me where he lived without the slightest interest.

'He wasn't there, of course, but it was his wife I'd wanted to see, not him. The woman who opened the door was a skinny plain-looking woman with kind eyes and a welcoming smile. I told her I had something important to tell her and persuaded her to let me in. Children's voices were coming from a room at the back of the house. I remember being relieved that she didn't bring me into the same room. Instead, she opened the door into a small stuffy sitting room that looked as if it were seldom used and invited me to sit.

'And there, in that twee over-furnished room, I told her exactly what her lovely husband had done; how he'd raped my friend and left her traumatised. I was so determined to make him pay, that I embellished the story and told her about all of the disgusting perverted things he'd made you do.' Joanne's smile was cruel. 'She didn't believe me at first, you know, but when I told her to check with the bar staff who would swear they saw you leaving with him, I could see doubt flicker in her eyes.' Joanne stopped speaking for a moment, the silence only broken by the sound of Megan's sobs.

'I felt sorry for her,' Joanne said. 'Sorry for any woman who had been so badly fooled. I told her you didn't want to go to the police but that I wanted to make sure she knew what a rotten filthy bastard she was married to. By the time I was finished, she was sobbing.' There was ice in Joanne's eyes when she glanced at Megan. Her voice scathing, she added, 'Much in the way you are now.'

'Enough!' Beth said. 'Stop it, Joanne. She's paid for her mistake.'

Joanne's eyes bored into Beth's. 'You think so, do you? But then, I haven't finished my story, have I?' She drained the glass and held it out for more, waiting until Beth poured before continuing. 'I organised to have the local Capel-le-Ferne newspaper sent to me. It's online now but it wasn't back then. I was convinced, you see, that a man who would rape so violently would do so again. When he did, when he was arrested for it, I was going to cut out the news story and send it to you, Megan, so you could finally, as I thought, get closure. Instead, a week later, what I saw was one of those clippings upstairs. *Local Man Missing*. I thought it was a good photo of him, he seemed so full of life.'

This time the silence lasted several minutes. Megan had stopped sobbing and there was no sound except their heavy breathing.

'It must have been a photograph that his wife particularly liked because they used it again in the next article, several weeks later. It was the report of his body having washed up on the shore.' Joanne swallowed a mouthful of brandy, the alcohol giving her strength to go on when all she wanted to do was sleep. 'The coroner's verdict was death by misadventure. His wife explained how he loved to walk the cliff path and must have slipped.' Joanne took a deep breath. 'But I knew... I *knew*... he'd killed himself because I'd told his wife about the rape. And I was glad!' Joanne's voice rose and she looked at Megan with a glint in her eyes. 'Glad he was dead.

'Everything I've done since, has been built on what I believed happened to you in Capel-le-Ferne, do you know that?' Joanne's smile faded as her lips narrowed and her eyes turned hard. 'Neither of you know what I really do for a living. I felt so sorry for his wife that day, not guilty for telling her, you understand, but sorry that she'd been fooled by her bastard rapist husband and I swore no man was ever going to treat me that way. Some men use sex as a power trip. I decided I could do that too. And I've done it very lucratively ever since.'

Beth squeezed her eyes shut and took a noisy breath between gritted teeth. She should have known, and perhaps somewhere, she had. That business website of Joanne's, for instance, hadn't she always thought it looked a little racy and more than a little ambiguous. Megan, she could tell, was oblivious, blank eyes looking from one to the other as she tried to understand. Feeling suddenly sorry for her, Beth took pity and said, 'I think what Joanne is trying to tell us is that she works as an escort.'

Megan still looked puzzled.

'I'm a hooker,' Joanne said bluntly, 'a prostitute, if you prefer that term. I sell my body for money.'

28

Joanne laughed at the look on Megan's face; surprise, shock, even disgust washing over it in waves. Beth's expression, on the other hand, had barely changed. Had she known? Had she guessed over the years that Joanne was something other than she'd said?

'A prostitute?' Megan said, still unsure if she had it right. 'You said you worked in corporate entertainment. I don't understand. You've always been the most honest person I've ever known and now you're saying that you've lied to us all these years?'

'Did I?' Joanne said, lifting both hands and grimacing at the stinging pain in her arms. 'Do I detect outrage coming from a liar? Honesty and prostitution aren't mutually exclusive. I didn't lie, I told you I was running a private corporate entertainment business, and believe me,' she said, arching an eyebrow, 'I'm very entertaining.' She ignored the expression on her friends' faces, especially the look of sympathy – or was it pity – on Beth's. Joanne didn't want either from them. She'd made her choice a long time ago. 'I charge an honest fee and provide an honest service,' she added. Wasn't that what she had told herself, time and time again over the years? She watched as Megan struggled to understand and to shift her thinking to incorporate this new version of her friend.

'You're a prostitute!' Megan said, the truth finally sinking in. 'It's not exactly the same thing as corporate entertainment. Far from it.'

'It's private, corporate, entertaining and *very* lucrative.'

Megan stood as if to leave but then sat again. 'Why aren't you saying something?' she said to Beth. 'Or,' she frowned, 'did you know?'

Beth took a sip of her brandy before answering. 'No, I didn't know... not really... I sometimes wondered what it was that she did.' She smiled faintly at Joanne. 'The private corporate entertainment business tag did make me wonder, you know, and your website is classy but a little bit... racy. But,' she hesitated, 'you seemed to be happy with whatever you were doing, so who was I to judge?'

Joanne shuffled in her seat. Blood had oozed through the makeshift bandages, small red circles appearing through the fine white cotton. Lifting her arms, she saw similar red circles marking the seat of the sofa. She couldn't bring herself to care. Lifting her chin, she stared at Megan. 'Anyway, you certainly can't criticise me for living a lie.' Joanne swallowed. 'If I hadn't gone to speak to Matt's wife that day, maybe I would have chosen a different path. When I got back to London, after Capel-le-Ferne, I had a call from Milcross and Batten offering me the PR position but all I could think of was what that man had done to you, and his poor pathetic wailing wife, so I turned it down.'

Megan's mouth opened and closed like a goldfish before she managed to speak. 'You're not putting this on me! Bloody hell, I take the blame for misleading you all those years ago but you made your own decision as to how you lived your life.' She looked to Beth for support. 'I'm right, aren't I?'

~

It was a freeze-frame moment; nobody moved or spoke. Finally, Beth answered Megan's question. 'The *law of cause and effect* states that every cause has an effect and every effect becomes the cause of something else. When you lied to us, you set a chain of events into motion. If you hadn't deceived us, Joanne would never have gone to Matt's wife. Because she did, that incident affected all the decisions she made from that moment on.'

'Yes,' Joanne said, 'and because I told her about the rape, she must have confronted Matt, leading to a breakdown in their marriage and his suicide.' Her anger faded as she saw Megan's look of horror grow and in a softer voice, she added, 'All because of your silly stupid little lie.'

'Cause and effect,' Beth said, emptying her glass and reaching for the bottle. She stood and filled all their glasses, stopping in front of Joanne and pointing at the sauce and the bloodstains. 'You've made a mess of the sofa.'

Joanne looked down. More blood had oozed through, red spots on the pillowcases and on the sofa. 'It doesn't matter anymore,' she said, lifting her glass and draining half in one mouthful, coughing as she swallowed, sending a spray of amber liquid over her pale pink pyjamas.

'You started something that affected all of us,' Beth continued, as she sat back in her seat. 'I–'

'Of course,' Joanne jumped in, 'that's why you joined the police, Beth, isn't it?'

'Yes and no,' Beth said, 'joining the police was something I had considered but it pushed me to make that final decision. It's, also, why I applied to join the Rape and Serial Sexual Offences Unit.'

'At least something good came out of it,' Megan said, a

childish remark that drew sharp glances from the other two. 'I just meant–'

'I know what you meant,' Beth said, 'and you're not completely wrong, some good did come out of my working for the unit; I've made it my priority to save as many women as I could from having to live with the same pain as I thought you'd been through.'

Joanne looked puzzled. 'Not that I particularly want to agree with Megan, but that *is* good, isn't it?'

'Do you know how many men get off from lack of evidence?' Beth asked, using the same argument she had used before, the same one she had used for years to justify what she did. She didn't expect an answer. 'Far too many. That's why I had to do something.'

Megan's gasp got both their attention. 'Oh no,' she said, a hand over her mouth. 'Oh please, no, don't tell me it's you.'

'What?' Joanne was beginning to think she'd had too much brandy, neither of the two women were making any sense. 'What are you talking about?'

Megan put down her glass. 'The Crown Prosecution Service is holding an emergency meeting tomorrow afternoon.' Her voice cracked as she spoke, her eyes fixed on Beth. 'It's you, isn't it?' She groaned when she saw the slight nod.

Increasingly confused, Joanne looked from one to the other. 'Will someone tell me what the hell is going on?'

'I was so determined to make the sexual predators we caught pay for their crimes, that sometimes I helped the case along.'

'Helped the case along?' Joanne put down her glass. Too much alcohol on an empty stomach, it helped dull the pain in her arms but it seemed to have addled her brain.

Megan explained, her eyes on Beth, her voice grim. 'Last week, the CPS was informed that a member of the police team had been passing crucial information to victims and victims' families in order to get a conviction. There was also speculation that the same member had been planting incriminating evidence on suspects. It's a disaster. As soon as it gets out, and it will, there will be any number of rapists and child molesters arguing their conviction is unsafe.' For a moment, Megan's eyes were full of pity. 'They're arguing for a stiff penalty, Beth. You'll get a custodial sentence. There's no doubt.'

Joanne's eyes filled with horror. 'No! Prison?' It was all too much to take in, too much to have to absorb. Glancing down at her mutilated arms, she wished she'd been brave enough to have carried out her plan, to have pressed harder. Everything was falling apart and she wasn't sure she could take any more.

No, that wasn't true. She knew she couldn't. She'd have to try again.

29

Prison! For the first time, the reality of her future hit Beth and a sudden wave of nausea sent her bolting from the room. In the hallway, disorientated, she hesitated before hurrying into the kitchen where she retched into the sink, turning on the tap to wash away the small amount of food and the large amount of brandy she'd consumed. She stayed with her head hanging over the sink for a few minutes as her stomach continued to spasm. The murmur of voices from the other room told her that at least Joanne and Megan were talking. Probably about her. Let them, Beth thought. They didn't know the half of it.

When the spasms eased, she turned and leaned back against the sink. She'd never cope with prison, but from what Megan said it looked as if that's what the future had in store for her. That officer from the Professional Standards department, she frowned as she tried to remember her name – Ling, DI Ling – she looked the type to lift up every stone and poke around in what lay underneath. There was no chance Beth's fellow officers would cover for her; they'd all be running scared and trying to remember if they'd said the wrong thing to the wrong person or hoping that the bright revealing light wouldn't shine on them.

'Are you okay?' Megan stood in the doorway. 'I'm sorry, maybe I shouldn't have told you.'

Beth rubbed her neck. 'My Fed rep said much the same thing.' She didn't add that she hadn't really believed him. 'Don't worry about it.'

'What are you going to do?'

Stupid, stupid question. 'I don't know. Leave it in the hands of fate, I suppose.'

Crossing to her, Megan put a hand on her arm and then, almost without thinking, they were holding each other. 'What a mess,' Beth said softly, her chin resting on her friend's head. 'What an utter mess.'

'It's all my fault. That one stupid foolish lie.' Megan pulled back to stare at Beth with tear-filled eyes.

She wanted to scream, *yes, all your damn fault.* But she couldn't. It wasn't true. Not really. Okay, Megan had started a chain of events with that awful deception but Beth and Joanne had chosen the paths they'd followed. 'We'd better go back inside.'

Arm in arm, they returned to the lounge where Joanne had obviously been thinking about what had been said. Her expression was grave, her voice weary, yet her words were sharp. 'I can't believe you were so stupid, Beth. How on earth did you think you'd get away with breaking the law?'

Beth sat and glared at her. Her life was a disaster, and now she was going to be lectured to by a prostitute? She guessed Joanne had read her mind when scarlet slashes appeared across her very pale cheeks.

'What I do isn't illegal,' Joanne said angrily.

'No,' Beth sneered back, 'you don't pick up kerb-crawlers, do you? You fuck strangers in posh hotels instead.'

The tension in the room was electric, both women glaring at each other, flint in their eyes, their mouths twisted into a snarl. Megan, hovering nearby with a look of desolation, held a hand out towards each friend. 'Please, let's not do this,'

Beth shut her eyes and let her breath out in a loud sigh. 'I'm sorry,' she said, her mouth twisted in regret. 'My life appears to have turned upside down.'

Megan reached for her hand and grabbed it. 'Tell her.'

Beth opened her eyes and looked at her blankly. 'Tell her what?' She saw the sympathy in Megan's eyes and realised what she meant. *Graham*. For a few hours, she'd forgotten about him. Of course, Joanne didn't know about him or, in fact, about Trudy. Beth gave Megan's hand a squeeze. 'Okay. I will, if you will.'

'What are you two on about this time?' Joanne said. 'Pardon me if I'm finding some of this hard to understand, I've had a bit of a difficult day.'

Beth looked at Joanne. Maybe she shouldn't put more stress on her.

'Tell me,' Joanne said. 'It can't make this day any more crap.'

'Graham's left me,' Beth said bluntly, there didn't seem any point in prettying it up. No matter what way she said it, it meant the same thing, he'd left her. *Left*. Such an ugly, horrible word.

The irritated tense look on Joanne's face faded and there was no anger in her voice when she spoke. 'Oh, Beth, I'm so sorry. You always seemed so good together. What happened?'

'You know what my hours are like. Erratic and long. He always thought I gave too much to the job, you know, he'd never have guessed how true that was.'

'Maybe now you can get back together?'

'You mean now I *won't* be a police officer? He can come and visit me in prison instead?' She held a hand over her mouth to stop the howl of anguish she knew was hiding inside.

'I'm not criticising, Beth, really, I'm not,' Joanne said, 'but what possessed you to risk your career by doing something so stupid as to plant evidence? You must have known you'd be caught eventually.'

Beth put her hand flat on her forehead. Her head ached but it wasn't migraine this time, just the stress of this hideous never-ending day. 'I've been doing it for years, maybe I got careless, I don't know. You've no idea how many times we had the right guy but couldn't prove it. The soul-destroying guilt when the bastard walked free. The devastation of the victims when we told them they'd not get justice.' Beth looked across at Megan. 'Every time,' Beth said, lifting her hand and pointing a finger at her, trying to make them understand why she'd done what she'd done, 'every bruised and battered person I saw, it reminded me of you that night, and I knew I had to do something. So, I did.'

Beth gave a shaky laugh. 'Now I wonder, how many of those injuries were self-inflicted, and how many times I was fooled by a desolate face.' Her voice trembled. 'I'm not blaming you, Megan, I made my own choices but I can't ignore the truth. How many innocent men did I help put away?'

30

Megan looked down. Beth wasn't blaming her but she didn't have to, she had enough blame for herself and the weight of guilt lay heavily on her shoulders. All of these things because of her deception. How could she bear it?

'I'm not blaming you, Megan,' Beth said. 'I made my decisions; they just happen to have been made for the wrong reasons. Anyway, now it's your turn.'

Megan blinked. Her turn? 'Oh, yes, yes, of course.' She glanced at Joanne and then looked back down, at her hands. 'There must be something in the air,' Megan started, eyes focused on her entwined fingers and on the diamond ring she still wore because she couldn't bear the finality of taking it off. Looking up with tear-filled eyes, she knew she didn't have to say more.

'Ah no,' Joanne said, 'not you and Trudy? That's impossible!' Her eyes narrowed as she tried to put it all together. 'But, wasn't it the reason you told us about that night, because Trudy insisted you had to be honest with us to have any future together?'

Tears gathered in Megan's eyes. 'It seemed it was too little too late. She called me a pathological liar.' Megan gulped. 'She was so cold, so hard, and looked at me with such contempt.' A tear ran down her cheek; she didn't brush it away.

'Oh no,' Joanne said, 'I'm so sorry. Maybe–'

'No,' Megan said firmly, 'there's no *maybe*. She asked me to move out by Friday. Insisted, in fact.' Rubbing her tear-filled eyes with one hand, she took a deep breath. 'It was as if she'd turned into someone else, someone I didn't know at all.'

'I've told Megan she can move in with me,' Beth rushed to say. 'It'll give her some breathing space until she sorts herself out.'

Megan hoped Beth didn't see her automatic look of horror at the thought of living in her tiny shabby home. It was an option she had to consider short-term. Long-term, she'd no idea what she'd do. She'd no savings; how incredibly stupid she'd been. The fact was she'd be lucky to be able to afford to *rent* anything as big as Beth's place. And buying wasn't an option. She caught Joanne's pitying glance. 'I'll be fine,' she said, wishing she believed it. How could she be, with the weight of all she had to bear? And to bear it all without Trudy.

'What about your parents?' Joanne asked. 'Couldn't they help?'

Megan shook her head. 'The fees for the nursing home they're in are astronomical. There's very little left.' She stood. 'I'm shattered, I need to get some sleep. Would it be okay if I stayed until the morning? I'll need to leave early.'

'You'll both need to stay,' Joanne said, shuffling unsteadily to her feet. 'There's a bed in the room where I've shoved my clothes, one of you can sleep there if you can make your way through all my stuff to get to it. The other will have to make do with this sofa.'

'The sofa's fine for me,' Megan said.

'You sure?' Beth said. 'I don't mind taking it.'

Megan gave her a grateful glance. 'Thank you, but it's a better fit for short people.'

As Beth and Joanne headed up the stairs together, Megan saw Joanne sway wearily and Beth slip an arm around her waist. 'Hang on to me,' Beth muttered, matching her steps to her taller friend. Megan took a deep breath and followed behind.

Minutes later, Joanne directed both women to the cupboard where she kept spare sheets and towels. There was no more talking, as if they'd said it all, and there were no more words left to try to make sense of things.

'I'll be leaving very early,' Megan said, with an armful of linen. 'I'll try not to wake anyone.'

Joanne stood in the doorway of her bedroom and lifted her wrapped arms. 'You won't wake me. I'm going to take a couple of sleeping tablets, otherwise I'd never get to sleep. Do either of you want one?'

'Yes, please. It might help,' Beth said.

Megan declined. 'I took two last night and couldn't wake up this morning so I'll pass, thanks.' She wanted to say more: to apologise, beg forgiveness, plead for mercy and understanding. Instead, she reached out a hand and rested it on each of their shoulders before turning and heading down the stairs.

In the lounge, she eyed the bloodstained sofa and with a shrug dropped the linen and sat down beside it. She could hear the low mumble of Joanne and Beth's voices and wondered if they were talking about her.

She swallowed a sob, afraid they would hear and come down to offer sympathy or pity. Neither would make her feel any better, neither would make everything all right again. And that was what she wanted. For everything to be okay. To be as it was. She wanted the life of promise she'd had only a few days before. It wasn't fair to be punished so badly for something stupid she had done so long ago. She flopped back on the sofa and stared at the ceiling.

Nothing was ever going to be the same again. Her life was over.

Matt Peters. Megan had not thought about him in years. If he'd tried to contact her, to insist she went back to clear his name, she'd have gone. Of course, she'd have gone. Her lie was never supposed to involve him; she'd made them promise, how could she have known they'd go back on their word. He had three children, according to that article Joanne had plastered around the walls. Three young children, left without a father because of her. She shut her eyes, swallowing the rush of bile that flooded her mouth. 'Oh God,' she murmured, wishing He were someone she believed in. Not that He could help. There was nobody who could turn the clock back twenty years and let her make a different choice.

Overhead, doors opened and closed, floorboards creaked and water rattled in the pipes. The sounds died away and silence settled over the house, broken only by Megan's ragged breaths.

She waited another hour for Beth and Joanne to fall into their medicated sleep before she stood. There was no way she was going to sleep, not with her head buzzing. Opening the door quietly, she climbed the stairs, placing her bare feet carefully, listening for any squeak or creak that might disturb them. Crossing the landing to the room Joanne had so bizarrely decorated, she went inside and shut the door behind her before switching on the light.

It must have taken Joanne hours, Megan thought, turning and looking around the room. Matt watched her from every angle. She reread both articles, they didn't tell her anything more. *Accidental death.* Megan murmured the words, grimacing. Now, unfortunately, she knew better.

She reached out and traced the man's smile with an unsteady finger. The harm she'd done. Too much to absorb. With a final look around, she left the room, closed the door quietly behind her and went back downstairs. She sat on the edge of the sofa for a long time... thinking of her future. There seemed, suddenly, no point in returning to London. With the weight of such guilt on her shoulders, how could she possibly prosecute the crimes of others? No, her career with the Crown Prosecution Service, her lifelong dream, was over.

She could have coped with that. It would have been difficult, but there were other avenues she could have gone down with Trudy by her side. Without her, she couldn't even contemplate such a long and lonely journey. The very thought frightened her. No, there was only one option left.

When the first streaks of daylight crossed the room, Megan stood and moved to look out the window. It was time to go. She picked up the bundle of clothes she'd brought down from the bathroom. They were creased and stained but she pulled them on without a thought. With her shoes in one hand, she opened the door and stepped into the hallway. She hesitated, before nodding slightly as if agreeing with the thought that had popped into her head, and went back upstairs to Joanne's shrine to the dead man. Inside, she very carefully peeled one article from the wall, folded it and tucked it into her jacket pocket.

Minutes later, she was in her car.

31

Beth slept heavily thanks to the two pills Joanne had given her and woke feeling groggy with her mouth dry and head thumping. Groaning, she held a hand over her eyes and wished she could make it all go away, everything: Megan, Joanne, the mess she'd made of her career. Everything. Except Graham, him she wanted back.

Crawling from the bed, she opened the bedroom door and listened. If either of the others were awake, they weren't making a sound. Beth crossed to the bathroom, turned on the cold tap and scooped a few handfuls of water to drink, a glance in the mirror telling her she looked as bad as she felt. Shaking her head, she returned to the bedroom and lay down, hoping a little more sleep would get rid of the fog in her brain. It was a lost cause; as soon as her head hit the pillow, images of Megan and Joanne's distressed faces flitted through her mind.

Giving up the attempt, Beth got up. She retrieved her creased dirty clothes and wondered about borrowing a clean outfit from Joanne. They were a similar size and she certainly had enough to spare. Of course, now she knew exactly why she had so many gorgeous clothes. 'Maybe not,' Beth muttered and, ignoring the stains and the distinctly unpleasant smell, she dressed and headed downstairs, hoping coffee would make her feel more awake.

The kettle had just boiled when the kitchen door opened and Joanne appeared, her skin an unhealthy shade of grey, eyes bloodshot. A silky white robe was belted loosely around her waist. She'd removed the makeshift dressings from her arms and there were flecks of fresh blood on the robe that said some of the cuts were still bleeding.

'You didn't sleep?' Beth asked, spooning coffee into two mugs and trying not to look at the criss-cross of scabbed cuts on her wrists.

Joanne sat at the table and rested both arms on top, wincing a little as she did so. 'Not for a long time, and not for long enough,' she finally answered. 'I feel pretty awful.'

Beth put a coffee in front of her. 'It's been a tough few days, Joanne.' She waited until her friend had drunk some coffee before asking, 'Are you going to be okay?'

Several sips later, Joanne looked at her with the hint of a smile. 'Do you mean am I going to try again?'

Beth put down her untouched coffee. There seemed to be no point in being subtle. 'Well, are you?'

'A man killed himself because of what I said–'

'That's not–' Beth started to say.

Joanne reached across and grabbed her hand. 'No, let me finish. He killed himself because of what I said. It didn't matter that I truly believed he had raped Megan.' Joanne lifted a hand to her eyes and wiped away tears. 'You think that's why I tried to kill myself but, you know, it wasn't really.'

Beth posed the obvious question. 'So why then?' She

watched Joanne's mouth twist as if the words were too difficult to say.

Finally, Joanne spoke. 'You said it was remembering what happened to Megan that night that made you determined to see that justice was done, even if you had to plant evidence to ensure it was. But it isn't Megan I've remembered all these years. At least, not only her.' She brushed tangled hair back and looked at Beth with a strange smile. 'It's Matt's wife who has haunted me. When I told her what he'd done, including all the filthy details that I made up, there was such pain and hurt in her eyes. It's her face I've seen all these years when men seemed to be sincere, the ones who wanted me to stop what I was doing and settle down. Maybe even have children. *Her* face that made me keep living the life I lead. Because why would I put myself in a position to feel such pain and disappointment?' Joanne lifted the coffee to her trembling lips and put it down without drinking. 'And now? I feel like I've wasted the best years of my life for a lie, and I'm finding it hard to live with that. But, no,' she said with an attempt at a smile, 'I'm not going to try again.'

Beth didn't believe her; she watched the way Joanne's gaze shimmied away rather than meet her eyes. 'It's not too late to change your life, Joanne. It's going to take a little time to absorb everything that's happened. Come back to London with me, stay with me for a few days, we can talk.'

Joanne gave an unamused laugh. 'I think your house is going to be a bit full, isn't it?' She tilted her head and gave a genuine smile. 'Do you really think Megan will move in with you? Even for a short while?'

Beth ignored the question. 'Fine, well, I've no need to rush back to London. Megan doesn't have to move out until Friday. Until then, I'll stay here.'

'Suit yourself,' Joanne said with a careless shrug. 'Speaking of Megan, did you hear her leave?'

'No. She's gone?'

'She said she had to leave early to get home to change and into the office by nine, so I assume so.' Joanne frowned. 'I hope she has; I really don't want to speak to her for a while.'

'Maybe I should check, she slept through yesterday and got into trouble,' Beth said, pushing her mug away. At the lounge door she listened before pushing it open. It was empty. Megan had gone. Good, she thought, because she didn't think Joanne could take any more angst and she knew she couldn't. She shut the door and turned to go back to the kitchen.

She'd taken a step when something drew her to the staircase. Had she heard something? She stared up, put a foot on the first step and then the next, pulled upward by a strange compulsion to keep going. At the top of the stairs, she looked at the door of the room where Joanne had made that terrible suicide attempt, remembering that awful moment when they'd opened the door and seen her lying there, the knife hanging from one hand. The knife... the knives, they were still in there.

They hadn't heard Megan leave.

Oh, dear God, maybe she hadn't?

Beth glanced down the stairs and opened her mouth to yell for Joanne to come up, but she shut it again. Joanne had been through enough. It would be better to confront whatever nightmare waited inside alone. She put her hand on the door, and held her ear to it. There was no sound. Was Megan lying in there, dead? Or dying?

Beth had seen dead people. After the first, the gaping jaws and wide clouded eyes hadn't really bothered her. But Megan was a friend, she'd known her forever. Grabbing the handle, Beth took a deep breath and flung the door open, braced to see whatever it was that waited for her on the other side. In her desperation, she opened with too much vigour, the door bouncing off the wall and almost shutting again. She reached a hand out and pushed it open, squinting to see into the dimly lit room, a sob escaping when she realised she'd been wrong. The room was empty, one bloodstained knife lying where Joanne had dropped it, the other still on the low table.

Beth stood in the doorway, her eyes running over the bloodstained carpet, the vicious knives and the terrifying decoupage. Megan was safe, but with sad certainty she knew Joanne would try again. Next time, she wouldn't use a knife and she'd probably succeed. Beth wasn't sure there was anything she could do to prevent it. She'd started to shut the door when something caught her eye. It puzzled her for a second, and she moved, one slow step after another until she was in front of it.

Her eyes searched the room, and came back to the same spot. A gap in the decoupage, just one. Had Joanne missed a spot? Peering closer, Beth saw a faint trace of glue. No, she realised, it hadn't been missed, a copy of the news article had been removed.

Beth was unsure what to make of it. She hadn't done it; she was sure Joanne hadn't. That left Megan. They'd been hard on her the day before. Beth had seen the distress in her eyes. And if losing Trudy hurt even half as much as losing Graham, Megan had already been in a lot of pain. Why on earth would she want a copy?

32

Feeling suddenly chilled, Beth spun around. Matt Peters, forever twenty-eight, forever with that inane smile, stared at her from every article. If she had her way, she'd tear them all off, not just the one. She turned back to the gap. It hadn't been torn off, she realised, it had been peeled away carefully. She was still trying to understand this turn of events when she returned to her seat in the kitchen. Picking up her coffee, she sipped it, putting it down again when she realised it was cold.

'She's gone?' Joanne reached over and took Beth's mug. Dumping it in the sink, she flicked on the kettle, took two clean mugs and made fresh coffee when the kettle boiled.

Beth was still worrying over what she'd seen. She took the coffee but put it down without drinking. 'There's a gap in your decoupage,' she said slowly, her head still trying to figure out why Megan would want to do such a thing.

'In my what?' Joanne spluttered her coffee.

'Decoupage... your artistry with those articles on Matt Peters. What would you call it?'

Joanne wiped away the spots of coffee that had sprayed onto

the counter with the flat of her hand. 'I wasn't thinking of any particular decorative effect when I did it.'

'Why *did* you do it?' Beth asked. It had been something she'd wanted to ask the previous day but it hadn't seemed appropriate. Now, she was curious, it had been a strange and beyond weird thing to do.

Giving a soft laugh, Joanne traced the line of cuts on her arm with a fingertip. 'I'd planned for it to be a place to face my day of reckoning. Does that make sense?'

Strangely enough, it did. 'But, on the day of reckoning,' Beth said, 'it's God who is supposed to judge everyone's actions and send them either to heaven or hell, Joanne. You're not supposed to judge yourself, especially not so harshly.'

'It felt right,' she said, her expression set. She waved a hand in dismissal. 'Never mind that now. What do you mean, there's a gap?'

Beth would have preferred to continue the conversation about Joanne's suicide attempt, to try to discourage her from another, but she could see from her shuttered eyes that she was wasting her time. She wasn't giving up though, she'd try again later. 'One of the copies has been peeled off. Very carefully too.'

It was Joanne's turn to frown. 'It wasn't me and it obviously wasn't you so it had to have been Megan. What a strange thing to do! She hardly wants a reminder of him.'

'Hardly.' Beth stood abruptly and left the room, returning moments later with her mobile. Tapping into her list of contacts, she found Megan's number and rang. It went straight to voicemail. 'Hi, it's Beth, ring me when you have a minute, okay?'

She cut the connection, put the phone down and immediately picked it up again, searching for another number. 'She's probably in court,' Beth said, 'admin will know. I have a good rapport with one of the secretaries, she'll tell me.'

It took a few minutes of waiting before Beth was able to

speak to that particular secretary. 'Sara, hi, it's Beth Anderson, Megan Reece's friend. I was trying to contact her and wondered if you'd be able to tell me when she'll be free.'

Beth listened for a moment. 'Okay, thanks, Sara, I don't know what's happened. When I find out, I'll get her to ring you.' She hung up and met Joanne's questioning look. 'She never turned up. Never rang. Sara said they're steaming.'

'How strange! She said she was going.' Joanne tilted her head. 'Didn't she? There was so much talked about yesterday that it's not all straight in my head.'

Beth tried to remember exactly what Megan had said. She couldn't remember the words; she could only remember her look of utter desolation. 'What exactly do the articles say?' Beth had only looked at Matt's picture and read the headings, not the details.

Instead of answering, Joanne stood and crossed to a bureau. Opening the top drawer, she took out a sheaf of papers. 'I wasn't sure how many I'd need,' she said, sitting and putting the bundle on the table. Matt Peters' smiling face looked up at them.

'I'm glad you didn't do the rest of the house,' Beth said, reaching to take the first sheet. 'It would have been even more creepy than what you did do.' She shot Joanne a quizzical look. 'What's with all the white anyway? If you don't mind me saying so, it's also a little weird.'

Joanne blinked. 'Weird? I suppose you're right. I hadn't really thought of it that way.' She picked up her coffee and sipped a little. 'When I bought the house, almost ten years ago, it was in bad decorative repair. I spent a lot of time and money getting it the way I wanted it.'

Beth watched as her expression grew sad and solemn. Joanne had always looked as though she hadn't a care in the world, always beautifully dressed and her make-up expertly applied. Perhaps now Beth understood why. Her appearance, her clothes, they were the uniform of her career choice, and her carefree manner was a polite façade. How well had Beth ever known her?

'It wasn't originally my intention to have everything white,' Joanne explained, 'but every time I had to choose something – paint, furniture, carpet – it seemed to be what I came away with.' She closed her eyes a moment and when she opened them there was a wealth of sadness in them that Beth had never seen before. She was sorry she'd asked. There was enough sorrow, she didn't really want to hear more.

But Joanne wasn't finished. 'I've never really acknowledged the truth, that my home is a direct contrast to the seediness of the lifestyle I chose.' She met Beth's eyes. 'Yes, seedy. I'm a prostitute, not a fool!'

Beth held her hands up defensively. 'I never thought you were. And anyway, I don't consider what you do *seedy*, as such.' She pointed to the robe Joanne wore. 'If I'm not mistaken, that's silk.'

The hand that ran down Joanne's arm was shaking slightly. 'Things aren't so bad now,' she said, her voice soft. 'I see mostly regulars these days, but in the beginning when I was filled with loathing for men because of the way I thought Megan and Matt Peters' wife had been treated, I charged them a fortune and let them do what they wanted with me.'

Joanne lifted one beautifully manicured hand and waved it round the room. 'How do you think I was able to afford this?' She gave a sad laugh. 'Do you know, I really thought, by making men pay, I was getting revenge for all the women who'd ever been abused and mistreated. When I think back on some of the things I did...' She gulped and shook her head. 'It makes me feel ill.'

Beth had visited enough women in the sexual offences unit to know the depths of depravity that men, and sometimes women, could stoop to. They may have paid Joanne well, but Beth didn't think her friend had got the best of the bargain. With each payment for services rendered, she'd have lost part of herself and it would have left its mark on her soul. Reaching out, Beth put a hand on her arm and could feel her tremble. 'It's not too late.' She wished she were able to put more reassurance into the words but it was hard when she didn't really believe them.

Joanne raised one eyebrow. 'Seriously?' She put her hand over Beth's. 'You know as well as I do, that it's way too late. For me,' she narrowed her eyes, 'probably for you too. From what Megan said, it looks like your career is over.'

Beth felt the warmth of Joanne's hand. She was probably right, on all accounts. 'I wonder if Megan felt the same.' The article was still in Beth's other hand, she lifted it, squinted slightly and read it. 'His wife said he walked along the coastal path most evenings. Her guess is that he slipped.'

'You don't believe that for a second,' Joanne said. 'The path is set a good bit back from the edge. He'd have had no reason to get that close unless he wanted to jump. I remember his wife's face, Beth, it was a picture of betrayal, she wouldn't have been able to hide that from him, even if she'd wanted to.'

Joanne waved the article. 'He was reported missing the next day and his body washed ashore some miles away a few weeks later. Whatever happened to him, she was wise to stick to her story that he fell because suicide cancels most insurance policies.'

'All these years she's spent hating him.' Joanne's eyes filled with tears. 'I often wondered what she'd told their children.'

Beth threw the article back on top of the pile. 'It can't have been easy for her. The children were only young. She had to cope with their grief but her own would have been tempered by what she thought he'd done.' Beth's eyes widened as an idea struck her. 'Would that be where Megan has gone? To his wife?

To tell her the truth and try to make amends, to apologise for her part in what happened?'

Joanne pulled her hand away and met Beth's gaze. 'I suppose it's possible, but she doesn't have to tell her, by now she already knows.'

33

J oanne saw Beth's look of shocked surprise and laughed, quickly slipping into hysteria. Joanne wasn't surprised. Ever since Megan's confession, she'd felt herself fraying at the edges. She'd probably have continued laughing for a long time if Beth hadn't stood and slapped her, hard. The blow staggered her but had the desired effect. Joanne sobbed once and fell silent.

After a moment, where neither of them moved, she rubbed her cheek. 'Thank you, although you might have pulled your punch.'

'I'm sorry,' Beth said, sitting back in her seat, 'I'm really sorry, but I couldn't handle a hysterical woman on top of everything else. Now, tell me, what did you mean about the wife already knowing?'

Joanne dropped her hands onto the table, wrapped her fingers around the mug of coffee, and took some comfort from the slight warmth. 'I wrote to her, when I'd decided to... you know...' She took a deep breath. 'I decided that the last thing I had to do was to tell her the truth. She deserved to know even after all these years. More importantly, her children deserved to know the truth about their father. So, I wrote a letter explaining exactly what happened that night.'

Colour drained from Beth's face. 'You told her everything?'

'I owed it to her.' Joanne was startled when Beth stood abruptly and with her hands curled into fists, moved away to stare out the window.

There was nothing in the backyard to hold Beth's interest yet she continued to stare, her hands clenched, her back rigid. They'd been friends for a long time. But Joanne wondered how much she really knew about Beth and gave a rueful smile – about as much as Beth knew about her. They'd been friends, but not, Joanne realised, confidants. They'd enjoyed each other's company, laughed and drank together but she didn't remember ever sitting down and having a heart-to-heart with either Beth or Megan. They'd all had secrets; it made deeper friendship impossible. 'You okay?' Joanne asked quietly.

'You posted it to her. When?' Beth asked without turning around.

Did it really matter? Joanne tightened the belt of her robe that had worked its way loose. 'Posted it? Of course, I didn't post it,' she admitted, raising an eyebrow when Beth turned immediately with a look of relief.

'Good,' she said, coming back and taking her seat again.

Joanne shook her head. 'No, you don't understand, who posts things anymore? I know I said *letter*, of course, I meant an email but I didn't send it to her.' She hesitated, her eyes fixed on Beth's suddenly alert face. 'I emailed it to the local newspaper, the same one that printed that article twenty years ago. I guessed they'd know how to contact her and I asked them to see she got it.' Joanne tilted her head, puzzled at the look of defeat in Beth's eyes. 'Don't worry,' she said quickly, 'I didn't name names, just what happened that night and how very sorry we were.'

Beth's laugh was hard and cynical. 'You didn't name names!

Are you serious? You've given the damn newspaper probably the biggest story they've had in years, maybe ever! They'll spread it across their paper, it might even be picked up by the nationals. Matt Peters was a local man, people will want to help and they'll think back, and remember. Somebody always remembers. The newspaper will contact the police, who will have no problem tracing the email you sent back to your computer, Jo, and it won't take them long to find out all the details. Twenty years isn't long enough.' She looked away and mumbled, 'Not nearly long enough.'

Tense moments followed before she turned back to Joanne. 'Megan knew you sent the email to the paper?'

Joanne slowly nodded. 'You'd run from the room. Megan was apologising yet again and I couldn't help myself, I blurted it out. She looked sick with guilt, Beth, and I was glad because if it hadn't been for her stupid deceit, my life would have run a different course. I wanted to hurt her,' Joanne said, meeting Beth's worried eyes.

'I think you probably succeeded,' Beth said. 'Why?'

'That's a stupid question!' Joanne stood and tossed her uncombed tangled hair back. 'You know why! If she hadn't deceived us, our lives might have been different. Megan should feel guilty, she should be hurting.' Joanne watched Beth's expression harden and turned from the derision in her eyes. But she couldn't escape the truth that was hurtling her way.

'You could have stopped her that night,' Beth said quietly. 'You saw her leave; I know you did.' The words fell into the silence and seemed to echo around the room.

Joanne spun round. 'I don't know what you're talking about!' But she couldn't meet Beth's eyes, because of course she knew, she just didn't want to admit it. The can of worms was open and everything was wriggling free and escaping.

'You lied that night,' Beth went on, 'when you said you didn't know where she was. I heard the lie, saw it in your eyes. And you pretended to look for her in the Ladies while I was asking the bar staff if they'd seen her, but I kept my eye on you, Joanne. You never went inside. You didn't need to because you already knew she'd gone.' Beth flung her arms in the air. 'Layers and layers of lies.' She began pacing. 'We're all at fault. It's time to stop pointing the finger at each other because we're equally guilty.'

And so, it was out. The lie that had been eating away at Joanne ever since Megan had told them the truth about what had happened. The lie Joanne had barely admitted even to herself. She'd seen Megan talking to the stranger that night, saw her picking up her coat and bag, getting ready to leave. Joanne had quickly averted her eyes when Megan had looked her way, she didn't want to be responsible for her, didn't want to have to tell her to wait for them. She could be an absolute drag, at times, and with her gone, it meant that Joanne and Beth could walk home together. Just the two of them, and they could talk about boys and sex and girly stuff without feeling the weight of Megan's dislike for such conversations.

The stranger hadn't looked threatening. In fact, he looked a little bored. She'd turned away, ignoring the little voice that told her she should be looking out for her friend, that she shouldn't let her leave with a strange man. But she was selfish and hadn't wanted to spoil her own night. That was the guilt that had haunted her day and night. Even Megan's confession didn't alter the facts. If Joanne had been a good friend, if she'd stopped her leaving with that man, the whole deception would never have occurred.

Joanne looked at Beth, her shoulders slumped with the weight of guilt and grief. 'Yes, I knew,' she said, her voice barely above a whisper. 'So, you were wrong. It wasn't Megan's action that set off a chain of events, it was that one action… or lack of… that did it. I'm responsible for everything that happened.'

Joanne held her hand up when Beth tried to interrupt. 'No, it's all out now. I was so cruel to Megan because I wanted to blame her for everything, for the choices you and I had both made, when deep down I knew '

Joanne stared at Beth with anguished eyes. '*I knew* I could have stopped it. Everything – my choices, yours, her split with Trudy – all of it could have been prevented if I had.'

34

Beth opened her mouth to argue with Joanne, to tell her she wasn't responsible, that no, it wasn't all out, and there was something she still didn't know. Before she had a chance to explain, her phone buzzed loudly. She was going to ignore it but thinking it might be Megan, Beth picked it up.

It wasn't her name that appeared on the screen but an unknown number. With a grunt of frustration, she answered, shutting her eyes when she heard a voice she recognised, sorry she'd bothered answering at all.

'It's Medwyn Kendrick.'

Beth wondered if it wouldn't be better to hang up.

'Medwyn Kendrick,' the caller repeated, and then, as if she might have forgotten who he was, as if his name might have slipped her mind, he added, 'your Fed rep.'

'Yes,' she said and felt a tremor run through her. She gripped the phone, sensing something colder in his voice, something more critical. He'd stay neutral, he was her Police Federation representative after all, but she guessed, whatever he'd found out, he'd made up his mind about her. Whatever he was going to

229

say next, she knew it wouldn't be good. 'Just a sec,' she said, and holding her hand over the phone, she looked at Joanne.

'It's work,' Beth explained. 'Do you mind if I take it next door?'

Without waiting for the nod she knew would come, Beth turned to leave the room. She closed the lounge door, her eyes immediately drawn to the sofa where the previous day's blood had dried, the dark red stains vivid against the white. There was a smell too. A slight metallic smell of blood, the stronger stink of despair. Was that coming from her? She sat on one of the chairs and lifted the phone to her ear. 'Okay,' she said, and didn't say anything more, pressing the phone tightly to stop the tremble in her hand, waiting for him to speak.

There was the distinct rustle of paper in the background before he spoke again, seconds when she was tempted to hang up. When he did speak, it was with an abrupt question. 'Do you remember Lydia Forest?'

Beth wanted to say that she didn't forget any of them, ever. They were in her head; the damaged living ones, the tragic dead ones. All of them, all of the time. Lydia, the fourteen-year-old with the almost translucent skin, pale blue eyes and dark blonde hair that fell in curls down her back. Beth remembered the vicious bites to her tiny breasts, the horrendous bruising to her thighs and genitals. And those pale blue eyes, vacant with shock. 'Yes,' Beth said quietly, 'I remember her.'

'And her father, Bruno?'

Beth's grip on the phone tightened, tips of her fingers whitening. Bruno. Had he told them? 'Yes, I remember him too.'

'He's awaiting trial for the murder of Arthur Lewis,' Kendrick said. 'DI Ling went to speak to him this morning. She'd read the transcript of his interview and noted that he'd admitted getting Lewis' address from the list of registered offenders. Lewis is the only one living within a two-mile radius so he said he suspected him. But Ling noticed, he hadn't been asked where he got the list from. There are so many vigilante groups out there, he might have said he got it from one of them. But DI Ling,' he continued, warmth in his voice when he spoke of her, 'is one of those excellent officers who doesn't like loose ends hanging about so she contacted his solicitor and got permission to go and ask him.' More paper crackled. 'DI Ling spoke to him at length and he eventually admitted he'd been given Lewis' address.'

Beth wondered what Ling had promised Bruno. A shorter sentence if he told her the truth; less time in prison meant more time with his daughter. Beth wouldn't have blamed him for taking that option.

Kendrick was still speaking. 'DI Ling asked him who gave it to him. And do you know what he answered?'

Had the Fed rep been beside her, she would probably have ripped the pages he was holding from his hands, she might even have punched him. She liked to think she'd have had the bottle. It was tempting to keep playing his little game. To say, *No, what did he answer*, but she was weary and tired of it all. 'I guess, he told her that I'd given it to him.'

There was a moment's silence, as if Kendrick didn't believe what he was hearing. That she was admitting to what she'd done. 'Yes. That's exactly what he said. You don't deny it?'

She probably could have argued that the tragic little man had picked her name at random from the officers he'd met, that he was so distraught over his poor Lydia that he'd have said anything to stay out of prison to be with her. Beth felt no resentment towards the very efficient DI Ling, although if she hadn't been searching with her suspicious mind, it possibly wouldn't have come out. But, after all, if she hadn't uncovered this particular incident, she'd have found a series of other infractions to bring Beth down. 'No,' she said to the patiently waiting Kendrick, 'I don't deny it. So, what happens next?'

'The CPS wants to throw the book at you, DI Anderson. There's a warrant out for your arrest.' His voice was cold and detached as he continued. 'The initial charge is that you inten- tionally encouraged or assisted an offence, which in this case is the murder of Arthur Lewis. In relation to the original charges, where it is alleged you provided evidence and information to victims and their families, you will be charged with perverting the course of justice. Other charges may be levied at a later date as the investigation unfolds.' There was another shuffle of paper before he finished, his tone a little kinder. 'It would be better for your case, DI Anderson, if you came in immediately.'

Beth wanted to laugh. Nothing she did was going to affect the outcome of her *case*. As he said, DI Ling didn't leave loose ends. Megan had said there was speculation that Beth had planted evidence, Ling would work through all her cases and find the ones where she had. It wouldn't be hard if you knew what to look for. It was over, the fat lady was singing in full voice, everyone could hear her.

'Fine,' Beth said. 'I'm in Royal Tunbridge Wells visiting a friend, I'll be back in a few hours.'

'I'll wait here in the station to meet you,' Kendrick said.

Beth was going to offer her thanks but he cut the connection without another word. Throwing the phone onto the seat beside her, she stared at the stained sofa without blinking. Joanne hadn't seemed to care that it was ruined. Maybe, now, Beth understood how she felt.

Grabbing her phone, she went back to see if Joanne had moved to get dressed. They should go after Megan. Beth frowned when she saw Joanne still sitting, clutching the half- empty mug of cold coffee in her hand as if she were really drinking it. 'Get dressed, Jo,' she said, reaching for the mug and prising it from her hand. 'I think we should follow Megan.'

'Follow Megan? How do you know where she's gone?'

Beth reached for the article she'd tossed aside. 'I think she's gone here,' she said tapping it with one finger.

'Capel-le-Ferne,' Joanne said slowly, and met Beth's eyes. 'To the coastal path?'

'We have to get there before she does anything stupid, Jo. I have to tell her...' She stopped and caught a breath. 'Get dressed, we need to leave.'

When Beth was alone, listening to the sound of footsteps on the wooden floor overhead, she sat and crumpled the article in one hand. Everything was over. She wasn't going back to meet her disappointed, shocked colleagues, to see them talking about her in hushed tones and listen to their snide *bent copper* as she walked past. And she wasn't about to sit in a courtroom on the wrong side, seeing all those eyes condemning her. Just like in Joanne's chamber of horrors.

Beth squeezed her eyes shut. She wasn't sure what she was going to do, but first she had to stop Megan.

When Beth's phone buzzed, she hoped it was her this time, hoped she wouldn't have to go tearing down to that God-forsaken town. But it wasn't Megan, it was Graham. Just a short text. *We should meet.*

We should meet? Not, I'm sorry for running out on you; not, I love you and miss you, I want to come back. It didn't matter anyway, he'd waited too long, her life was a mess and it was too late. She quickly typed two words.

Sorry... Goodbye.

35

'Was the phone call about your suspension?' Joanne asked twenty minutes later as Beth pulled out of the driveway onto Grove Hill Road. The traffic on the main road was bumper to bumper and it was a few minutes before a flash of headlights indicated she could move out.

'Something like that,' Beth said, giving the car behind a wave of acknowledgement.

'Not good news though?'

Beth turned her head briefly to look at Joanne and then concentrated on the traffic, negotiating the twists and turns until she was on the road to Capel-le-Ferne. She could feel Joanne's eyes on her, knew she was waiting for more details and shot her another quick look. 'They're charging me with intentionally encouraging or assisting an offence.'

'That doesn't sound too bad.' Joanne reached a hand out and patted her shoulder.

Joanne didn't understand and Beth didn't want to go into details but she felt she owed her some explanation. 'It's serious. The offence in this case is murder. There's no differentiation in the sentence between assisting or actually doing the act.' She gave a soft laugh. 'Actually, the poor soul, Bruno, who did the deed, has strong mitigating circumstances. The bastard he killed, raped and sodomised his fourteen-year-old daughter. His legal team may even plead temporary insanity. There's no shadow of a doubt he'll get a far lighter sentence than me.'

Beth felt the hand on her shoulder tighten and gave her friend a glance. 'If I go back, they'll throw the book... probably several books... at me. They're not keen on police officers letting the side down.'

'If you go back?' Joanne's voice was husky.

'That's the thing. *If I go back.* There's a warrant out for my arrest. They're expecting me to turn myself in, of course, like the well-behaved police officer I was supposed to be.'

'But you're not going to.' It wasn't a question, just a sad statement of fact. Joanne dropped her hand, turned away, and stared out the passenger window.

There was no further conversation, both women lost in their thoughts as the car sped towards the coast.

Echoing their mood, the sky grew darker as they reached their destination and by the time they drove through Capel-le-Ferne it was raining heavily. Beth automatically slowed as they passed the pub where everything had started, both women craning to look, their eyes bleak.

Wind buffeted the car as they drove on, the windscreen wipers swishing manically backward and forward trying to clear the deluge of rain that hammered the car.

Almost half a mile further on, when the sign for the car park loomed, Beth indicated and pulled in. The gloomy wet day, low visibility and howling wind hadn't encouraged others to venture out and there was only one other car. Beth pulled up as close to it as she could and looked through the rain-streaked windows to where Megan sat, staring straight ahead. Beth waved and beeped her car horn but there was no reaction.

'Perhaps she can't hear,' Joanne said. 'It's windy out there, sound gets blown away.'

Maybe, but there was something about Megan's unnatural stillness... maybe they were too late. It was a struggle to open the car door, the wind fighting to keep Beth inside and pulling the door from her grasp when she finally succeeded. Pushing it shut behind her, she hurried across the short distance to reach the passenger door of the other car.

The rain was coming down in straight rods. Soaked in seconds, Beth's wet hands fumbled with the door handle before she wrenched it open and fell into the passenger seat. 'Bloody hell!' she shouted, struggling to close the door. She wiped the rain from her face and turned to her friend.

Megan sat, pale and still, staring straight ahead. Wet hair was plastered to her head, clothes stuck to her skin. Was she breathing? Looking closely, Beth couldn't decide but there was no blood, no sign of self-inflicted violence. 'Megan,' she said quietly, the single word lost in the wind that battered the car, forcing her to say it again, louder, more desperately pleading, 'Megan!'

Megan's lips parted. 'It seems Joanne and I are more alike than I thought.'

'What?' Relieved her initial fears were wrong, Beth leaned closer, putting a hand on her friend's arm.

Megan turned her head slightly as she raised her left hand. Clutched in it, wet and crumpled, was the copy of the newspaper cutting she'd so carefully peeled from the wall. 'It seemed only fair to follow him,' she said, forcing Beth to lean even closer to catch her words. 'I wanted to jump and end it all; to close that damn chain permanently. But,' her eyes lowered, 'I didn't have the courage.'

After a moment, she looked back to the windscreen. 'Maybe if I went out now, the wind would help me. I could stand near the edge and wait for a gust.'

'Oh, Megan.' Beth's hand tightened its grip but, pulling away, Megan pushed open the door and ran. 'Wait,' Beth cried, jumping out and running after her, startling Joanne who'd come to see what was happening. There was no point in trying to explain. 'Come on,' she said, shouting to be heard. She picked up speed, determined to catch Megan before she left the path.

Beth was taller than Megan, her legs longer, so it didn't take long to catch up. 'Wait,' she said, grabbing hold of her jacket and holding on to her arm when Megan tried to pull away, clawing at her fingers, trying to prise them open, snarling at Beth when she failed.

'I have to do this,' Megan shouted into the wind. 'You said it yourself, I started a chain of events, I have to close it, Beth. My end will finish it all.'

'You don't understand,' Beth said, tugging on her arm. 'Come back to the car, there's something I have to tell you... to explain what really happened.'

Joanne arrived breathless and clutching her chest, hair whirling around her head, panicked eyes looking out towards the grey heaving sea, the edge of the cliff only a few feet away. 'For God's sake, Megan,' she said, grabbing hold of her other arm. 'As I've learned, it's not that easy to kill yourself.'

Between them, they led their struggling friend back to Beth's car, forcing her into the back seat, Joanne slipping in beside her while Beth sat into the driver's seat and quickly locked the doors. The silence inside was palpable, made all the more so by the shrill wind that howled and whooped outside the car, the stronger of the gusts buffeting it and making it shudder.

Turning in her seat, Beth looked at the bedraggled woman. 'Oh, Megan,' Beth said again, wishing she could find words of reassurance and comfort. She was used to offering them to the sad broken women she met during the course of her work, to trotting out a ream of platitudes, but she'd never been in a situation like this where words seemed meaningless.

Joanne appeared to be having the same problem but, sitting as she was beside Megan, she reached out and grabbed her in a hug instead. When she pulled away, all three women spoke at the same time.

'I need–'

'I want–'

'I'm sorry!'

They stopped and gave a quick laugh. Beth took a deep breath, steeling herself. It was time for the truth, the only words that might make a difference. But before she could get them out, Joanne squeezed Megan's hand and said, 'No, I'm the one to be sorry, it was so much easier to blame you than to admit the truth about that night.'

Megan blinked in surprise. 'I don't understand.'

'There's no need,' Beth said, reaching out for Joanne who pulled away.

'There's every need. She deserves to know the truth. No, please don't try to stop me,' Joanne said when Beth again attempted to interrupt. 'I need to do this.' She turned to Megan. 'That night, I saw you chatting with Matt and leave with him. I could have stopped you.' She wiped raindrops from her face with a shaking hand. 'I *should* have stopped you but I was having a good time and you could be such a…'

'Bore?' Megan said when Joanne stopped.

'I was going to say drag but that will do.' She squeezed her arm. 'You were always so convinced you weren't as pretty or as interesting as us, and frowned so grimly when we talked about boys and sex, it did put a dampener on things. So,' Joanne shrugged, 'I let you go off alone with that man, and when we couldn't find you at the end of the night, I pretended to Beth that I hadn't seen you.

'When we got home and found you, the guilt hit me. I felt responsible. That's really why I went to his wife, I was trying to make some form of recompense for *my* lie.' She lowered her head. 'And all these years, I've felt guilty for what you'd gone through, for not having been a better friend.'

Megan shut her eyes. 'And then I told you the truth.'

'Yes, and I was stunned, but don't you see, Megan, I didn't go to his wife because I thought you'd been raped. You'd made us promise not to do anything, remember? No, I'd gone trying to make myself feel better. Matt Peters' suicide is on me, not on you.'

Opening her eyes, Megan managed to put a smile in place. 'Perhaps we should share it then. Equal blame for an innocent man's death.'

The wind, stronger, howled and rocked the car. The sea wasn't visible from where they sat, but dark clouds hurled across the sky and rain streaked the windscreen. 'It's wild out there now,' Joanne said, with a shiver, before looking back to Megan. 'Yes, I agree, we should share the blame.' She reached out a hand. 'If I'd been a better friend... I'm sorry.'

Beth watched them, her insides twisting. This was the moment for the final lie to be revealed. There was no reason not to tell the truth, she had nothing to lose that she hadn't already lost. Nothing at all. 'No,' she said, the word barely heard. Clearing her throat, she tried again. 'No.' Waiting until both women looked at her, she smiled. 'No, you can't share the blame for something that didn't happen.'

She waited, watching as they thought about what she'd said, puzzled lines creasing their foreheads, eyes blinking rapidly, neither of them wanting to be the first to ask, *what do you mean?* Wind whistled around the outside of the car, but inside, there was a silence heavy with expectation.

Into it, she dropped what should have been said a long time ago. 'Matt Peters didn't commit suicide.'

36

B eth waited for one of them to speak. The final lie, her lie. It was time the whole truth was out to put a stop to all the misplaced guilt.

Megan frowned and exchanged confused glances with Joanne before both looked at Beth. 'I don't understand,' Megan said. 'Are you saying he's still alive? That it wasn't his body they found?'

Beth watched Joanne's eyes brighten as she clutched at this hope, her hands clasped together under her chin, as if she were saying a prayer. 'Is that it?' Joanne asked and there was the same note of hope in her voice. 'Seriously? Did he run away? Is that it?'

Looking at the suddenly alert women she'd known half her life, Beth wanted to laugh, scream and have the same hysterics as Joanne had had earlier. It would be so much easier if she could say, yes, that Matt Peters was sunning himself on some tropical island surrounded by a bevy of beautiful women. She could say it; she was a very, very good liar. She saw their expressions fill with expectation, looking relieved, almost happy, ready to believe, *desperate* to believe that the huge burden from their past could be so easily erased. Her mind spinning, she rested her forehead against the seat. She *could* say it. What was so wonderful about the truth anyway? It certainly hadn't worked for Megan and Trudy.

Raising her head, Beth met her friends' eyes. She could have spun a tale about it not being his body they'd found, that he'd been seen since in Jamaica or somewhere. It might have worked except for one big problem: Joanne's email. The shit was going to hit the fan when that came out and Beth didn't want to be around for it.

Anyway, lies had got them into this mess in the first place. 'That night, Megan,' Beth said. 'You were so convincing, I never for a moment doubted what had happened to you.' She reached out to Megan, grabbing her hand when she saw her mouth twist in anguish. 'I'm not judging, not at all, I'm just trying to explain. I rang you every day, remember? You always sounded so sad, so lost.' Beth turned her focus onto Joanne. 'And I saw that guilt was eating away at you, Jo. Maybe I should have told you then that I knew you'd lied but, there was a bit of me that thought it served you right for not stopping Megan from going off with that man.'

Wind had reached a crescendo, battering the small light Suzuki and drowning out Megan's sobs. They sat, the three of them, linked by hands, shared memories and deep regrets. 'I came back a day later,' Beth said so quietly her words were almost lost.

'What?' Joanne said, leaning forward, Megan's hand clenched once more in hers. 'What did you just say?'

'I came back,' Beth said again, raising her voice to be heard. 'You were both so sad, so lost, I couldn't rest until I'd made him pay.'

She saw a look of puzzled disbelief appear on her friends' faces. 'He might have come across as a loyal family man to you,

Megan, but I had no problem persuading him to come for a moonlight walk with me.' Beth gave a harsh laugh. 'You know better than any of us, Jo, how much you can persuade a man to do with the promise of a great blow job.'

Lifting her free hand, she jerked her thumb towards the coastal path. 'I brought him here. He was a bit impatient to get down to the nitty-gritty and tried to persuade me to do it in the car, but I told him I had a thing about doing it in the open air and persuaded him to walk with me. It was a lovely night; balmy with a clear sky sparkling with stars.' Her laugh was cynical. 'A night for romance, really, but he was only interested in one thing. He kept grabbing my hand and holding it against his bulging dick.'

'Oh God,' Megan gasped, her hand going to her mouth. 'Oh God, don't tell me–'

'Don't tell you?' Beth interrupted her. She saw the truth dawning in Megan's expressive eyes and squeezed her hand. 'It's time it came out. It was easy, actually, he was so obsessed with what I was going to do for him, his brain firmly lodged in his genitals, that he wasn't even aware we'd wandered off the path towards the cliff edge.' Beth's eyes narrowed. 'I remember he was fiddling with his zipper, desperate to release his erection. I whispered into his ear that it was almost time and asked him to take a couple of steps backward.' Her mouth twisted in a wry smile. 'He didn't hesitate. For a fraction of a second, he seemed to hang there suspended, his eyes wide in absolute horror, hands reaching out for me, his mouth opening in a pathetic scream for help and then, *puff*, he was gone. I was convinced I heard the splash his body made when it hit the water but I was probably imagining it.'

'You killed him!' Joanne's voice was hardly more than a whisper. 'All these years, I thought I was to blame, and no matter how many times I tried to convince myself that he deserved to die for what he'd done to Megan and for causing his wife such pain, in the back of my mind the guilt at being responsible for his death ate at me. All these years!' She looked at Beth with tear-filled eyes that narrowed with anger.

'We never spoke about it so I didn't know you'd gone down and talked to his wife, did I?' Beth said defensively. 'If you'd told me, I'd probably have–'

'Probably?' Joanne said with a sneer stretching her mouth. 'You'd probably have told me you'd murdered a man? Lured him up here and pushed him off the cliff. I think not!'

Beth gave a sad half-smile of acknowledgement. 'No, maybe not.'

Megan looked bleak and stunned.

'That's why I couldn't let you kill yourself today, Megan. Or you, Joanne,' Beth said, reaching out to grab Joanne's hand and hold it tightly. 'The guilt is all mine. And if anyone is going to finish it tonight, it's going to be me. I've nothing else to lose.' She looked directly at Megan. 'You were right, my Fed rep rang before we left. They're charging me with intentionally encouraging something or other.' She waved a hand. 'Whatever it is, they're waiting for me to turn myself in. I'll do time, probably a lot of it, there's no question.' She glanced through the window at the dark threatening sky. 'This is a good place to end it.'

Without another word, Beth released both their hands and opened the car door. Instantly, the door was grabbed by the wind and wrenched from her hand. Ignoring it, and the alarmed shouts from her friends, she crossed to the coastal path and ran along it, battling the wind to stay on her feet. She knew the exact spot she was looking for. It had stuck in her memory, just a few yards beyond an information board where the path widened slightly.

Twenty years had passed but she found it without a problem.

'Stop,' Megan said, hurrying to catch up behind her, Joanne trailing a few yards to the rear. 'There's no need for this.'

Beth smiled and unbuttoned her coat. 'Go back to the car, this is right for me.'

'You won't be able to,' Megan said. 'I couldn't. I stood there for ages.' She looked out to where foam-topped waves raced across a heaving grey sea and back to where Beth was removing her shoes. 'Joanne,' she said desperately, 'tell her!'

Joanne laughed, a wild look in her eyes. 'I couldn't do it either, Megan, but maybe together?' She unbuttoned her jacket as she spoke, folding it neatly and laying it down at the side of the path. She picked up Beth's discarded coat and, folding it, laid it beside hers.

Beth smiled at her. 'Tidy to the end, Joanne.'

'Can't let our standards slip,' her friend replied, unbuttoning her shirt, wincing as she pulled a scab free, looking at the blood on her arm with a wry smile. 'At least I'll never have to explain the scars.'

Laughing, Beth pulled off her jumper, dropped it on top of her coat and then undid her bra. With a chuckle, she held it up. Watching as the cups filled with wind, she let it go and laughed as it blew away to dance in the breeze before dropping down, down and out of view. Naked, goosebumps rising on her arms and legs as the rain lashed, ropes of wet hair swirling in the wind, she watched Megan shuffle from foot to foot, mixed emotions crossing her face.

And then with a sigh, she shouted, 'I couldn't live without Trudy anyway.'

In all the years they'd been friends, Beth had never seen Megan naked. Even now, when she'd peeled off her sodden outer clothes, she was shy about taking off her bra and the surprisingly sexy thong she wore. Unlike Beth, she held her underwear tightly, folding and placing them under her clothes.

'I don't want people to think I wasn't wearing any,' she said with such a serious look that Beth smiled, leaned closer and kissed her cold wet cheek.

When the wind threatened to blow their clothes away, Joanne insisted on moving them to a nearby natural indentation surrounded by grassy clumps. Beth wanted to shout at her that it didn't matter but, instead, she wiped the rain from her eyes and watched Joanne fold all their clothes neatly and place their shoes tidily on top to anchor them. Beth laughed when she picked up her red flats and raised an eyebrow at the scuffed heels.

'I never did get you into Louboutins, did I?' Joanne said, putting the shoe down neatly.

'You failed dismally in your mission to smarten me up,' Beth said, slipping an arm around Megan's waist. 'Luckily, Megan was smart enough for the two of us.'

Beth watched Joanne scrutinise the piles of clothes.

'It's not quite right,' she said and then, with a wink for Megan and Beth, she reached down, pulled a sleeve from the middle pile and tied it to a sleeve from the pile on either side so the three were linked. 'Better,' she said then stepped backward.

All three were shivering. Beth looked up and down the coastal path. Rain still fell heavily and it was hard to see more than a few hundred yards. It was unlikely anyone was going to be walking along the path, unlikely anyone would try to stop them.

'This is it, isn't it,' Beth said, reaching to pull first Megan and then Joanne into a hug.

The three women stood like that for several minutes, their hair intertwining, their arms wrapped around one another, rain running down their naked bodies. But there were no worried looks, no awkward words of doubt. Each face was set, resolved, determined.

'What will they think when they see them?' Megan said, nodding to the tidy piles.

'Perhaps that there were three friends who'd had enough?' Joanne suggested.

Beth stared at their clothes. Joanne had not just tied loosely; she'd knotted the sleeves together. 'They'll think that there were three women who shared something that kept them together, in life and in death,' she said. Pulling away, she turned slowly, making a complete circle and taking in a final look at their surroundings. She slicked her wet hair back and with a dreamy expression looked out to sea. 'Time to go,' she said, reaching a hand out to her friends.

'Just one more thing,' Megan said. 'I wasn't sure whether I should take it with me or not.' She held her left hand to her mouth and kissed the engagement ring before sliding it from her finger, and with a final lingering look, dropped it into her shoe. 'That's it.' She took Beth's right hand.

Joanne took Beth's left one and together they walked across the rough ground to the edge of the cliff, the howling wind buffeting them, rain lashing their bodies. In front of them, the grey sea and sky blended together so that there was no beginning, no end.

'Goodbye,' Beth said, squeezing their hands.

Megan squeezed back. 'God speed.'

Joanne waved towards the sea with her free hand. 'Despite everything, it's been great,' she said, 'but now our future awaits.'

They smiled at each other one last time and took another step forward, their toes curling around the edge of the cliff, their hair blown back by the force of the wind, rain continuing to wash them so that their bodies were slick.

Beth gave a final squeeze to each of the hands she held. 'Still time to change our minds,' she said and felt their hands tighten in response. It seemed nobody was having second thoughts.

'Okay,' she shouted into the wind, 'let's go.'

And they went soaring.

37

The call came through at 8am. A man walking his dog had seen something strange on the coastal path just outside Capel-le-Ferne and phoned it in. The duty sergeant seeing PC Bourke trying to avoid his eyes, barked, 'Bourke!' He waited until the man raised his head to look at him before saying in a more controlled voice, 'Go and find out what this guy is talking about. He won't say anything other than "It's strange". He's waiting for you in the coastal path car park outside town.'

PC Miller hid a grin as Bourke scowled. They'd been sitting around since they came on shift an hour before, Bourke citing paperwork every time Miller said they should go and see what was happening in the world. It would be good to get out and find out what had concerned the man. Something strange could be anything. Recently, she'd been called out for a dead animal that was frightening children and for obscene and offensive graffiti scrawled across the noticeboards along the cliff path.

Bourke was probably the laziest officer she'd ever had the misfortune to work with in her short year as a police constable. She listened to him grumble all the way to the car where he insisted, as usual, on doing the driving. It didn't bother her, she much preferred to sit looking out the window at the scenery, this part of the country still being new to her. Not that there was much to see that morning, the heavy cloud hiding the sun, slowing the daybreak. At least, she thought, the rain had stopped and the wind had died down to a gentle breeze.

Ten minutes later, they pulled into the car park, seeing the man waving frantically as if they, for some reason, were going to pass him by. Bourke pulled over and stopped beside him.

'Mr Rumsey?' Miller said, getting out. She knew Bourke would stay in his seat unless she needed him, which suited her just fine.

The man who stood waiting was trying to control a large dog straining at the leash, tongue lolling, breath coming in large odorous pants, slobber hanging from the corners of its wide mouth. 'Yes, that's me,' Rumsey said and indicated the path just behind. 'It's not far, shall I show you?'

'If you wouldn't mind, sir,' Miller said politely and fell into step beside him, steering clear of the dog. Not that she minded dogs, but she wasn't keen on slobber. Rumsey, she was glad to see, was right about the distance. It was only a few hundred yards from the car park. She stopped him with a raised hand as he pointed towards something unidentifiable a few feet ahead. 'Did you touch anything?'

'No,' he hurried to say. 'I had Brandy on the leash, he was heading towards it but I pulled him away. I knew immediately there was something not right.'

Miller could see why as they moved a little closer. Just beside the path, in a small natural hollow, sat three piles of clothes. Each was tidily done, the garments folded and placed one on top of the other. Finishing off each, a pair of shoes sat neatly facing the same direction. They'd been there a while. The clothes were wet, the shoes holding a layer of rainwater. Debris had blown in to decorate the piles with dead leaves, twigs and even a crumpled crisp packet.

'Is it okay if I go?' Rumsey asked. 'It's exhausting holding Brandy like this.'

Miller saw the strain on his face that was due in some measure to the dog's continuous attempt to get away and the knowledge that was clear in the sadness of his eyes. 'Yes, of course,' she said gently. 'We will need to get a statement, if you leave my colleague your address we can come and take it later, if you'd prefer.'

With a final glance at the sad collection, Rumsey headed back to the car park, leaving her alone. Squatting down, she looked more closely at the clothes, drawing a quick breath when she noticed something odd. At first, she thought it was accidental that the piles of clothes seemed to be joined, something done perhaps by the wind. But, after examining them from each side and noting the unusual neatness, she realised a sleeve had been unfolded and extended to touch a sleeve from the next pile. Not just touching, they were knotted so that each was linked to the other. 'Like holding hands,' Miller muttered, standing up.

Looking down, she saw that the shoes had more than rainwater in them. Items of jewellery had been put inside, the early morning sun making what looked like a diamond ring in one shoe sparkle. Miller squatted down again. Three women. Friends.

Raising her eyes, Miller looked across to the sea where white-topped waves raced in the breeze. She'd been taught not to leap to conclusions but it seemed clear what this was. A suicide pact. Three friends had come here and had jumped. From their belongings, she could tell at least two of the women were well-to-do. Miller wondered if she'd ever discover why they did such a terrible thing.

Taking out her phone, she took a few photos. She'd send them to the detectives who would be investigating. They'd come out themselves, of course, but just in case, it was always good to have photos of what they found on arrival. Three women. Miller wondered again what their story was, what had driven them to such a sad end. There was only one car in the car park; she guessed that belonged to one of them. It would give the investigators a head start in identifying who they were. She was relieved it wasn't her job to notify family and friends.

She stood, the wind picking up once more to toss her short hair and howl in her ears. Brushing the hair from her eyes, she took a last look at the clothes before walking away, turning back with wide eyes as she heard a sibilant whisper that seemed to drift on the wind. She wasn't a woman given to flights of fancy but, later, she would tell her partner that she was sure the word she'd heard hissed was *lies*.

EPILOGUE

Barbara Adcott kept still for the obligatory photograph and waited while her passport was checked, concentrating on breathing normally, keeping her eye on the passport control officer, a slight smile curving her lips.

'Are you here for business or pleasure?' The officer's eyes flicked from the photograph on the passport to the attractive brunette standing in front of him.

'A bit of both,' Barbara said, increasing the intensity of her smile. 'I've been moving about a bit recently. I'm planning to settle here permanently if things work out.'

'Have a good stay and good luck.' With a nod, the officer shut Barbara's passport and handed it back to her.

A taxi took her to her central Toronto hotel. Within minutes she'd checked in and was shown to her luxurious fifth-floor room where floor-to-ceiling windows gave a stunning view of the city. 'Very nice,' she said, handing the porter a folded five-dollar bill.

Leaving her luggage where it was, she moved to the window and stared out. Toronto had been a good choice. Big enough to get lost in, big enough to offer her opportunities. Her reflection in the window made her smile. It was surprising how different she looked with short dark hair, she had to look twice sometimes. Reaching a hand up, she tucked a strand behind her ear and stared through her reflection to the city below.

The flicker of regret that she'd felt on and off since that clifftop drama sparked into flame again. Could she have done it any differently? As soon as she'd let the words out about killing Matt Peters, she'd regretted them, but they weren't words she could take back. For all their lies and deception, even taking into account Joanne's career choice, both she and Megan were law-abiding decent people. They wouldn't have been able to let it go.

The realisation she'd made a huge mistake was immediate, as was her response. She was used to thinking on her feet, to making snap decisions to deal with potential threats so she hadn't hesitated, running from the car, the plan forming in her head as she moved.

The view of Toronto faded as her eyes filled. Resting her forehead on the cold window, she shut her eyes, feeling hot tears run down her cheeks. Had Joanne and Megan realised that she hadn't jumped with them? Letting their hands go at the last moment, she'd thrown herself backwards for safety, hugging the cold wet ground as raindrops bounced off her skin. The wind whistled in her ears. If they'd called out as they fell, she wouldn't have heard and she was glad. She wouldn't have wanted to hear their last words, to know if they were aware that she'd lied one last time. Anyway, at that stage it was too late for words.

It had been such a risky strategy, her daring made her gasp even now, two months after the fact. With a glance around to make sure the coast was still clear, she'd scrabbled to her feet, left her clothes where they were and run, naked, back to the car.

There was an old rug in the boot. She'd dragged it around her wet body and jumped into the driver's seat.

Beth had sat shivering, partly from the cold, more from what she'd just done. It wasn't sensible to stay there but it was several minutes before she was able to shake off the numbness. Then she did, because it was done, and she needed to make sure it hadn't been done in vain. Leaning over the passenger seat, she'd searched for a moment, her eyes narrowing when she'd found what she was looking for, one of Joanne's long blonde hairs.

With it clutched in her hand, Beth had checked outside to ensure she was still alone in the car park and hurried from her car into the back seat of Megan's, the wind grabbing at the thin blanket and whipping it around her as she moved. Inside, she leaned forward and placed the blonde hair on the passenger seat and pulled a hair from her head to lay on the headrest behind. She opened and closed the seatbelt, touched the window, opened the door and dashed back to her own car. That should give them enough evidence that they'd all travelled there together. There would be none of Joanne's fingerprints in the car, but that couldn't be helped. The lone hair would have to suffice.

With a last glance at Megan's car, Beth had reversed quickly and driven from the car park.

There was only one place she could go. Joanne's house. With the weather as it was, nobody was going to discover their clothes for a few hours. They'd identify Megan first from her car, but it would take longer to place Beth and Joanne. She guessed she'd be safe in Joanne's house for a night anyway. And getting in would be easy, after all, she'd done it before.

In Royal Tunbridge Wells, she'd found parking a short distance from the laneway she needed to access. The blanket covered her but it would have drawn attention she didn't want or need, so she snuggled down in her seat and waited for darkness and the quiet of night.

It took only minutes to get to the back gateway, her bare feet slipping on the mossy ground, biting her lip to stop the automatic squeal of disgust when she walked on something live and gelatinous.

The crowbar she'd used to lever the window open was still where she'd dropped it and she was soon inside. She couldn't resist a grin and cheer of satisfaction, but the *woo hoo* echoed in the silent house, her grin fading on the first tiny flicker of regret and the sudden almost overwhelming sense of loss.

She'd padded upstairs, pulled on a pair of pyjamas, and set about preparing for her future, keeping herself busy, refusing to dwell on what had been done... what *she* had done.

Finding a suitcase, she opened it on the floor of the spare bedroom and stared at the array of clothes hanging on stands or piled on the bed. She was lucky for although Joanne had been inches taller, they'd been the same build and into the case went trousers she could turn up, shirts, skirts, underwear and a couple of Joanne's less-revealing dresses. A couple of jumpers, a jacket and she was set. Joanne had slightly bigger feet than Beth but she found a couple of flat pairs of shoes that would do for a while. Lastly, because she couldn't resist, she added a pair of Joanne's precious Louboutin shoes. With a quick check to make sure she'd everything she needed, Beth shut the case.

She slipped on a pair of gloves she'd found in the wardrobe. It was a sensible precaution, they'd find her fingerprints in various parts of the house, but they might be suspicious to find them on the bedside lockers. There she found what she'd been looking for – a jewellery box. Joanne had some very nice pieces and Beth knew she would need every penny to make her plan work. It didn't take her long to go through it and remove the good stuff – the diamonds and the gold.

She left her car where it was. They'd find it out on the street and assume she'd left it there to travel with Joanne. But there was something she needed to take from it. Throwing a coat over the pyjamas, she'd opened the front door, locked the latch to ensure it didn't shut her out, and hurried to the car. With the boot open, she'd pulled up the mat that covered the spare wheel and felt around the space, grunting when she found the packet she was searching for.

Back in the house, she'd opened it and taken out the contents. She had been honest with her friends, she'd always known there was a possibility she'd be caught someday and she wasn't a fool, she'd made plans. In the packet was a passport and references from a now-defunct private investigation company, all in the name of Barbara Adcott. The references were a few years out of date; that wasn't a worry, she'd come up with a cover story. More importantly, the passport was in date.

Next morning, grabbing the suitcase and her bag, she'd pulled a beanie over her hair, walked to the train station and paid cash for a ticket to Manchester. Her mind stayed blank as the train chugged along. Changing trains in London, she'd kept her eyes on the ground in front of her feet, the collar of her jacket turned up, and tried to stay in the middle of large groups of people.

It wasn't until she'd checked into a cheap Manchester hotel in the early afternoon that she allowed herself to relax. A local supermarket had provided all she needed for the next step, and two hours later, her hair cut and dyed, she checked it against the passport photograph. She'd done a good job.

It was a few weeks before she'd managed to sell the

jewellery. She'd carefully sussed out suitable shops before approaching them. With some compromise and bargaining, she was three thousand pounds better off. It wasn't much but it was enough. Money had been the weak part of her plan, the two hundred pounds she had managed to put away wouldn't have lasted long. It certainly wouldn't have got her to Canada.

But now, thanks to Joanne, here she was.

Beth pushed away from the window. It was a nice hotel; she'd stay for a couple of nights before moving somewhere cheaper. Her friends' faces came to her again as she sat with whiskey from the minibar and looked out over the lights of Toronto. She'd done them a favour, really, they'd nothing to live for. Neither had she, as Joanne had rightly pointed out, but she'd never been the type of person to give up. And she'd made it. New country, new identity.

She'd thought about a change of career, would have done so but for the final text she'd received on her phone from DS Kadam. Beth and Sunita Kadam had known each other for years, and Beth knew she'd have been stunned to hear the allegations against her. So, expecting Sunita to cut all ties, she was surprised to hear from her. Then she read the text.

The forensic team searching Arthur Lewis' house found hundreds of pornographic photographs of young girls, among them photos of Lydia Forest. I hope this helps, good luck, Sunita.

It had indeed helped. It had made her reconsider her future. She hadn't lied; what she'd thought had happened to Megan all those years ago had set her on this path, but what had kept her on it was getting justice for girls like Lydia. Beth was good at what she did. Being a police officer had provided her with good training and knowledge but she'd had to bend rules to get the job done. There had been a wobble when she'd learned the truth about Megan, wondering if Beth had put innocent men away. But her colleague's text had straightened that out. Her instincts were spot on. Perhaps, here in Canada, she could carry on what had become more of a mission than a job.

Tomorrow, she had an interview with a private investigation firm and she was confident she could convince them to give her a position. They weren't offering much money but they weren't asking too many questions, and initially she wouldn't be doing anything of importance. She had it all planned. First, she'd do a Private Investigator Training course, a necessary step if she wanted to apply for a Private Investigator Licence.

Once she had that, she could set up on her own and get back to what she did best. And this time, within reason, she could make her own rules and regulations. She imagined Megan sniffing the word *vigilante* and Joanne's laugh as she told Beth to go for it. Their voices and laughter echoed in her head and made her smile.

Megan and Joanne... sometimes... half-awake in the middle of the night... Beth would swear she felt their hands in hers. Maybe, she wasn't going on this new journey entirely alone. Was it a coincidence that her short dark hair was a little like Megan's; and in Joanne's clothes, hadn't Beth acquired a little of her glamour?

They were dead... Beth was too... but Barbara Adcott had an exciting life ahead of her. She'd make sure she lived it for all three of them.

ACKNOWLEDGEMENTS

Grateful thanks to the Bloodhound team, in particular to the director of Bloodhound Books, Betsy Reavley, who had faith in me: Tara Lyons, Editorial and Production Manager, for getting this book organised: Heather Fitt, Publicity Manager, for ensuring it got out there, and my editor, Morgen Bailey, for making it better.

A huge thanks to readers, reviewers and bloggers who spread the word and make writing worthwhile.

Thanks to my friends and family for the ongoing support, for listening, encouraging and cheering me on.

The writing community is so supportive and I have made some good friends who are generous with their time and encouragement. Grateful thanks to the author, Leslie Bratspis, who read an early ARC and gave me editorial advice. To the author Jenny O'Brien, for your unfailing support and encouragement. To the authors Vikki Patis, Jim Ody and Pam Lecky for your friendship – thank you all.

A big thank you to Sam MacInnes of Edwards Stationery shop in Melksham who was happy to answer questions about photocopying.

I love to hear from readers – I can be contacted as follows:

Facebook: https://www.facebook.com/valeriekeoghnovels
Twitter: @ValerieKeogh1
Instagram: valeriekeogh2

Printed in Great Britain
by Amazon

42071570R00158